Praise for the Josie Marcus, Mystery Shopper Series

Accessory to Murder

"A funny, laugh-out-loud whodunit. Elaine Viets has created characters that you can identify with. . . . This is one book you don't want to miss."   —The Romance Readers Connection

"A well-thought-out whodunit starring a sleuth who is totally believable and a bit quirky."   —*Midwest Book Review*

"A very interesting series. . . . I'm looking forward to the next book."   —*Deadly Pleasures*

High Heels Are Murder

"[A] laugh-out-loud comedic murder mystery guaranteed to keep you entertained for any number of hours—the perfect read for a rainy day. . . . Shopping, St. Louis culinary treats, and mayhem abound, providing for a satisfying read."
—Front Street Reviews

"*High Heels Are Murder* takes Josie into the wicked world of murder, mayhem, and toe cleavage. From the sweat and toil of having to work three jobs to afford a Prada knockoff to the glamorous world of stiletto shopping, Viets spans the female psyche with panache and wit."   —*South Florida Sun-Sentinel*

"Viets has written one of the funniest amateur sleuth mysteries to come along in ages. Her protagonist is a thoroughly likable person, a great mother, daughter, and friend. . . . The strength and the freshness of the tale lies in the characters."
—*Midwest Book Review*

Dying in Style

"Finally, a protagonist we can relate to."
—*Riverfront Times* (St. Louis, MO)

"Laugh-out-loud humor adds to the brisk action of *Dying in Style* . . . with an insightful look at the bonds between mother and daughter, the challenges of living in a multigenerational household, and the rewards of nonjudgmental friendship. Viets's fast pace is complemented by realistic dialogue and well-drawn characters in believable relationships. Viets affectionately uses her native St. Louis as the backdrop for this new series."
—*South Florida Sun-Sentinel*

continued . . .

Also by Elaine Viets

MURDER WITH ALL THE TRIMMINGS

Josie Marcus, Mystery Shopper

Elaine Viets

AN OBSIDIAN MYSTERY

OBSIDIAN
Published by New American Library, a division of
Penguin Group (USA) Inc., 375 Hudson Street,
New York, New York 10014, USA
Penguin Group (Canada), 90 Eglinton Avenue East, Suite 700, Toronto,
Ontario M4P 2Y3, Canada (a division of Pearson Penguin Canada Inc.)
Penguin Books Ltd., 80 Strand, London WC2R 0RL, England
Penguin Ireland, 25 St. Stephen's Green, Dublin 2,
Ireland (a division of Penguin Books Ltd.)
Penguin Group (Australia), 250 Camberwell Road, Camberwell, Victoria 3124,
Australia (a division of Pearson Australia Group Pty. Ltd.)
Penguin Books India Pvt. Ltd., 11 Community Centre, Panchsheel Park,
New Delhi - 110 017, India
Penguin Group (NZ), 67 Apollo Drive, Rosedale, North Shore 0632,
New Zealand (a division of Pearson New Zealand Ltd.)
Penguin Books (South Africa) (Pty.) Ltd., 24 Sturdee Avenue,
Rosebank, Johannesburg 2196, South Africa

Penguin Books Ltd., Registered Offices:
80 Strand, London WC2R 0RL, England

First published by Obsidian, an imprint of New American Library,
a division of Penguin Group (USA) Inc.

First Printing, November 2008
10 9 8 7 6 5 4 3 2 1

Copyright © Elaine Viets, 2008
All rights reserved

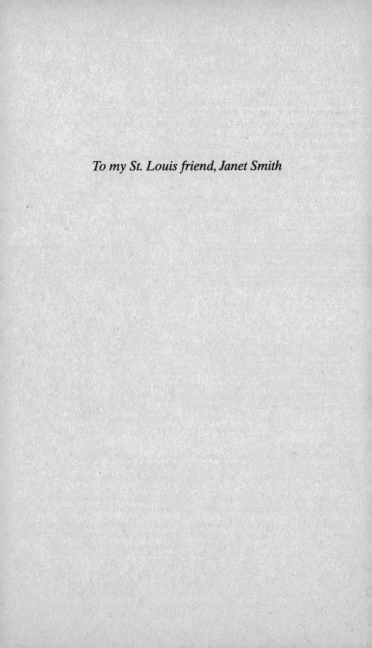

To my St. Louis friend, Janet Smith

Acknowledgments

So many people helped me with this book; I don't want to forget anyone. Thanks to my St. Louis experts, Jinny Gender, Karen Grace, and Janet Smith. Thanks also to Valerie Cannata, Colby Cox, Susan Carlson, Kay Gordy, and Anne Watts.

I also want to thank Emma, my expert on nine-year-olds. She used to be one last year. Emma gave me deep background on what it's like to be nine years old. I wish I could use her real name, but the world is a dangerous place these days for little girls.

As always, thanks and love to my husband, Don Crinklaw, for his extraordinary help and patience. It's not easy to live with a writer, but he manages.

My agent, David Hendin, is still the best.

My editor, Kara Cesare, devoted long hours to editing and guiding this project. Thanks also to Lindsay Nouis and the ever-careful Obsidan copy editor and production staff, and to publicist Leslie Henkel.

With thanks to Book Tarts—Nancy Martin, Michele Martinez, Harley Jane Kozak, Kathy Sweeney, and Sarah Strohmeyer—you've been true blog sisters on The Lipstick Chronicles.

Many booksellers help keep this series alive. I wish I had room to thank them all. I really appreciate their efforts.

Thanks to the librarians at the Broward County Library and the St. Louis Public Library who researched my questions, no matter how strange, and always answered with a straight face.

Thanks to public relations experts Patti Nunn and Jack Klobnak.

Thanks to super saleswoman Carole Wantz, and to the many members of the mystery community who were so kind to me when I was sick.

Special thanks to the law enforcement men and women who answered countless questions on police procedure. Some of my police and medical sources have to remain nameless, but I want to thank them anyway. Particular thanks to Detective R. C. White, Fort Lauderdale Police Department (retired).

Any mistakes are mine, not theirs.

Chapter 1

"Mom, can I see your wedding pictures?" Amelia Marcus asked.

"My what?" Josie Marcus hit the gas and nearly smacked the Hummer parked in front of them. Great. It was owned by the PTA president. Josie gave the woman an insincere smile and a little wave.

"Your wedding pictures," Amelia said. "You know. When people get married, they get pictures taken. Woman in a white dress. Man in a black tux."

"Don't get sarcastic with me, Amelia Marcus," Josie said.

The air seemed to be sucked out of the car. Josie felt an odd, still silence, as if she'd just survived a bomb blast. She'd been dreading this question from her nine-year-old daughter for almost a decade, since the moment Josie knew she couldn't marry Amelia's father.

"Put your seat belt on," Josie said.

Amelia had thrown her winter coat in the backseat, dropped her monogrammed backpack on the floor, and flopped down on the front seat. She must have had a difficult day at the Barrington School for Boys and Girls. Amelia's hair stuck up at odd angles and her socks slid down into her shoes. Again.

My daughter has inherited the slippery-sock gene

from me, Josie thought. Amelia's rich, dark hair and long nose were from her father, Nate. The sprinkling of freckles, like tiny flecks of chocolate, was all her own.

Josie thought her child would be a dramatic-looking woman. She was glad Amelia hadn't inherited her mother's ordinary looks. As a mystery shopper, Josie needed to blend in to the crowd when she went to the mall. But her daughter stood out, even in the throng of schoolchildren.

Not that I'm prejudiced or anything, Josie thought.

The school grounds were filled with yelling, shrieking children, running in the pale December sun. It was sixty-two degrees, unusually warm for winter in St. Louis. Tender green plant spears were poking out of the mulched beds and the trees were budding. The new buds would die in the next frost.

Josie eased carefully out of the school driveway, praying she wouldn't hit any kids darting heedlessly in front of her moving vehicle. With her luck, she'd clip the child of a lawyer. Worse, two lawyers.

"Mom," Amelia said. "I was asking about your wedding pictures. You've never showed them to me."

"My wedding pictures . . ." Josie repeated as she sailed through the stop sign at the end of the school drive. Horns blared and brakes screeched.

"Mom, that lady in the black SUV flipped you off."

"Shame on her." Josie gritted her teeth and tried to delay the inevitable. "Why do you want my wedding pictures?"

"We're doing a family tree for class," Amelia said. "Grandma showed me her wedding pictures. She has a leather photo album with gold letters. She got married in 1953 and wore a white lace Cinderella dress. She was really skinny."

Grandma Jane had been a fairy-tale beauty. Too bad

her marriage to my father didn't have a happy ending, Josie thought. That particular prince turned out to be a toad in a pin-striped suit. He walked out when I was Amelia's age. Mom worked herself half to death to put me through school. And she wonders why I didn't want to get married.

"Mom," Amelia nagged, "where are your wedding pictures?"

It was hard to think straight with horns blaring and Barrington parents glaring.

"Uh, I don't have a wedding album," Josie said.

"Were you too poor?" Amelia said. She was a scholarship student at a rich kids' school.

"No," Josie said. She'd considered creating a fake album by Photoshopping pictures. But she'd promised herself she wouldn't lie to her daughter.

"Why not?" Amelia said.

"It got lost in a flood," Josie said. The lie just sprang out of her mouth.

"What flood?" asked Amelia. "We live on a hill in Maplewood."

"The Great St. Louis Flood of 1993. It happened before you were born."

"Jarred said his parents didn't have any wedding pictures because they didn't get married. His mother said marriage was middle-class. Zoe called Jarred a little bastard. She got detention from Ms. Apple."

"Good," Josie said.

"Ms. Apple said that Zoe was judgmental. That's *so* last century."

"She's right," Josie said.

Zoe was nine going on thirty-nine—the first girl in Amelia's class to tongue-kiss a boy, drink a martini, and smoke cigarettes. She dressed like Britney Spears on a bender and dispensed wildly inaccurate sex information.

She told Amelia that Coke was a contraceptive douche and that girls couldn't get pregnant the first time they had sex. Josie was amazed how many of the dangerous myths of her youth still survived.

Amelia seemed to be measuring Josie's loud silence. "Mom, did you marry Dad?"

"Uh," Josie said.

"I'm a bastard, aren't I?" Amelia said.

Josie wanted to cry. "No, sweetie. That's a terrible word. Don't ever use it. Children are not to blame for what their parents did—or didn't do."

"You didn't marry Dad, did you?"

"No," Josie said.

"Why did you lie to me?"

"Because I didn't want to hurt you. I was wrong, honey," Josie said. "I loved your father very much. But I didn't want to marry him."

"Why not?" Amelia said. "You told me you should wait until marriage to have sex."

"That's the ideal," Josie said. "But sometimes people don't live up to the ideal."

"I bet Grandma was pissed when you got pregnant."

"Amelia! You know better than to talk like that. Yes, Grandma was angry when I failed to live up to her standards. But then you were born. When she saw how cute you were, she forgot all about being mad."

"What about Dad?" Amelia said. "Did he think I was cute?"

"I'm sure he would."

"Would? Did he ever see me? Was he dead when I was born?"

"Yes." A second lie. Sort of. As soon as Nate was arrested for selling drugs, he was dead to me, Josie thought.

"Where's he buried?" Amelia asked.

"What?" Josie said. More horns blared.

"Mom, that was a red light," Amelia said. "You drove through it."

"I know that," Josie said. Damn, her daughter was persistent. The kid could be a telemarketer.

"Is he buried in Arlington?" Amelia asked. "Zoe's grandfather fought in World War Two and he's buried there."

"No, he's not buried in Arlington," Josie said. "He's buried in Canada."

That was the truth. Nate was buried in a Canadian prison. Josie considered his crime worse than murder.

She'd known this conversation was coming. She'd had plenty of time to invent a good answer. Josie had rehearsed this scene in her mind, with all the wise and tender things she'd tell her daughter, but the time never seemed right.

Josie's mother had wanted Josie to marry Nate, then divorce him. "At least give the baby a name," Jane had said when Josie announced her pregnancy.

"She'll have a name," Josie had told her mother. "If she's a girl, I'll call her Amelia, after the woman pilot."

"Are you nuts?" said her mother. "Amelia Earhart vanished. They've never found her body."

"She's still a good female role model."

"If it's a boy, will you call him Wilbur, for the Wright brothers? How about Orville?"

"If the baby is a boy, I'll name him Richard, after Grandpa."

Andy, Josie's ex-fiancé, had offered to marry her and raise the baby as his own. But the man had made his proposal sound as if he were royalty offering to marry a peasant. After all, she was damaged goods. A ready-made family would look good on Andy's résumé, Josie decided. It would show he was solid corporate material, prepared to settle down. But Andy didn't really love her. Josie would never let her child be a springboard for anyone's career.

Her cell phone rang, and she pulled into a parking lot to answer it. It was Mike, the hunky Dogtown plumber she'd been dating.

"Hello," she said.

"Josie, what's wrong?" Mike said.

Josie could picture his fabulous slate blue eyes and broad shoulders. "Why do you think anything's wrong?" she said, dodging.

"I can tell by your voice. Hmm. School has just let out, so I'm guessing Amelia is in the car and she's the problem."

"Riiiiiight," Josie said. She sounded fake-cheerful. "I'll tell Amelia you asked after her. She's working on a school project and she asked for my wedding pictures."

"What did you tell her?" Mike asked.

"The pictures were lost in a flood."

"We've talked about this, Josie. You ought to tell her what happened. She has the right to know the truth."

"I told her that I loved her father very much and my life has never been the same since he's been gone," Josie said.

"Is that true?" Mike said.

"Yes. No. I don't know anymore," Josie said.

Amelia was staring at her mother.

"You want to go out for warm gingerbread tonight?" Mike said.

"Always," Josie said. "Where is it?"

"The new Naughty or Nice shop on Manchester Road."

"Someone was dumb enough to open another Christmas shop near Christmas All Year Round?" Josie said.

"Yeah, my ex-girlfriend, Doreen."

"Oh, sorry. She's your daughter's mother, right?"

"Right. And it was a dumb thing for Doreen to do. I don't think that area can support three twelve-month Christmas stores, and Doreen has an 'alternative' Christmas shop."

"What's that?" Josie asked.

"You'll have to see it to believe it," Mike said. "I can't explain it. But I want Doreen to succeed, so I thought I'd go tonight and buy gingerbread. Pick you up at seven?"

"Mike, I don't think it's a good idea for me to meet your ex."

"Doreen isn't the jealous type," Mike said.

"Right," Josie said. "I believe in Santa Claus, too."

Chapter 2

Mike pulled up in front of Josie's flat at seven that night. She could see his red Ford pickup shining under the bright streetlight. She was touched that he'd cleaned it for her.

"Good-bye, Amelia," she called, and kissed her daughter. "Go on upstairs and see Grandma."

Josie waited until her daughter was inside Jane's flat, then ran out to see Mike. Josie's mother didn't approve of her dating a man who drove a truck, but Josie didn't have that kind of snobbery. Plumbers made good money. Their work was useful. One of the nastiest men she'd ever dated was a paper pusher who had a Lexus, so Josie didn't think the right car was the key to anything.

Josie liked everything about Mike, even his truck. There was a holly wreath on the front grille.

"You've cleaned your truck," she said. "It looks nice. And you decorated it for Christmas."

"I did?" Mike looked puzzled. "Oh, the wreath. Heather did that."

Mike looked a bit embarrassed, but Josie knew if his daughter put that wreath on there, it would stay for the entire holiday season. Whatever Heather did was fine with her daddy.

Josie climbed in, kissed Mike, and snuggled beside

him in the roomy seat. He smelled of soap, hot coffee, and something indefinably manly.

She waved at her nosy neighbor, Mrs. Mueller, who was peeping out her upstairs window, one slat of her blinds lifted by a fingernail. The old snoop quickly dropped the blind.

"Did you get a cat?" Josie asked.

"No," Mike said. "Maybe I should. My fat Lab, Chudleigh, likes to chase cats. He needs the exercise. Not that he could ever catch one."

"Your truck bed is stacked with sacks of cat litter," Josie said.

"A winter storm is supposed to be coming in soon," Mike said. "I use the litter if I get stuck on ice. Some of those back streets never get plowed."

"That's the St. Louis attitude toward snow," Josie said. "God put it there, and God can take it away."

"It sure doesn't seem like Christmas is only three weeks away," Mike said. "It's too warm."

"I'm not in a holiday mood, either," Josie said. "The trees are budding and the spring flowers are coming up. It doesn't feel natural. Do you like Christmas or do the holidays depress you?"

"I'm okay," Mike said. "Christmas used to be more fun when Heather was little and she believed in Santa Claus. I loved to watch her eyes light up when she tore into her presents. I have the cutest Christmas-morning videos. But her mother ruined it all."

"What happened?" Josie asked.

"When Heather was eight, I asked her what she wanted for Christmas. She said she wanted me to marry her mommy so she could be like the other kids at school."

"Ouch," Josie said.

"Right," Mike said. "I know Doreen put her up to it.

She'd been pressuring me and then she started using our daughter."

"It's not fair to drag a kid into a grown-up fight," Josie said.

"Anyone but an eight-year-old would know that marriage to Doreen would be a disaster," Mike said. "Doreen lied to me from the first. She told me she couldn't get pregnant. Well, she did. I did the honorable thing—I said I'd support our baby and send her to college. But marriage was not on the agenda."

"I'm sorry," Josie said.

"Hey, I'm a big boy. I take responsibility for my actions. Heather was a cute baby. She's going through her surly teenage phase now, but she'll snap out of it."

Josie wasn't so sure. She thought Heather's bad mood was permanent.

"What about you?" Mike asked. "How do you feel about the season?"

"I've been looking at Christmas decorations for months. I'm sick of grinning Santas and simpering angels."

"I don't blame you. The malls put them up after Halloween," Mike said.

"Are you kidding? Most malls start the Christmas push right after Labor Day. The beach chairs are barely packed away before the Christmas trees come out. How can Doreen stand Christmas twelve months a year? I'm turning into Scrooge already. All that phony holiday cheer.

"Is Doreen a sweet, Mrs. Claus type, round and jolly with a gray bun and twinkling eyes?"

Mike laughed. "Doreen doesn't twinkle. She also doesn't give a reindeer fart about Christmas. Her favorite color is green, but only if it's money. You'll meet her tonight, so you can see what she's like. Brace yourself. We're heading into a holiday zone."

The blinking colored lights made the upcoming block look like the Las Vegas strip. Christmas All Year Round had a giant Santa waving from the roof and yelling, "Ho, ho, ho."

"Bet the neighbors love that," Josie said.

"They don't care. They get a twenty percent discount if they live in the area."

"It must work. Look at that line. It's halfway down the block," Josie said.

"Too bad it's not Doreen's shop," Mike said.

Across the street at Naughty or Nice, a winking Mrs. Claus was showing a lot of leg for the chilly North Pole. This Mrs. Claus was a temptress. Josie wondered if she belonged on the store's sign.

"Doreen figures it's smart to open her franchise across from an established store, because she'll get the people who are tired of waiting in line," Mike said. "So far her theory hasn't worked."

"Waiting in line is a city ritual," Josie said. "That's where you see your friends. Christmas All Year Round gives free hot chocolate while you wait. Besides, what is Doreen going to do after the holidays when all the decorations are on sale at the big stores?"

"Doreen thinks her place can thrive all twelve months."

"I hope so. But I've never heard of the Naughty or Nice stores."

"She gets mad when I say that," Mike said. "Doreen says I want her to fail. She couldn't be more wrong. We both want Heather to go to college. If her mother is making money, it will be easier to send my daughter to a good school. Doreen has invested more than a hundred thousand dollars in the franchise. She got eighty thou after her aunt Milly died, and the rest came from me."

One hundred thousand dollars, well invested for another four years, could send Heather to a good local college, Josie thought, but she kept silent.

"There's the problem," Mike said, pointing to a fake Tudor cottage next door to Naughty or Nice. "That shop, Elsie's Elf House, is owned by Doreen's rival. There are now *three* Christmas stores in the space of two blocks. One of them is sure to fail."

"Survival of the fittest," Josie said. "Now there's the real spirit of Christmas. Why did Doreen choose this location?"

"She didn't. The franchise chose it. She opened her store and Elsie's Elf House moved in two weeks later. Doreen was furious. Those women have some history."

Doreen's building looked like it had been built by Elsie's elves. It had a steeply pitched roof, plastic mullioned windows, and wooden icicles on the eaves. An inflatable Santa butt and legs were hanging out of the chimney, as if Saint Nick were smothering headfirst in the chimney.

Josie shivered. "Nice," she said. "That should make the little children feel good."

"I think it's mean," Mike said. "But the Santa butt is one of her best sellers. Wait till you see the inside."

A tinkling bell sounded when Mike opened the door, and odors of warm cinnamon and spice floated out. Josie stared at the tacky Christmas displays. There was a kitschy print of the Edward Hopper painting set in the late-night diner, *The Nighthawks*. On one stool, a world-weary Mary held a howling Baby Jesus. A tired Joseph sipped coffee. A donkey was tied to a parking meter. Three kings, dressed in gold and gangsta bling, approached bearing gifts—a set of gold mag wheels, a bottle of Crown Royal, and a jewelry box overflowing with diamonds and pearls.

"Uh," Josie said. She was distracted by an inflatable

Homer Simpson in a Santa hat leering at a simpering Christmas angel who looked like Barbie with wings.

A herd of moth-eaten deer heads hung on the walls, red noses flashing.

"Looks like someone shot Rudolph," Mike said.

Josie said nothing, but it took all of her restraint.

Hanging from the ceiling by gold threads were hundreds of angels, elves, Santas, snowflakes, and star ornaments, each one seeming gaudier than the last.

A felt banner embroidered DEFINITELY NAUGHTY covered a doorway. Josie lifted it. The banner hid a floor-to-ceiling display of "pornaments"—pornographic Christmas ornaments. They included snowmen and reindeer in awkward positions, and an elf with a body part that definitely wasn't elfin called SOUTH POLE. Mrs. Claus had her face in Santa's lap for a SNOW JOB.

Josie dropped the banner in disgust, backing into a shelf of crocheted angels with toilet-paper rolls hidden under their full skirts, like heavenly shoplifters. The angels teetered but didn't fall.

"What are those?" Mike asked.

"Toilet-paper covers," Josie said.

"What's wrong with naked toilet paper?" Mike said.

"Beats me," Josie said. "I'm not ashamed to display mine."

"It's classier if you hide it," said a woman stirring a cauldron of apple cider behind the counter.

Doreen, Josie guessed. Anyone who sold pornographic Christmas ornaments had no business talking about class.

"This is Doreen, Heather's mother," Mike said, stepping awkwardly between the two women.

Doreen glared at Josie. Her long thin nose, wild gray-black hair, and shapeless dark outfit reminded Josie of a witch. All she needed was a wart to complete the ensemble. Doreen's expression was Scrooge-sour, and the lines around her mouth pointed down in permanent disapproval.

How did cheerful Mike hook up with this unhappy woman?

"This is Josie," Mike said, as if presenting a rare jewel. "Doreen, we came in for your cider and warm gingerbread."

Doreen looked Josie up and down, an aristocrat sizing up a housemaid. "So you're Mike's latest?" she said. "Good luck, honey. When you hang around a plumber, you get a lot of shit."

Doreen slung two stingy pieces of gingerbread and two cups of cider on the countertop. Josie sipped her cider. It was sticky. The gingerbread was stale and left grease spots on the cheap paper plate.

"Amazing," Mike said through a mouth full of gingerbread. Josie thought he was astonishingly tactful.

"Better than that stupid chocolate snowman cake *she* sells next door," Doreen said. "Who ever heard of a chocolate snowman? They're supposed to be white."

"How's Heather?" Mike asked.

"Your daughter is icing cakes in the back," Doreen said. "She's not happy."

Like mother, like daughter, Josie thought.

If only Mike didn't have a sullen teenage daughter, Josie would marry him tomorrow. Heather was big-boned and brawny like her father, but she had her mother's bitterness. She was mean to Amelia. Josie had no desire to be Heather's wicked stepmother. Single motherhood was hard enough.

Heather came out of the back room wearing a green felt elf hat and carrying a spatula covered with frosting. Heather's baggy jeans and stretched-out sweatshirt made her look heavier. Her wild brown hair needed a good cut and her pale skin was sprinkled with zits.

Heather burst into tears when she saw Mike. "Daddy, she's making me work here. I'm stuck slaving in this store and I have to wear this stupid hat."

The kid was right to cry, Josie thought. It was a stupid hat and a terrible place to work. No daughter of hers would work in a shop that sold pornaments.

Mike turned bright red. Steam seemed to come from his ears. "Why are you using my daughter as your cheap help?" he asked Doreen. "You get good child support. Are you putting that money into this store instead of using it for Heather? Look at her clothes. She's dressed like a bum."

"She's fourteen," Doreen said. "They all dress like that. Heather has a work permit. It's time she learned there's more to life than IM-ing her friends and listening to her iPod."

"She should be having fun," Mike said. "She has the rest of her life to work."

Amen, Josie thought, but again she said nothing. It wasn't her child or her fight.

Chapter 3

Heather was pouting. It was not a pretty sight. She'd set her elbow on the frosting knife, and it left a grease spot on her sweatshirt sleeve. Josie could see—and smell—that Doreen was not spending money on new clothes for the girl. That sweatshirt was faded and faintly musty. Josie wondered if Doreen had bought it at a garage sale and neglected to wash it.

Heather's lower lip stuck out like a shiny tumor. Her blue eyes were small, hard stones. How could any child who looked like hunky Mike be so homely? It was a cruel joke by Mother Nature that Mike's daughter had his manly chin, strong frame, and broad shoulders, topped by her mother's unruly hair.

"Come on, honey. Working at a Christmas store is not that bad," Mike said. "You're one of Santa's helpers."

"We sell pornaments, Dad. You know. Porn. Little elves with big dicks. Ho fucking ho."

Mike winced. He didn't like his daughter talking dirty. "Heather, honey," he said mildly.

Heather's voice rose to an angry screech. "What if my friends see that South Pole elf? They'll think I'm a freaking perv."

She's right, Josie thought. The tumescent elf would make the girl's life miserable at school. The boys would torment her and offer to show her a bigger pole. The girls would giggle and make cruel remarks. Josie felt sorry for Heather, even if she was obnoxious.

"The shop isn't really busy in the evenings," Mike said.

"Or the mornings. Or the afternoons." Heather's sarcasm could make the plastic angels blush.

"How about if I pick you up at five tomorrow night?" Mike said. "You could come by Josie's and see Amelia." He gave his most fatherly smile.

Heather rejected it. "That sucks out loud." She stuck out her lip like an Ubangi princess in an old *National Geographic*.

Josie suppressed a sigh. Heather and Amelia didn't get along. All they had in common was working moms and absent fathers. Mike desperately wanted the girls to be friends. He was like his big, clumsy Lab lumbering into a delicate situation and thumping around.

Too bad any friendship was hopeless. Heather and Amelia had hated each other from the moment they were introduced.

Amelia had spent one night at Heather's home. She'd complained so much that Josie had had to bribe her daughter with a new sweater to get her to go. Amelia had called her mother at six the next morning to come pick her up. Amelia never got up that early on a weekend. She even refused Doreen's homemade waffles for breakfast. She wanted to leave—immediately.

All the way home in the car, Amelia complained. "Heather is mean, Mom. She called me a snob. Just because I don't go to public school like she does. She made fun of the way I talked. She said I was a baby because I don't have a cell phone."

About half of Amelia's class had their own phones. Amelia had been campaigning for one.

"And the dog next door barked all night. I couldn't sleep."

Josie refused to expose her daughter to more of Heather's snide remarks, even at Mike's suggestion. "Uh, I'll see if Amelia has plans," she said.

"She doesn't have plans," Heather said. "Who'd want to hang with a dork like her?"

Josie longed to slap that sneer off the kid's face, but she didn't believe in hitting children.

"That's enough," Mike said.

"She's lame, Daddy," Heather whined. "She's a baby. I'm five years older. I should be paid to babysit."

"I'll drive by the shop tomorrow night, if you want to go to Josie's house," Mike said.

Doreen poked her witchy face between her husband and daughter. "Right. Don't consult me. What do I know? I'm only her mother. Don't teach your daughter any responsibility, Mike. Let her grow up to be shiftless shanty Irish like your family."

Mike was shiftless? Josie resented the slur on Mike's ancestry. His family worked hard. His mother was a cleaning woman. His brothers were in the family plumbing business with Mike. Mike was on twenty-four-hour call at least twice a week for plumbing emergencies.

Not your child, not your fight, she reminded herself. But Josie hated her silence. In her mind it was cowardly. Josie believed if you didn't speak out against prejudice, then you agreed with it.

"I'd better go," Mike said. He threw down more than enough cash to cover their food. "I'll take the rest of my shiftless Irish money with me." He slammed out of the shop. The tinkling bell jarred Josie's nerves.

"Thank you for the cake," Josie said, and followed him outside.

Mike was sitting in his truck, taking deep, calming breaths. "I can't believe I got suckered into fatherhood by that woman," he said. "My daughter will grow up as nasty as her mother."

"She's just a teenager," Josie said, though she secretly agreed with him. "Mike, it would be good if our girls got along, but it's not going to work. Not at this age. Five years is nothing to adults, but it's an unbridgeable gulf at fourteen. Heather is embarrassed to hang around with someone as young as Amelia. She wouldn't want her around even if they were sisters."

"It wouldn't hurt Heather to be nice," Mike said.

"Don't try to force this friendship," Josie said. "Heather is welcome to sit at my house and watch TV tomorrow night. I'll order pizza."

"Really?" Mike said. "I'm on standby tomorrow. I have to be by the phone for all those clogged toilets. I'd love to hang out at your house and eat pizza with you, but I know I'll get an emergency call. Are you sure you won't mind having her?"

"Of course not," Josie lied. "I feel sorry for her. If the kids at her school ever see those pornaments, Heather will never live it down."

"That's going to stop," Mike said, gritting his teeth. "My daughter isn't going to hustle porn."

"Can we stop at Elsie's Elf House and get Amelia a chocolate snowman?" Josie asked. "She loves them."

"Uh, now is not a good time," Mike said. "If Doreen sees me going over there, I'm a dead man. She watches that parking lot like the military patrols the Iraqi border."

"She must hate what she sees," Josie said. "All those cars stopping at someone else's shop."

"Some people have the nerve to park in Doreen's

lot," Mike said. "She runs out and screeches at them. They leave and never come back. That's why she has all those empty parking spaces. Tell you what: Is there something else that Amelia likes besides the chocolate snowman?"

"Cotton candy ice cream from MaggieMoo's."

"Then let's go get her some," Mike said. "Does the ice cream really have cotton candy in it?"

"Yep. All that sugar makes my teeth ache," Josie said. "But Amelia loves it."

"Then she'll have it," Mike said. He bought Amelia four scoops of her favorite flavor.

When they got to Josie's home, Mike walked her to the door and kissed her. Josie felt a tingle that started in her suede boots. She gave a little sigh.

"I love that sexy sound. It's what keeps me coming back." Mike kissed her again. "I love you."

Josie could see the night stars over his shoulder—and the dark cloud of Mrs. Mueller at her upstairs window. Josie's neighbor was peeking out her blinds.

"I've got to go," Josie said.

"Are you angry at me?" Mike said.

"No, we're putting on a show for my nosy neighbor," Josie said.

"Then let's give her something to really watch," Mike said, and kissed Josie until she was breathless.

Watch that, you lonely old bat, Josie thought. I bet Mr. Mueller never kissed you half so hard.

She pulled away reluctantly.

"I have to go inside. Amelia's ice cream will melt," Josie said.

"Are you sure?" Mike asked.

Josie was sure. If the ice cream didn't turn into a puddle, she would.

"Why don't you drop off the ice cream and come back to my place?" he asked.

"I can't tonight. But later in the week, Amelia can sleep upstairs at Mom's and I can stay with you."

Josie kissed Mike again and waved to Mrs. Mueller. The blinds snapped shut as Josie escaped inside, hair tousled and face pink. She ran smack into Amelia, hovering on the other side of the door.

"Looks like you've been having fun," her daughter said. Josie could hear her disapproval.

"Look what Mike got you," Josie said, holding out the bag of ice cream.

Amelia tore the lid off the container. "Cotton candy! My fave," she said.

"He'll have something a little less fave for you tomorrow night," Josie said.

"Oh, no. I am not spending any more time with Heather." Amelia made gagging motions.

"Look, Amelia, I know she's not your best friend," Josie began.

"Best friend! She's a loser face, Mom."

"Loser face" was Amelia's latest condemnation. Josie had no idea what it meant, but she wanted to head off criticism of Heather before she ended up agreeing with her child.

Josie rummaged in the hall closet among the old umbrellas and tote bags and pulled out a worn photo album. "You can take these pictures of your father to school if you want," she said. "For your class project."

"Don't need them now," Amelia said. "The teacher dropped the project. Too many blended families. The parents protested."

Josie felt cheered. She wasn't the only one with an unconventional family.

"Mom, are you sure Dad is dead?" Amelia asked. She was scraping the last ice cream out of the container.

"Positive," Josie said.

"You're not lying to me?"

"Why would I do that?" Josie asked.

"Because it's easier," Amelia said.

Chapter 4

"I'm bored."

Only a teenager could put that much anguish into two words. You'd have thought Heather had been in solitary confinement for decades.

Mike's miserable daughter had been at Josie's house exactly fifteen minutes. She commandeered the TV remote, flipped through the cable channels without asking permission, sighed dramatically, and complained.

"Where'd you get this cheap cable?" Heather asked. "This TV is a friggin' antique. Who used to watch this piece of crap, Looey the Fifteenth?"

"Louis the Fifteenth didn't have a TV, loser face," Amelia said.

"Thank you, Miss History Channel," Heather said.

Josie wanted to set Heather out on the porch like a surly cat. She wished Mike were here. He'd shown up with his daughter and two pepperoni pizzas, hoping to settle in for the evening. His cell phone rang before he could even sit down.

"Sorry," Mike had said. He slid the pizzas onto the coffee table and took the call in the kitchen. He came back into Josie's living room looking disappointed. "Sounds like a busted stack pipe in one of those big old houses on Utah Place in South St. Louis. This could be an all-nighter."

"My dad, Captain Shithead," Heather said. "Savior of toilets in distress."

Josie waited for Mike to reprimand his daughter. Instead he gave a sickly smile, grabbed a slice of pizza, and said, "Sorry, have to go." Josie got a greasy kiss on the cheek and he was out the door, leaving his daughter behind.

After insulting Josie's TV, Heather flopped on the couch and started texting her friends at school. Amelia stared at her in disbelief.

"What's the matter, Baby?" Heather said. "Mommy won't let you have a cell phone?"

"I don't want one," Amelia said. "I have a life."

"Fucking liar," Heather said. "You don't have any friends to text."

"That's enough," Josie said. "We don't talk that way in this house."

"We don't talk that way in this house," Heather mimicked.

"Would you like to go back to your mother's Christmas store?" Josie said. "I'll be happy to drive you there."

"Good idea," Amelia said.

Heather stood up, pulled on her hoodie, and crammed a slice of pizza into her mouth. "I'm going for a walk," she announced.

Seconds later, Josie could hear the girl rummaging in her fridge.

"May I help you?" Josie called from the living room.

"I'm getting myself a drink," Heather said. "Is that okay with you?" She slammed the back door so hard the glass rattled.

Josie didn't stop her. She looked out her back window and saw the girl slouched by Josie's garage. It was about fifty degrees, so Josie didn't have to worry about Heather freezing to death.

Josie heard glass breaking and saw Heather toss a bottle at Mrs. Mueller's back fence. The streetlight revealed liquid splashed on the fence and running down the wood.

Oh, great, Josie thought. Now I'll have to paint Mrs. M's fence. She opened the back door and said, "Heather, stop throwing bottles this minute, or you're out of here."

"Good," Heather said. "That's where I want to be—outta here." She lobbed another bottle at the neighbor's fence. The girl had a good arm.

Josie burst out the door and stood in front of Heather. "I said, 'Stop.' Or do you want to go to your mother's store right now?"

"All right, all right. Just leave me alone, okay?" Heather said.

My pleasure, Josie thought. But she stopped to look at the broken bottle. It was brown glass.

"Were you drinking beer?" Josie asked.

"No," Heather said. She belched loudly. Josie could smell the bitter beer on the girl's breath. She went inside for a dustpan and broom. She couldn't have a neighbor driving over broken glass and getting a flat tire.

"What was loser face doing?" Amelia asked. "Was she drinking my Diet Dr Pepper?"

Josie opened her fridge and stared at the empty space on the middle shelf. "I think she took the four beers I kept for Mike."

"She must be trashed," Amelia said.

This is my fault, Josie thought. I should have been watching Heather. But I never have to lock up the booze around Amelia. There's going to be hell to pay with Mrs.

Mueller. Sure enough, red lights strobed down the alley. Two police cars were parked behind Josie's house, lights flashing.

"It's the cops," Amelia said. "Did somebody rob a house?"

"No, this is a much bigger crime," Josie said. "Heather threw beer bottles at a fence, and Mrs. Mueller called the police."

"That old lady will go apeshit."

"Amelia!" Josie said.

"Sorry. But Mrs. Mueller will want the death penalty for the crime against her fence," Amelia said.

Josie grabbed a thick sweater out of the hall closet and went out to face the police and her irate neighbor.

Two uniformed officers were in the alley, standing between a slouching Heather and an angry Mrs. Mueller. The old woman glared like an enraged cat. One officer was a woman in her thirties who looked strong but chunky. She had short brown hair and a stern expression. Towering over her was an older officer with silver in his hair and the beginning of a gut.

"You can see the beer running down the fence, officers," Mrs. Mueller said. "She threw at least two bottles. I believe the child has been drinking."

"Ain't no child, bitch," Heather said, and belched again. "I'm fourteen."

"She is definitely underage," Mrs. Mueller said.

Josie ran up to the little group. The chill in the air wasn't entirely due to the cool night. "Is there a problem, officers?" she asked.

"Are you the parent or guardian of this girl?" the officer asked.

"Fuck, no," Heather mumbled.

Mrs. Mueller gave a stagy gasp at Heather's language.

"I'm not Heather's mother, but I am watching her while her father is at work," Josie said.

"And doing a poor job of it," Mrs. Mueller added.

"We have a situation with an intoxicated minor, ma'am," the older officer said to Josie. "We'll have to take her into custody unless you can locate a responsible party."

"Her father is on a job in South St. Louis," Josie said. "I can call him. He'll be here in twenty minutes."

"What is the nature of her father's work?" the officer asked.

"He does shit jobs," Heather said.

"Must be in law enforcement," the older officer said.

"He's a plumber," Josie said. "He's one of the owners of Mike's Dogtown Plumbers."

"I know that company," the woman officer said. "They fixed my mom's toilet Thanksgiving Day when she had a houseful of guests."

"Go ahead and call him," the older cop said. "It will save us the paperwork for taking an intoxicated minor into custody."

"Humpf!" Mrs. Mueller said, at this apparent dereliction of duty.

"My cell phone is in the house," Josie said, and ran inside before they could follow her.

She was relieved when Mike answered on the second ring. "What's wrong, Josie?" he said.

"It's Heather. The police are here and—"

"Is she hurt?" Mike said. "Is my girl hurt?"

"No. She's fine. She snuck some beer out of the fridge. She drank two bottles and threw two more at Mrs. Mueller's fence. The old lady called the cops. They won't haul Heather to the juvie division if you'll take custody of her."

"I'll be there in ten minutes," Mike said.

"Drive carefully," Josie said to his disconnected phone. She went back to the grim group in the alley. "Heather's father is on his way," she said.

"What about my back fence?" Mrs. Mueller said.

"I'll repaint it," Josie said.

"Is that an acceptable solution, ma'am?" the older police officer asked Mrs. Mueller.

"Well, if she does a good job," Mrs. M said reluctantly.

"How about if I paint the fence tomorrow, weather permitting, and you drive by and inspect it, officer?" Josie needed a referee. Mrs. Mueller was never happy with anything she did.

"And what about this young woman?" Mrs. M said. "She should be taking some responsibility, too."

"Heather can scrub down the fence and sweep the glass out of the alley right now," Josie said.

"In the dark?" Heather said.

"You can see by the streetlights," Mrs. M said.

Josie handed Heather the dustpan and broom. "I'll go get you some paper towels and spray cleaner," she said.

"I'm not a maid," Heather said.

"How'd you like to spend the night in juvenile custody?" Josie said. "I hear they make you clean toilets."

Reluctantly, the kid started to work.

"You missed a spot over there," Mrs. M said, pointing to a shard of broken glass near her gate.

Heather snarled. "I'll get it."

There was a squawk of static on the radio. "We'd better go," the male police officer said.

"I'll call if there are further problems," Mrs. M said.

I bet you will, Josie thought, but she heard a chime.

"That's my doorbell," she said. "It must be Mike, Heather's father."

"He got here awfully fast," Mrs. M said. "I hope he didn't break any speeding laws." The old snoop was itching to start more trouble.

Josie ran for her house. *Ding-dong. Ding-dong.* The doorbell rang wildly. Amelia had strict orders never to open the door at night without her mother being present.

"Coming!" Josie called breathlessly. "I'll be right there!"

She flung open the door and stared at the man on her porch. He wasn't wearing a coat. The buttons strained at the lower half of his plaid shirt. His gut drooped over the top of his pants. His khakis were stained and his socks hunkered down in his shoes. His greasy dark hair was almost gone, but a few strands clung to his shiny scalp like survivors on a raft. His face was damp with sweat.

Josie studied his face. It was bright red with grog blossoms—burst blood vessels—and his nose was so covered with booze-inflicted lumps and bumps, it looked like an exotic gourd.

"Josie!" he said, spraying her with beer-scented breath.

"Do I know you?" Josie asked.

"In the biblical sense," he said, and hiccuped. "Where's my li'l girl?"

Josie didn't recognize the man, but Amelia did. "Daddy!" she cried, and wrapped her arms around his stained khakis. Josie's daughter and the man had the same dark hair and arched brows. This sloppy drunk was Josie's daredevil lover, Nate. It was like looking at a ruined portrait. Under a layer of boozy bloat was her Nate.

"Daddy!" Amelia cried. "You're not dead."

Chapter 5

"Josie, don't you know me?" the man asked. Big blubbery tears ran down his drink-ravaged cheeks.

Josie stared at him. Was this beer-sodden lump really Nate? Josie thought she could see the outlines of her impetuous lover: A few less pounds, a little more hair, and maybe this man was Nate.

Amelia wrapped her arms around him and cried, "Daddy, Daddy, I knew you weren't dead."

How did Amelia know Nate was her father? Josie wondered. Sure, her daughter had seen his photos. But this flabby drunk bore little resemblance to the dashing helicopter pilot Josie had loved a decade ago.

This can't be happening, Josie thought. I put my life back together after you wrecked it, Nate. I have a good job, a new man, and faithful friends. Now everything is unraveling.

"No," Josie said, "I don't know you." Not anymore, she thought.

"Josie, how can you do this to me?" Nate wept. "Why didn't you tell me we had a bootiffall, a beautiful daughter?"

"Why didn't you tell me you were a drug dealer?" Josie said.

"I thought you knew," Nate said. "How did you think I could afford all those gifts?"

"I thought you had money," Josie said. "You flew a helicopter."

"Piloting a copter doesn't pay that much. Not enough to take you to Bermuda, Aruba, and the Cayman Islands," Nate said. "I wanted to give my Josie the best." His voice wobbled with self-pity.

"So you sold drugs," Josie said, failing to keep the disgust out of her voice.

"I didn't hurt anybody," Nate said. "If they didn't buy drugs from me, they'd go somewhere else."

"The oldest excuse in the world," Josie said.

"Drugs killed my friend Zoe's sister," Amelia said.

"Drugs have ruined a lot of lives," Josie said. "Including ours, Nate. We could have married, if you hadn't been arrested for dealing."

"Aw, baby, don't be mad at me." Nate swayed slightly and clung to the back of Josie's worn couch.

"Mad? I'm furious. And you're disgusting. How did you find us?"

"Through my detective abili-bili—" Nate gave up on the word. "I'm a good detective, and you're still living in the same house."

"Oh," Josie said.

Josie heard the back door open. Heather materialized at the door to the living room, watching Nate and Josie's fight as if it were a play staged for her personal entertainment.

"Is that drunk your father, Amelia?" Heather sneered.

"Aw, don't talk that way, honey," Nate said, hiccuping. "I'm not drunk. I'm happy."

"You should talk," Amelia said. "You're drunk, too, Heather."

"Fuck you," Heather said, and threw up on the living room carpet.

Wonderful, Josie thought. Now the carpet is DOA.

She slid between the two girls. "Amelia, go to your room," Josie said.

"But I just met Daddy," her daughter whined.

"Yeah," the drunken Nate said. "We just met. We missed the last eight years."

"Nine," Amelia corrected. "I'm nine now."

Nate started crying. "Another year without my little girl. How could you be so cruel, Josie?"

Josie ignored him. "Heather, you need to freshen up," she said.

"Yeah, you smell gross," Amelia said.

Josie took an elbow and towed the reluctant Heather to her own bathroom. She gave the girl fresh towels and a clean T-shirt.

"A U2 shirt?" Heather said. "Those guys stink."

"Not as bad as you do," Josie said. "You'd better clean up before your father gets here. He's going to be angry enough."

"So what?" Heather said. "He's too much of a wimp to do anything. I don't take orders from him. I live with Mom."

Josie shut the bathroom door and went into the kitchen for more paper towels to pile on the worn carpet. She'd have to shampoo the rug, and she wasn't sure the pizza stain would come out. It was in the middle of the doorway, so Josie couldn't hide it with a plant stand or a table.

Nate followed Josie around like a lost duckling. "Let's go out to dinner," he said, a sickly half-smile on his face. "I came by so we could catch up on old times, get acquainted again."

"No," Josie said. "I'm sorry, Nate. I'm seeing someone else."

"You can do more than see me, baby," Nate leered. He wiggled his thick hips and nearly fell down. Too many six-packs had ruined his six-pack abs. It was pathetic, like watching an aging actor try to recapture his sexy youth.

Josie was grateful when her doorbell rang. Mike was on her doorstep, looking impossibly handsome. His blue uniform shirt brought out the blue in his eyes, and his sleeves were rolled up to reveal muscular arms. He moved inside with athletic sureness.

"Where is she?" he asked. "Where's Heather?"

"Taking a shower. She got sick and threw up on the rug."

"Oh, Josie, I'm sorry," Mike said. "I'll get you a new one."

"This rug is so old, one more stain won't make a difference," Josie said.

"Who's this?" Nate demanded in a belligerent tone.

"Who are you?" Mike asked.

He towered over Nate. The two men sized each other up warily, teeth bared like angry dogs.

"This is Nate," Josie said.

"I'm Amelia's fa-fa-father," Nate said, stumbling over the word.

"Is this true?" Mike said.

Josie blushed in shame. "I haven't seen him in ten years," she said.

"A deadbeat dad, huh? Where's he been?"

"In prison," Josie said. "I thought he was locked up for life and barred from the United States. I don't know what he's doing out of jail."

"They let me out on a tech—on a techni—on a techni-calla-lily," Nate said.

"And now it's time for you to leave," Josie said. "Did you drive here?"

"We can't let him drive drunk," Mike said.

"No, I'll call a cab," Josie said.

"Doan wan no cab," Nate said. "Car right outside. Red car. Rental." His arm made a wide sweep and nearly knocked over the lamp on the end table.

Josie caught the lamp before it fell, then looked out the door. "Oh, Lord, he's parked in front of Mrs. Mueller's house and his car is halfway up on her lawn. When she sees those tire tracks in her grass, I'll never hear the end of it. We've got to get him out of here. Give me your keys, Nate."

"They're in my pants pocket. You can feel around for them." Nate tried to roll his eyes roguishly and failed.

"I'll get them," Mike said, and pulled the keys out of Nate's right front pocket.

"Hey!" Nate said. "That's awf'y personal. I don't even know you."

"Where are you staying, Nate?" Josie asked.

"Hotel. Downtown."

"Which hotel?" Josie said.

"The one across from Tony's. We used to eat there, 'member? I bet he doesn't take you to Tony's."

"I'll drive Nate to the hotel," Mike said. "Why don't you follow behind us in his car? We'll leave it with the hotel valet and I'll bring you back home."

"What about Heather?" Josie said.

"I'll pick her up when we get back," Mike said. "This shouldn't take long."

Heather walked in, wearing Josie's U2 T-shirt, wet hair stringing down her back. "I'm not babysitting the kid," Heather said.

"I'm not asking you to," Josie said.

She also wasn't leaving her daughter alone with that teenage werewolf. Josie shut her bedroom door and called her mother. Jane answered with a sleepy "hello."

Josie suspected Jane had dozed off in front of the television again.

"Mom, I have a problem. Could you watch Amelia for an hour?"

"Of course, Josie. Send her upstairs."

"I can't, Mom. Heather is here and I don't want to leave Mike's daughter alone in my house. I need you downstairs."

"Amelia is no trouble," Jane said. "But that other one—"

"I'm sorry to do this to you, Mom. Heather has already been in the beer. Mrs. Mueller caught her drinking out by the garage and throwing bottles at her fence."

"Josie!" Jane said. "How am I going to hold my head up in this neighborhood?"

"You're not the one drinking," Josie said.

"I'll be right down," Jane said. "I hope you're not serious about that plumber, Josie. Marry that man and you'll marry his problems, too."

"Heather lives with her mother," Josie said.

"Then why is that obnoxious girl drinking beer at your house?" Jane said.

"Mom, please. The quicker you come downstairs, the faster I can get rid of her."

Josie could hear her mother clomping down the stairs that connected the two flats. She opened the back door and reintroduced Jane to Heather.

"This is my mother," Josie said.

Heather didn't bother to look up from the television. Jane saw Mike coaxing Nate out the front door.

"Josie, what is Mike doing with that man?" Jane asked.

"The guy isn't feeling well," Josie said.

Jane sniffed the air. "He has a bad case of beer flu, judging by the stink."

"He showed up here drunk. Mike is taking him back to his hotel. I'm following in his rental car."

"Do I know this person?" Jane asked.

"Yes, but you haven't seen him in a while," Josie said. "I'll explain as soon as I get back."

Mike marched the drunken Nate to his pickup and practically threw him in the passenger seat, then slammed the door. Josie watched Mike struggle to buckle Nate into his seat while she started the rental car. Finally, Mike's pickup roared and the headlights came on.

Nate's rental car was big and square and felt stiff after Josie's little Honda. Josie drove as carefully as she could, moving slowly off Mrs. Mueller's lawn. The car drove over the curb and landed in the street with a chassis-rattling thump. Josie winced at the tire ruts in Mrs. M's carefully tended grass. Would she have to reseed the lawn tomorrow, as well as paint the fence?

Josie drove in a daze, trying to wrap her mind around the fact that the sodden drunk in her living room was Nate. What had happened to her ex-lover in ten years? Nate drank when they dated, but only a few beers. He wasn't an alcoholic then. Not that she noticed.

How did Amelia instantly know this man was her father? Josie had hardly recognized Nate. Amelia had never seen her father when he was young and vital. What made her cry, "Daddy!" the first time she saw him?

Tears blurred Josie's vision as she followed Mike's truck. They were downtown now. The silver bend of the Gateway Arch soared over the night sky, softly reflecting the city lights. Well-dressed diners waited for their cars outside Tony's restaurant. Homeless men shambled through the park across from the domed Old Courthouse.

Josie left the rental car with the hotel valet and helped Mike half carry Nate to his room. She fished Nate's room key out of his shirt pocket. Nate was snoring when they dumped him on the bed. Josie stuck the valet parking ticket in the bathroom mirror, where Nate would see it when he woke up. She pulled off his shoes.

"I'm not going to undress him," Mike said.

"Me, either," Josie said.

Nate rolled over and mumbled something. His night-stand was cluttered with empty beer bottles and spicy-chip bags.

"Let's go," Josie said. She shut Nate's room door. Josie and Mike walked in strained silence through the lobby and out to his truck.

"I can't believe you dated that alcoholic, much less had a kid with him," Mike said when Josie was seated beside him.

Josie felt a hot flare of anger. "Your choice of mates wouldn't win any prizes," she shot back. "And your drunken daughter ticked off my nasty neighbor."

They drove to Josie's home in angry silence. Mike collected his daughter and refused to kiss Josie good night. Heather looked pleased at her father's snub.

Once they were gone, Josie looked in on Amelia. Her daughter was asleep in her bed, touchingly young and innocent. Josie tucked her in and turned off the room light.

Jane was sitting on the living room couch. "Was that drunk really Nate?"

"Yes," Josie said. "He came back here to see Amelia. He's become an alcoholic."

"Josie, he drank too much when you dated him. I warned you, but you didn't listen. Now that he's back, maybe he could join a rehab program. St. Louis has some wonderful recovery centers."

"Mom, I'm not dating a hopeless drunk."

"You don't know if he's hopeless," Jane said.

"Excuse me," Josie said. "I must have problems with my ears. The same mother who said a sober, hardworking plumber wasn't good enough wants me to marry a falling-down drunk."

"Only if he can be cured," Jane said.

"Cured? He's not a ham, Mom. The cure rate for alcoholism is low."

"But it does happen. It's not completely hopeless. And he's a pilot, not a plumber."

"Mom, what's with you? You hated Nate when we were dating," Josie said.

"It would be good for Amelia if you married her father."

"The right man would be good," Josie said. "The wrong drunk would not."

Chapter 6

"This store sells abominations!" the preacher cried. "It perverts the Lord's birthday. Its profits are obscene. God hates Naughty or Nice!"

The skinny black-suited man in the Roman collar pointed dramatically at Doreen's elfin shop. Picketers circled the store chanting and waving homemade signs. Josie saw badly lettered versions of PUT CHRIST BACK IN CHRISTMAS! SAY NO TO NOEL PORN and NAUGHTY OR NICE IS NASTY. The naughty Mrs. Claus winked wickedly at the protesters.

The TV in Josie's bedroom displayed six X-rated ornaments purchased by the TV reporter. One was the South Pole elf, now wearing a black modesty bar. The video did not display any part of the infamous Snow Job ornament.

Josie turned up the sound as the blond reporter interviewed the irate preacher. He was a tall man with a thin, ascetic face, evangelist's silver hair, and a black frown.

"This godless filth is on the same street as our church," he ranted. "It's time we throw the money changers out of our temple. These ornaments insult Christians. What's next? Elves molesting the Christ Child? This woman is Satan's handmaiden. She must be stopped."

Josie shuddered at the preacher's unholy venom. His

eyes were crazy with rage. If women could be burned at the stake, she was sure the witchy Doreen would be in for a hot time.

Mike's ex glared at the camera through the locked front door, as if she were under siege. Was she flipping the preacher the bird? Josie couldn't tell. The video had been shot at night and her hands were in the shadows.

Josie picked up her cell phone and called Mike. He needed to know. Mike answered, even though he could see her number on the lighted display. Maybe he didn't blame me for Heather's misbehavior, Josie thought.

"Sorry to disturb you at ten fifteen at night, but I think there's a problem," she said. "Do you have your television on? No? Then you'd better turn on Channel Seven."

Josie heard Mike rummaging around, and then a sudden burst of sound. The reporter stood in front of the store saying, "The shop owner refused to be interviewed by Channel Seven, but she did issue a written statement saying there is nothing wrong with a little fun at Christmas. She insists she does not sell pornography and her product is protected under freedom of speech. A spokesperson for the Naughty or Nice franchise said they do not endorse sales of offensive ornaments in their stores."

Mike groaned. "Just what we don't need. The franchise will force the shop to close, thanks to those picketing fanatics. I'll lose my twenty thousand and Doreen will be out her eighty thou investment. Nobody will buy that shop after this publicity."

"I'm sorry, Mike." Josie was genuinely sorry if the shop had to close and Mike lost his hard-earned money, but she thought Doreen had brought this problem on herself. "At least Heather wasn't at the store when this happened. Your daughter won't be embarrassed on television."

"I've got to get Heather out of that store," Mike said.

"Can't you just forbid her to work there?"

"She has a work permit and I'm not the custodial parent," Mike said. "But this controversy should help. Maybe it has a bright side after all."

"I hope so," Josie said. She wished him good night and hung up.

The next morning, Josie read the *St. Louis City Gazette*. The front page featured a story and photos of the Naughty or Nice church picketers. One shop window was boarded up. A protester's brick had smashed the glass. Josie wondered if Mike was right. Would the shop stay open now after this publicity?

Do I care? Josie thought.

Doreen had caught one break: It was Saturday, a low-circulation day for the newspaper, so her shop's shame would not be spread throughout the whole metropolis— unless people had watched TV Friday night.

Today was also Josie's day off. She had to deal with her daughter. Josie regretted her cowardly lies about Nate. All night she'd rehearsed make-believe conversations with Amelia. In each one, Josie sounded wise and protective and her daughter wept a few tears, then flung her arms around her mother and forgave her. Josie knew that was pure fantasy. Amelia was as stubborn as her mother.

Josie peeked into Amelia's room. Her daughter was still asleep, one foot flung out of the covers. Josie rearranged the blanket, so Amelia's foot wouldn't get cold. Then she went to the kitchen and put on the coffee. While it was perking, Josie dressed in her oldest clothes. She had to paint Mrs. M's fence after she'd had some caffeine. Luckily it was a sunny day, but the temperature had slipped to thirty degrees. The sleet was supposed to hit later.

Josie had to hurry if she was going to get the fence painted before the bad weather arrived. She drank a cup of coffee, rummaged in the basement for leftover white house paint and a roller, and went outside.

The paint rolled on the fence smooth and creamy. Mrs. M came out to supervise. She wore a short gray jacket and looked like a Russian prison matron. Mrs. Mueller made Josie put on three coats of paint and still complained that she could see the beer stain.

"I can smell it, too," Mrs. Mueller said. "My fence has the rank odor of old beer."

All Josie could smell was the powerful odor of fresh paint.

"Tell it to the cops when they come by," Josie said, packing up her paint, tray, and roller. "Three coats are enough. I'm finished."

Mrs. Mueller huffed, but Josie ignored her. She was certain Mrs. M hadn't discovered the ruts in her front lawn yet. If she had, she would have given Josie another earful.

Josie found Amelia having breakfast at the kitchen table, scarfing down toast, grape jelly, and milk. Her daughter was reading a book. Josie smiled. Her mother used to reprimand her for it, but Josie didn't mind if Amelia read at breakfast. She never understood why her mother hated it.

"Good morning," Josie said.

Amelia ignored her.

Josie was spoiling for a fight after dealing with Mrs. Mueller. "I said, 'Good morning.' " She raised her voice a few notches.

Amelia still didn't respond.

Josie took the book out of her daughter's hand. "Excuse me. When did I become invisible? And is that a backpack I see on the floor by the front door? Who's going to pick it up before someone trips over it and breaks her neck? The maid. Oh, wait. We don't have a maid. That must be me! I have a new title. Josie Marcus, mystery shopper *and* maid."

"Moooom," Amelia said, dragging the word out for at least four syllables.

"Don't Moooom me," Josie said. "You sound like a sick cow."

Amelia mumbled something that Josie couldn't hear. "I missed that," Josie said. "Were you apologizing?"

"No," Amelia said defiantly. Tears leaked out of her dark brown eyes, but she was too proud to give in to them. "I said your new title should be 'liar,' because that's what you are. You lied about Daddy."

Ah. Now the ugly facts were out in the open. Josie had to tell the truth this time, no matter how difficult. She poured herself another cup of coffee with shaking hands and sat down next to her daughter. She could hardly bear to look at Amelia's tearstained face.

"I'm sorry, Amelia. I thought I was doing the right thing, but obviously I wasn't. I didn't know that your father was a drug dealer when we were dating. By the time I found out, it was too late. I was already pregnant with you. I wanted you more than anything in the world, but I didn't want you involved with anyone who'd been in prison."

"Why?" Amelia cried. "What's so bad about prison? Todd's father went there for embezzling. Todd said it was like a country club."

"Prison is never a country club," Josie said. "In a country club, people wait on you and call you 'sir.' You can come and go as you please. You dine in pleasant rooms and eat good food.

"You can't leave prison until you've served your sentence. The food is worse than your school's cafeteria and there's an open toilet in your room. Guards watch you all the time. You have no freedom. Todd could only see his father on certain visiting days. Todd's father went to his own mother's funeral with two marshals guarding him like he was with the mob. He wore handcuffs in front of their friends and family. Todd's mother was so embarrassed, she looked like she wanted to crawl into her mother-in-law's coffin.

"Some prisons are not as bad as others, but none are vacations. You go to prison for punishment, and it's filled with bad people, and you cannot avoid them. I didn't want you dragged into that world. That's why I said your father was dead. I lied. I was wrong. I can see you were hurt and I didn't protect you after all. I'm sorry for the pain I caused you. It was a poor decision on my part."

"What's wrong with being dragged into that world?" Amelia said.

"Drug dealers break the law. Some of them kill people to get their money. When your father sold drugs, he put us all in danger." Josie wondered if she'd been watching too many *Miami Vice* reruns.

"Did Daddy kill anyone?" Amelia said.

"I don't think so," Josie said. But she wasn't sure anymore. "The man I knew was kind and generous, and I loved him more than anything in the world, except you."

But whether the man I loved was the real Nate, or I'd idealized him, I'll never know, Josie thought.

Chapter 7

"Did you love Daddy when you were young?" Amelia said.

Josie's daughter was methodically spreading grape jelly on a second piece of toast, making sure all the corners were perfectly purple.

Josie wanted to yank the knife out of her daughter's hand, but she sat still. This was a lull in their battle. She knew another shot would be fired soon.

"Oh, yes," Josie said. "I was crazy about your father." She didn't add *I'm still young.* By Amelia's standards, thirty-one was ancient.

"Why?" her daughter said.

"Because he was so funny and energetic. Because I never knew what he would do next. One weekend he would whisk me off to Aruba to scuba dive. We'd go to New York for dinner the next. I never knew what to expect. I liked that."

"But besides taking you places, did you love him?"

Josie winced. "Yes," she said.

It was a good question, and one Josie had never honestly answered before. Nate had kept her off guard their whole courtship. If she'd married him, would their wild romance have withstood the daily grind of grocery shopping, jobs, light bills, and taking out the trash? Not to mention her mother, Jane? Would Nate have become an alcoholic if he'd lived with Josie? There was no way to answer those questions.

"I loved your father," Josie said.

"Do you still love him?" Amelia picked up on that past tense—"loved"—immediately.

Josie tried to give her nine-year-old as much honesty as she could handle. "Part of me still loves Nate and always will. But living with an unpredictable man who has a drinking problem is asking for trouble."

"Is it me?" Amelia asked. "Is that why you broke up with Daddy?"

"No, sweetie. I stopped seeing Nate when he was arrested in Canada for dealing drugs. He was barred from this country. I'd just learned I was going to have you, and I thought it was better to break off our romance. Children need stability, and he couldn't give you that in his situation."

"What if he reformed?" Amelia said.

"It's hard for grown people to change their ways," Josie said. "It's not impossible, but it is difficult. I'm not that much of an optimist that I believe he'll simply stop drinking. I have a question for you: How did you know Nate was your father the first time you saw him?"

"I just knew," Amelia said. The toast had reached her desired level of perfection. "I always knew he wasn't dead, or I would have seen his grave. He's old like you, but he has my eyes and hair. He looks like my daddy."

"Yes, he does," Josie said.

"He found me because he's my daddy. Zoe got a pink Love hoodie for her birthday," Amelia said, abruptly changing the subject as she crunched her toast.

"That's nice," Josie said. She recognized this as another bid in Amelia's Christmas gift hint campaign.

Zoe dressed like a junior hooker. The principal called

in Zoe's mother to discuss her child's fashion choices. Zoe's mom showed up wearing clothes even more revealing than her daughter's outrageous outfits, and the discussion ended quickly.

Amelia was smart enough to know Zoe was not high on Josie's list of favorite people. "Paris Hilton was photographed wearing a pink Love hoodie," Amelia said, as if this touch of stardust would persuade her mother.

Josie remained silent.

"Emma's getting one for Christmas," Amelia said.

Josie liked Emma and respected her mother. "I doubt that," Josie said. "Emma's mom doesn't think Paris Hilton is a good role model."

"Emma's grandmother is buying it for her. Do you think Grandma—"

"Your grandmother cannot afford an overpriced hoodie," Josie said firmly. "Don't even mention it to her."

"It's only sixty dollars," Amelia said.

"Grandma lives on Social Security and a small pension," Josie said. "Sixty dollars is too much money for something you'll outgrow in a couple of months."

"What about a cell phone? Those are free."

"Only if you sign up for a plan that bleeds you dry," Josie said. "You are not getting a cell phone."

"It's important for my safety," Amelia said. "That's why the other kids have them."

Nice try, Josie thought. "I drive you to school and to Emma's house. You don't roam the malls or walk to the bus stop. Why do you need a cell phone?"'

"So I can text my friends," Amelia said.

"You already spend hours sending them instant messages."

"It's not the same, Mom. Everyone has a cell phone. I'm nothing but a loser face without one."

"Somehow, Amelia, I doubt that."

Amelia gave a pained sigh. Josie was tempted to sigh along with her, but she was interrupted by a knock on the door.

Josie opened it to find Nate on her front porch. He was a different man from the one she saw last night—at least a clean and sober one. Nate was dressed in a fresh white shirt, open at the collar, and neatly pressed pants. The shirt gapped across his burgeoning beer belly. But some things couldn't be cleaned up. Nate's complexion was crisscrossed with spidery veins. His eyes were red and the skin under them was puffy. His nose—Josie used to love to trace its noble dimensions with her finger—still looked like an exotic gourd. He was carrying a shopping bag of Christmas-wrapped packages and a big bouquet of red roses.

"Presents for my girls," Nate said. He handed Josie the flowers. He paused, as if he'd prepared a little speech. "I came to apologize. I should have called first before I showed up last night. I shouldn't have let my little girl see me drunk. I didn't mean to drink, Josie. I got nervous. I knew you would be angry when you saw me and I started drinking and couldn't stop."

Ah, an alcoholic's excuses. Josie hated them. Somehow Nate's drinking problem was her fault. He was a long way from recovery.

"Daddy!" Amelia came running out of the kitchen in her pink robe. "What did you bring me?"

"Open your packages and see," Nate said, handing his daughter the shopping bag.

Josie didn't like this, but she let Amelia tear open the brightly wrapped presents. Her daughter ripped into them like a young lioness opening an antelope.

"My hoodie!" Amelia said. "It's exactly what I wanted! And a cell phone. This is the cool RAZR phone, too. Even Zoe doesn't have one."

Josie didn't like the greed gleaming in her daughter's eyes.

"Thank you," Amelia said. "Thank you, thank you." She threw her arms around her father.

"Aren't you going to open your present, Josie?" Nate asked. He handed her a flat box about the size of a floor tile. It was Tiffany blue. Josie was relieved to see the box was too big to hold an engagement ring.

"I have something to do first," Josie said. She went straight to Amelia's room and switched on her daughter's computer, then studied the SENT MAIL queue. Amelia had written to an e-mail address Josie didn't recognize. She opened it.

"Dear Daddy," Amelia's e-mail began.

I'm so happy you came home 4 me. I'm having a big problem-o. Mom is dating this plumber, Mike, and I think she's going 2 marry him. He has a loser face daughter named Heather. If Mom marries him I'll be like Cinderella, and have 2 do all the work and wait on horrible Heather. Mike lets her do whatever she wants. She's mean.

You have 2 save me. I could live with you in Canada. I like cold weather.

My fave color is purple and my fave ice cream is cotton candy. What's yours? Do you like chocolate? I like the chocolate snowmen with extra sauce at Elsie's Elf House, but I can't go there now that Heather's mom owns the Christmas shop nearby. She gets crazy if we spend money there instead of at her lame place, and her gingerbread sucks out loud.

All the girls at school are rich except me. I'm the poor kid, and they laugh at me. They laugh at Mom's car, too. Zoe says it looks like something her housekeeper drives.

I wouldn't look so poor if I had a new Love hoodie like all the girls wear but it's sixty dollars and Mom won't buy it. E-mail me soon and tell me all about yourself.

It was signed "Love, Amelia, your daughter."

Josie was so furious that she wanted to smash the computer screen.

Cinderella indeed. Where did Amelia get this fairy tale? It's true Josie was serious about Mike and hoping for marriage, but not at Amelia's expense. She would never turn her daughter into Heather's servant. Servant, hell. Josie could barely get Amelia to set the table, much less wait on Heather.

Josie called Jane from her own room. Her hands shook so badly, Josie could hardly punch in her mother's number.

"Josie, what's wrong?" her mother said. "You don't sound like yourself."

Josie said in a low voice, "Mom, Nate's here. We have problems we need to hash out, and one of them is Amelia. Can she stay with you before I kill her?"

"Josie, send the child up here this instant."

"Will do," Josie said.

"And be careful with that man. He can make trouble for you. He never signed over his parental rights."

"He was in jail when Amelia was born."

"But he's out now and you don't know why," Jane said.

"He said it was a technicality," Josie said.

"If he was pardoned, he could sue for custody and take Amelia back to Canada. Then where would you be? You need a lawyer. Nate could take her now and just disappear. Don't upset him."

"Thanks, Mom, that's good advice. I'll find someone

who knows international law. I'll ask Alyce's husband, Jake, for help. He owes me."

Josie took a deep breath to calm herself, then called Amelia way too sweetly. "Can I see you a minute, dear?" she said.

Amelia came in wearing the pink hoodie over her robe and danced around her room, showing it off. "It's perfect, Mom," she said. "It's just what I wanted. It's the right size, too."

"And how would your father know that?" Josie asked through clenched teeth. She wanted to tear the pink sweatshirt off her daughter. It took all her strength to restrain herself.

"I don't know," Amelia lied.

"It wouldn't have anything to do with an e-mail you sent your father, would it?"

"You read my e-mail," Amelia said, outrage in her voice.

"That's my privilege as long as you live in this house. Where did you get Nate's e-mail address?"

"He gave me his card last night, while barfing Heather took a shower," she said. "Daddy said I could e-mail him anytime."

"Give me that hoodie," Josie said.

"It's mine," Amelia said.

"Give it to me, or I'll rip it off your back and put it in the Goodwill donation box."

Amelia reluctantly peeled off the hoodie.

"You're grounded, young lady," Josie said. "No computer except for schoolwork. Now get dressed and go upstairs to your grandmother. You have exactly five minutes to be out the door."

Amelia was furious at her mother. "I hate you. You're a liar," she said. "I'm going to live with my father."

Suddenly, Josie felt like a hostage in her own home.

Chapter 8

Deep breaths, Josie told herself. You can't come out screaming at Nate. That will only drive Amelia closer to her newfound father.

When she felt calmer, Josie went out to face her ex. Nate was pacing her tiny living room. Suddenly, the room that had seemed so homey looked small and shabby. Was the couch starting to sag? She spotted a cobweb on the table lamp and brushed it away. Amelia's pink backpack was still abandoned by the front door, and the new stain Heather had added to the worn carpet seemed radioactive.

Josie wondered if she looked slightly worn, too, and then brushed that thought away like the cobweb. Concentrate, she told herself. You have to save your daughter. What if Nate wants to take Amelia back to Canada? If he sues, you can't afford a good lawyer. Your mother will have to get a second mortgage on this place.

"Is Amelia okay?" Nate asked.

"She's fine," Josie said too cheerfully. "She has to see her grandmother now."

Nate looked disappointed. "Oh," he said. "I thought we could spend some time together."

"When we work out some ground rules," Josie said.

"Wait a minute," Nate said. "She's half mine."

"That's what we need to talk about," Josie said.

"How about lunch at O'Connell's Pub?" Nate said.

That's where Josie and Nate had first met. Josie didn't want to encounter the ghost of their former romance—or any of their old friends. Too many of them would be happy to start Nate on a Saturday bender.

"What if we grab a burger at Ruley's Tavern on Manchester?" Josie said.

"I've never been there," Nate said.

"It's a neighborhood joint," she said. "Very quiet." With no painful memories.

They walked two blocks to the little bar. The day was growing chilly. Nate wore a leather jacket. Josie wondered if it was the same bomber jacket he'd had when they were dating. She doubted Nate could zip it over his belly.

"The area looks good," Nate said.

"Believe it or not, Maplewood has become hip," Josie said.

"I believe it. It's like a small town in the middle of a big city."

Ruley's was an old-fashioned tavern, with a pool table, a pinball machine, and beer cases piled almost to the ceiling. Regiments of booze glowed in the backbar mirrors. A fat bartender wearing a stretched-out T-shirt was polishing glasses. An old man dozed on a barstool. He was the only customer.

The sun lit the dust-filmed windows, and Josie saw that her nice neighborhood place was sliding into a dive. The old tin ceiling was yellow with grease. The bathroom doors had dog silhouettes marked POINTERS and SETTERS. The air was scented with sour beer and Pine-Sol.

Nate and Josie took a battered table in the corner. The large, brassy-haired waitress said, "What can I get you, hon?"

"A draft Bud," Nate said.

"Coke for me," Josie said.

They both ordered cheeseburgers. "Lots of onions on mine," Josie said, hoping that would kill any lingering thoughts of romance.

It didn't. As soon as the waitress disappeared through the kitchen door, Nate pulled out the blue Tiffany & Co. box and handed it to Josie.

"Open it," Nate said.

Inside was a diamond and platinum Elsa Peretti teardrop necklace, so finely made it was like a miniature sculpture. Josie did enough mystery-shopping to know she was looking at ten thousand dollars' worth of jewelry.

"It's lovely," she said.

The necklace glowed in the dingy bar.

"Put it on," Nate said. "I want to see how beautiful you look wearing it."

Josie carefully closed the velvet-lined box and said, "Nate, I can't accept it. I'm seeing someone else. I'm serious about him."

She handed back the box.

"And what does that mean for us?" Nate asked. He finished half a beer in one gulp.

Us? Josie thought. There hasn't been any "us" for a decade. You didn't even send me a letter in all that time. You never called. You just disappeared. In the dark bar, she could see vestiges of the man she had once loved, but Josie was a different woman now, too worldly-wise to fall for Nate again.

"We've both moved on, Nate," Josie said gently. "We're different people now. We live in different countries. Let's stay friends for the sake of our daughter."

"You mean the daughter I just found out about?" Nate had a belligerent edge to his voice. He downed the beer and signaled for a second one.

Josie hoped the waitress had tunnel vision. But the woman put another cold glass near Nate's hand. Nate drank it in two gulps.

"Remember when we flew to New York?" Nate asked. "It was a day almost like this one."

Josie dreaded playing "remember when." But now it all came flooding back. In her mind's eye, she saw Nate the way he was then: young and strong, before alcohol ruined him. It was a crisp fall St. Louis morning, and they were walking in Forest Park. The grand old trees were a blaze of orange and yellow and the sky was china blue. Josie was crunching dry leaves.

"What a gorgeous day," Josie had said.

"Not as gorgeous as you," Nate had said, and kissed her.

"Oh, Nate, I know what I am," Josie had said. "I'm no *Vogue* model. I'm plain old Josie."

But Nate was in one of his reckless moods. "You're not plain," he'd told her. "Not by a long shot. You need to be treated like a *Vogue* model. Let's go to New York for dinner at the Four Seasons."

And so they did. Josie made a quick phone call to her mother and told her she'd be home late. Josie didn't add that they were going to New York. She didn't want to hear the "you're heading for trouble, young woman" lecture again. Jane disapproved, but she always disapproved

Josie and Nate were in Manhattan by three that afternoon, and Nate took Josie on a shopping spree.

"You always thought you were plain," Nate said, bringing her back to the present. "I never understood that." He gave her hand a squeeze.

"Nate, there's nothing distinctive about me. It's why I make a good mystery shopper. I can melt into the crowd as Mrs. Ordinary."

"That's not how I remember it. You were worried you didn't have a dress for dinner. I bought you that black dress in Manhattan. You were a knockout."

Josie looked around the dingy neighborhood bar and couldn't believe she was the same woman who'd run off for a magical night in Manhattan. She still remembered the dazzling interior of the Four Seasons, with its mid-century spaciousness. Nate had whispered in her ear, "Did you see that fat guy by the window? His eyes are bugging out, staring at you in that dress. *Vogue* should be so lucky."

Josie did notice. She also noticed that Nate ordered a steak that cost more than her poly-sci textbook. Nate paid cash for their meal and their suite at the Pierre Hotel, but that barely registered. Josie was bewitched.

The magic was gone when she arrived back in St. Louis. Jane was waiting at home, arms crossed, body bristling with indignation. She immediately spotted Josie's dress bag.

"So, you let a man buy you expensive clothes like a kept woman," Jane had said. "I bet you were drinking, too."

"Only wine," Josie said.

"Well, isn't that sweet," Jane had said. "Only wine. You broke your engagement to a good, decent man so you could live like a drunken tart."

"I broke up with Andy because he was boring. He loved his job better than he loved me," Josie said.

"All men are like that," Jane said. "The rest will leave you in the lurch."

"Like my father left you?" Josie said.

Jane slapped her daughter.

"I'm young and I want to have fun," Josie had screamed at her mother. "What's wrong with that?"

"Josie?" Nate said. "Did you hear me? I said I'm talking to a lawyer about Amelia. I want to know why you didn't contact me when you had her."

"Because you were in jail," Josie said, raising her voice.

The old man sleeping on the barstool woke up, blinking.

"Don't be angry, baby. It wasn't my fault," Nate said.

It's never your fault, Josie thought, but she didn't say it. "You were arrested for drug dealing," Josie said, lowering her voice.

"But my lawyer got me out. I'm innocent." He batted his eyes. He looked guilty as all get-out.

"Nate, yesterday you said you got your money selling drugs. How did you get out of jail?"

"Medical marijuana is legal now in Canada. They even have a marijuana spray called Sativex. One of my clients had multiple sclerosis and took marijuana for the pain. I gave her the weed free. She testified that I helped her feel better."

"Really?" Josie said. "So you weren't selling drugs. You were doing charity work."

"I did help people," Nate said. Again his voice had that nasty edge. "I don't know how my lawyer did it, but I'm free. I contacted my old friends in St. Louis. They told me I had a daughter. I didn't hear that from you. Amelia's a cutie. She has my hair and nose. No need for any DNA tests."

His nose? Not anymore, Josie thought. She tried not to stare at his drink-ruined nose. She prayed that Amelia's elegant nose would never look like her father's tumorous honker.

"Why this sudden interest in your daughter?" Josie said. "Haven't you been out of prison a year?"

"Two years," Nate said. "I was serious about someone, and she didn't want children. So I had a vasectomy.

Now the urologist isn't sure it can be reversed, and my father wants grandchildren."

Hot anger flared through Josie. Nate didn't love Amelia. He was trying to avoid surgery with a ready-made child. Typical drunk's selfishness. She tried to remember her mother's advice to be nice to him for Amelia's sake.

Nate produced a box wrapped in Christmas paper from his leather jacket. "Here's another present for my girls," he said. "Waitress, another beer."

The waitress brought it before Josie gingerly unwrapped the box. Inside was a stack of U.S. currency. Josie looked at the hefty denominations and did some quick calculating. She thought there was nearly ten thousand dollars cash in the box. The money smelled slightly moldy.

While she examined the cash, Nate pounded down his third beer and ordered a fourth. The waitress brought it without comment.

"Where did you get this money?" Josie demanded.

"I had it around," he said.

"That's what you kept in that storage unit by the airport," Josie said. "Cash and drugs. Look at the dates on this money. It's ten years old at least. You didn't come back to see me or your daughter. You came to pick up your drug money. You have to pay your lawyer." She stopped herself before she added, *so you can steal my daughter.*

"Josie, how can you say that?" Nate said. He gulped the fourth beer like it was cold water on a hot afternoon.

"Because you are a drunk and a liar," Josie said.

"That's harsh," Nate said. His voice wavered as if he were about to cry.

"Here you go, hon." The waitress put two plates of burgers and fries in front of them. "Anything else I can get you?"

"Ketchup," Josie said.

"Another beer," Nate said. His voice was slightly slurred.

That made five beers in less than fifteen minutes. Josie was seething. Nate was starting another binge. She waited until the waitress left, then said, "You're still selling drugs, aren't you?"

"Why would you say that?" Nate asked. He didn't deny her charge.

"You're throwing money around," Josie said. "Ten thousand dollars on a necklace for me. Ten thousand in cash. Dealers never believe drug money is real. You think the supply is endless."

She handed him back the money with regret. She still had feelings for the young man she'd loved. She missed his wildness, his unpredictability. Now her life revolved around her work and Amelia's school. There was no time to rush off to Manhattan for dinner.

"Josie, think of everything you could give Amelia with this," Nate said. "And yourself. Your home could use some sprucing up. You could buy a decent used car. Your daughter is embarrassed she doesn't have as much money as the other girls in her school."

"My car is fine," Josie said. "We're fine. Amelia will survive without a sixty-dollar hoodie. She needs a sober father with a decent job. The other kids' parents are lawyers, doctors, and business owners. They can say how they make their money. You can't. I won't let my daughter live on drug money."

"She's my daughter, too," Nate said. "My money spends like any other cash. Do you think those doctors and lawyers make only honest money? All money is dirty, Josie." He gulped down the fifth beer and signaled for a sixth.

"This cash has blood on it," Josie said.

"Whoa," Nate said. "Aren't we dramatic?" He fanned a stack of fifties. "See, no blood. Just a little dust. Let's go back to your place and be friends, huh? Get reacquainted?"

"No," Josie said. "It's over, Nate. I'm sorry it turned out like this, but we can't see each other anymore."

"Aw, come on, Josie. Don't be like this."

"I have to get back." Josie stood up, threw some money on the table, and began walking toward the door.

"Josie, don't do this," Nate said.

"Good-bye," she said. "I'm sorry, Nate."

"No, you're not," he said. "But you will be when I get through with you."

Josie tried to hold her head high as the bartender, the waitress, and the old man at the bar stared her out the door.

"Can I get you anything else?" the waitress asked.

"Another beer," Nate said defiantly. He was so loud, Josie could hear.

She nearly cried. Nate had made his choice.

Chapter 9

Josie took the side streets home, stomping through the dry leaves in the gutter. She crushed sycamore leaves, big as dinner plates. Josie took a childish pleasure in their rustling crackle. A beer can blocked her way, and she gave it a swift kick into the street.

She wished she'd kicked Nate instead.

Josie argued with Nate in her head all the way home:

Threaten me, will you, you worthless drunk? You'll be sorry. If you loved me so much, why didn't you call me ten years ago when you were arrested? You've been out of jail two years. You've had plenty of time to contact me. You could have called before you showed up drunk on my doorstep. But no, you just reappeared, after a decade. Now that you can't have a child, you want mine. You're ready to resume our romance as if nothing happened.

Mostly Josie was mad at herself. How could I have been so stupid? Why didn't I see a lawyer to ensure I had custody of Amelia? Now I could lose my little girl. *My.* She is no longer our daughter, Josie thought. Amelia was *hers*. Any memories of the tender lover she'd had ten years ago were burned away by her anger. She realized how little she knew about Nate. When did he become a hopeless drunk? Did he have an alcohol problem when they were dating? Josie didn't know.

She'd had no idea he was a drug dealer back then. He never used or sold drugs around her. He always had cash for their outrageous adventures, but she'd never asked where the money came from. Were you dating Santa Claus? she asked herself. Did it ever occur to you to ask Nate where he got the money?

I was stupid, she thought. I knew nothing about this man. Nothing. I jumped into bed with him and had a child. Now he wants her back. Over my dead body, she thought. No, over *your* dead body, Nate.

Josie did know one thing for sure: Nate had a daredevil streak. He could kidnap Amelia and disappear into Canada and Josie would never find them.

Worse, Amelia might help her father. Right now, a new father who bought expensive gifts was more fun than a working mom who made her clean up her room. Amelia was too young to feel threatened by living with a drunk's uncertainties.

Go home, Josie told herself. Calm down. Fix some coffee and consider your options. You need a plan. Anger is an indulgence you can't afford. She marched into her home and nearly tripped over that blasted backpack. It was still plopped by the door.

"Amelia!" she called.

No answer.

Josie felt a flash of panic, then remembered her daughter was upstairs with Jane. She dialed her mother's phone.

"She's right here," Jane said. "We're making brownies."

"Oh," Josie said.

"You sound subdued," her mother said. "Is there a problem?"

"A big one," Josie said. "Nate has threatened to take Amelia away from me."

"Then we'll have to watch her extra carefully," Jane said. "One of us will always be there to pick her up and take her to school."

"What about if she's home alone while I'm at work?" Josie didn't trust her daughter to obey her "don't answer the doorbell" command if Nate was on the porch with presents.

"Then I'll watch her," Jane said. "I'll ask Mrs. Mueller for help, too."

"If anyone has the talent for this assignment, it's Mrs. M," Josie said. "She's a first-rate snoop."

"Josie, that's not nice," Jane said. "You know she's my friend."

Josie could never understand why her mother worshiped Mrs. Mueller. The iron-haired woman ruled the neighborhood's major organizations. Mrs. M appointed her friends to choice assignments and banished her enemies to dreary workhorse committees. But Josie had to force her to give Jane her fair share of the good slots.

Mrs. M had made Josie's teenage years a misery. She'd caught young Josie smoking cigarettes back by the garage and ratted her out to Jane. Josie was grounded for a month. She had retaliated by leaving a burning bag of dog doo on Mrs. Mueller's porch. Mrs. M had stomped the smoking bag with a sturdy shoe, and Josie had been grounded for what seemed like the rest of her teenage life.

Mrs. M still regarded Josie as a juvenile delinquent. Josie thought the old woman was a witch with a capital *C*.

The kitchen coffeemaker had erupted into "just finished" gurgles when Josie's cell phone rang. She checked the display. Her boss, Harry the Horrible, was calling on a Saturday. This was not good news.

"Josie, I need you to work this weekend," Harry said.

Josie could hear slurping noises and a football game in the background. She was afraid to ask what Harry was eating. Harry claimed to be on the Atkins diet, but that was mainly an excuse to chomp big chunks of meat. He lost the same three pounds over and over.

Sloop! Slurp! Josie imagined Harry gnawing a mastodon rib. He'd have grease spots on his shirt and clumps of chest hair peeping out between the buttons like baby birds. In the background, Josie could hear a crowd cheering. Josie hoped the cheers were for the TV team, not Harry's eating capacity.

"This is a seasonal job and it has to be done fast," Harry said. "I need you to mystery-shop two Christmas store franchises this weekend."

"Which ones?" Josie asked cautiously. She was sure she'd have to doom Doreen's enterprise.

"Elsie's Elf House," Harry said.

Josie breathed a sigh of relief. "No problem-o," she said, sounding like Amelia.

"And that ditz with the dirty ornaments. I can't think of the store name. Wait a minute, let me look it up."

There was a hollow clattering sound, as if Harry had dropped a large bone, followed by the rustle of paper. Josie's heart pounded while he searched. Please don't let it be Doreen, she prayed.

"Here it is," Harry said. "Naughty or Nice. The franchisers want to know just how naughty the store is. It could be in violation of their agreement. They may have to shut down the store if it's offending the Christian community."

"I can't mystery-shop that store," Josie said. "I know Doreen."

"How well?" Harry said. "You neighbors? Eat over at her house three nights a week? Are you godmother to her kids? Is she a relative?" His questions were punctuated with smacking sounds and an ugly bone crack.

"No, nothing like that," Josie said. "I've never been inside her house."

"Then you're okay."

"No, I'm not," Josie said. "My boyfriend used to date her."

"He still going out with her?" Harry said.

"No. But they have a kid."

"I don't see what the problem is," Harry said. "In this town lots of people know each other."

"Harry, I can't do that assignment," Josie said. "It's a conflict of interest."

"I'll rule on conflicts. I don't see one."

"But—" Josie said.

"Butt is right. Get your cute little butt over there this weekend if you want to keep your job. I'll fax you the questionnaire."

"Harry, I don't think—"

"You're not paid to think," Harry said. "That's my job. You asked for extra hours, so I gave them to you. For some reason, headquarters likes you. But if you're not available, there are other mystery shoppers looking for work during the holidays, even members of my own family."

That was a dig at Josie. She'd reported a sales clerk for rude behavior at a store she'd mystery-shopped. The clerk was fired. She was also Harry's niece. Rudeness ran in the family.

"My niece is working at Wal-Mart these days, no thanks to you." Josie heard a chomp and a distant cheer as her awful boss slammed down the phone.

My cute little butt, indeed, she thought. If I'd had my tape recorder on, I'd sue his double-wide rear and retire.

She giggled at the idea of his haughty niece working at a humble Wal-Mart. She wondered how long this retail mismatch would last.

Josie was not about to shop alone at Doreen's store. She needed a witness. Her best friend, Alyce, didn't like phone calls when her husband was at home. Saturday and Sunday were Alyce's family time. But this was a shopping emergency. Josie dialed Alyce's number.

"What's wrong, Josie?" Alyce asked. "Why are you calling on a Saturday?"

"Harry's making me shop Doreen's store. She's Mike's ex."

"That rat," Alyce said. "I mean Harry, not Mike."

"I'll lose my job if I don't go," Josie said. "For this assignment, I want a witness. It doesn't take a crystal ball to know that store probably won't pass."

"I can't do it today," Alyce said. "How about tomorrow if I can find a sitter? I'll drive to your house about one o'clock."

"Fine with me," Josie said. "We can go for tea at the Kerry Cottage. They have Irish soda bread. My treat."

"Thanks," Alyce said. "But I've been baking all day. I don't need more temptation. If I can't get a sitter, I'll call. Otherwise, I'll see you tomorrow."

For once, Josie was relieved when Mike didn't call. She couldn't tell him she was mystery-shopping Doreen's store. He'd know it would never survive a professional evaluation.

Josie was going to send back the pink hoodie Nate gave Amelia. Her daughter was not wearing clothes bought with drug money. She found the precious hoodie tossed on Amelia's unmade bed. Josie carefully packed it away in her own closet, along with the new cell phone.

She heard a rattling sound on the windows. The

promised sleet storm had started. The sky was the color of old iron.

Amelia came downstairs an hour later with a plate of warm brownies sprinkled with powdered sugar. "Have one, Mom," she said.

Josie bit into the brownie and said, "Yum. Nice and moist. You have your grandmother's gift for cooking."

Josie reached for a second brownie, but Amelia pulled the plate away. "That's all," she said. "I'm saving the rest for Daddy."

Daddy, Josie thought resentfully. Never mind that I fed and clothed you for nine years. Now it's Daddy. Josie smothered her jealousy. Besides, she didn't need the calories.

"Have you seen my hoodie?" Amelia asked.

"I've put it away," Josie said.

"Where?" Amelia asked.

"Where I can send it back," Josie said.

Amelia turned purple with fury. "You can't do that," she said. "It's mine."

"Your father didn't ask my permission to give you that hoodie," Josie said.

"He doesn't have to get your permission. He's my father." Tears leaked out of Amelia's eyes. Amelia's fists were clenched and her jaw had that stubborn bulldog look she got from her grandmother. "You're just jealous because Daddy has money and you don't."

Her words were a knife in Josie's heart. Was she jealous? Maybe. A little. Okay, a lot. "Amelia, I know you're happy that your father came to see you, but he doesn't get his money from a regular job. He sells drugs. The same drugs that killed your friend Zoe's sister."

"Liar," Amelia said. "He'd never do that. He's not dead and you said he was. Now you say he's a drug dealer. Daddy would never sell drugs."

"He has. He does. Until he gets an honest job, you can't have his money."

"Liar! Liar! You're just saying that because you're jealous." Amelia marched into her room and slammed her door so hard the house shook. Josie followed her down the hall. Somehow, she'd lost all moral advantage over her daughter. Josie was a liar and Amelia knew it. Worse, Amelia rubbed Josie's nose in her lies.

"Open this door, young lady."

"Go to hell," Amelia cried. "That's where liars go."

Josie rattled the handle. The door wasn't locked. She threw open the door so hard, the handle buried itself in the plaster wall behind the door.

Amelia sat cross-legged on her bed, biting her lips to keep from smiling.

"Say something," Josie said.

"You broke the wall, Mom," Amelia said.

Josie walked out of the room, closing the door behind her. She was too afraid to answer.

Chapter 10

Each year, Alyce waited for Christmas with a child's delight. She decked the halls, the walls, and the lawn. She unpacked her mother's antique ornaments and brought out her own Christmas china. Mistletoe hung in the doorway. Artfully arranged holly, pinecones, and poinsettias brightened tables. Swags of evergreen draped the stair railings.

Alyce had every kind of ornament—except Doreen's pornaments.

Alyce's house smelled like cinnamon for the entire month of December. She made cookies, fruitcakes, and pomander balls out of cloves, oranges, and green velvet ribbons. Christmas morning was a feast, with cranberry bread, spicy gingerbread logs, fruit stollen, shirred eggs with red and green peppers, and a spiral-sliced ham. Dinner included a crown roast and a flaming plum pudding. Just hearing about Alyce's holiday plans made Josie feel like she'd walked into a *Gourmet* magazine spread.

"I love Christmas stores," Alyce said. "Maybe I can pick up some new ornaments."

"Where are you going to hang them?" Josie asked. "Every inch of your tree is covered already."

"There's always room for new ornaments," Alyce said. "Justin is at the grab-and-chew stage. I can't put any of my mother's handblown glass ornaments on the lower branches where he can reach them. Oh, this place is so cute."

Elsie's Elf House looked like a fairy-tale cottage, right down to the thatched roof.

"Are those real kittens peeking out of that thatch?" Alyce asked.

Josie stood on tiptoe for a closer look. "They're plastic, just like the thatch," she said.

Josie opened the holly-wreathed door. Bells jingled merrily, and they could hear the tinkling wind-chime sound of hundreds of ornaments twirling on their gold ribbons. "White Christmas" oozed out of the speakers, sweet and smooth as eggnog.

"This is lovely," Alyce said, her eyes as wide as a child's on Christmas Day. Even in the cramped store, Alyce managed her odd floaty walk. Her silky white-blond hair shone in the soft light.

She browsed the ornaments and bought simple stuffed cotton ones for the lower branches of her tree. They were pretty, practical, and not destined for heirloom status. Justin could grab and chew them all he wanted.

Josie asked the clerk to take down six different ornaments from the displays, as her mystery-shopping instructions required, before she bought an iridescent glass ball. Josie planned to keep that one.

The red-haired clerk was a tiny woman wearing a green elf suit. Even in a green belled cap, she was barely five feet tall. Josie wondered if the faux elf was Elsie herself or some poor saleswoman forced to wear a silly costume.

The things we do for money, she thought.

"Oh, look," Alyce said. "They have a crème brûlée torch on sale. Nice price, too." Alyce was addicted to arcane kitchen instruments, including citrus trumpets and herb mills.

"You should buy it," Josie said.

"I've sworn off single-use gadgets," Alyce said. "I can heat the topping under the broiler just fine."

But she looked longingly at the tiny blowtorch. Josie vowed she'd go back and buy it for Alyce for Christmas, along with the butane inserts.

"That was fun," Alyce said as they left Elsie's.

"Brace yourself for the next shop," Josie said. "Naughty or Nice is going to be nasty."

"Oh, Josie, how can anyone be unhappy at Christmastime?"

"You haven't met Doreen," Josie said. "That woman can start a fight in an empty room. Look at the picketers she's stirred up."

The two women threaded their way through the church picketers circling the steep-roofed building with the wooden icicles and the winking Mrs. Claus. Either the protest had grown since the TV report or more people were available on Sundays. Women in sensible wool coats and knit hats carried condemnatory signs and chanted "Naughty or Nice makes Baby Jesus cry." "Naughty or Nice is nasty."

"Stay away from this godless cesspool, women! Your souls are in peril," commanded a skinny scarecrow with bristling black eyebrows. The preacher who'd been on TV Friday night looked even scarier in person.

Alyce ducked her head and tried to make herself invisible. Josie lifted her chin and brushed past the vitriolic man of God.

Bells jingled and they were inside the store. Josie's heart sank when she saw Heather behind the counter. The last hope that Naughty or Nice could survive a mystery-shopping test was dead. Heather was alone in the store, with the chanting churchgoers circling outside. What kind of mother left her daughter in the middle of an ugly controversy?

A bad one, Josie decided.

Alyce examined a shelf of porcelain figurines. Josie pasted a smile on her face and said, "Hi, Heather. I'm Josie, remember?"

"Yeah. You're fucking my father," Heather said.

Alyce nearly dropped a china Christmas angel.

"Is your mother here?" Josie asked.

"No, she left me by myself to sell to the pervs," Heather said.

Josie almost felt sorry for the unpleasant girl. "Is the adult section still hidden behind the DEFINITELY NAUGHTY banner?"

"You get off on that porn crap?" Heather said. Her scorn could have melted the Christmas candles.

Josie moved the banner aside and signaled to Alyce, who slipped into the nook and stood face-to-face with the South Pole elf.

"Eeuww," Alyce whispered. "That's disgusting."

"I have to buy one," Josie said. "It's my job."

"Better you than me," Alyce said. "You're right. This store is nasty." She stepped away from the South Pole ornament as if it were a tiny demon. Alongside it were curvy topless female figurines wearing Santa hats, fishnet stockings, red heels, and tiny, strategic holly leaves. A hand-lettered sign said, SANTA'S HO, HO, HOS.

Josie put the South Pole ornament by the register. "I'll take this and a slice of warm gingerbread," she said.

"It's your money," Heather said, and shrugged.

"Alyce, would you like some gingerbread or cider?" Josie asked.

"No, thanks," Alyce said.

Heather plopped a greasy hunk of cake on a paper plate. Josie bit into the gingerbread. It was stale.

Alyce was staring at Josie's cake as if she'd never seen gingerbread before. "Josie, what's that in your cake?"

"A chopped raisin," Heather said.

"Raisins don't have legs," Alyce said.

Josie nearly gagged. Half a cockroach was hanging out of her cake. She threw a paper napkin over it and said, "I'd better go. Please ring up the ornament."

"Does Mike know you buy that shit?" Heather asked. She didn't apologize for the roach.

"Ring it up, please," Josie said.

"Twenty dollars," Heather said.

Josie realized the girl had charged her for the insect-infested cake and the ornament.

Heather threw the ornament in a bag, not bothering to wrap it in tissue. The girl started to toss the cake slice in the trash, but Josie grabbed it. "I'll take that with me," she said.

"Why?" Heather said.

"I paid for it," Josie said.

The two shoppers tottered out of the store. Josie breathed in the fresh, clean air and prayed she wouldn't throw up in the parking lot. Once inside her car, Josie tucked the cake in a zip-top bag.

"I don't think I'll ever eat gingerbread again," Alyce said. "If I do, it won't have raisins in it."

"That was awful," Josie said. "I nearly barfed in the store."

"Why are you keeping it?" Alyce asked.

"It's exhibit A if Doreen raises a fuss. And trust me, she will."

"Should we call the health department?" Alyce asked.

"No," Josie said. "This place will be closed before Christmas. Between the picketers, Doreen, and that surly child behind the counter, there won't be any customers."

"Josie, I'm no prude, but those ornaments are disgusting. How can anyone defile Christmas? It's a children's holiday."

"You missed the edible crotchless panties marked A SPECIAL TREAT FOR SANTA. The panties were peppermint flavored. The spearmint of Christmas."

"No, please," Alyce said. "No jokes. This is sad."

"I agree," Josie said, "and I'm burned out on Christmas. I've looked at holiday decorations since Labor Day. I'll have to give this store low marks and take the flack when it closes."

"You're joking. People will cheer when that store closes."

"Not Mike," Josie said. "He's an investor."

"Your Mike? The plumber? He's too classy for that," Alyce said.

"He sank twenty thousand dollars into that loser to help Doreen."

"Do you really think it will hurt your relationship?" Alyce asked.

"Mike will try to take the high road. But he invested in this store so Doreen could make enough to send their daughter to college. When it closes, it will hurt him—and us."

"Can you tell Mike now and prepare him?"

"I'm not allowed to discuss assignments with people who have a financial interest in them. I tried to get out of mystery-shopping this store, but Harry the Horrible said I had to do it—or lose my job."

"Mike will understand," Alyce said.

"I hope so," Josie said, but she'd never felt more hopeless. "I need a favor from your husband, Jake."

"Anything," Alyce said. "He owes you. We both owe you."

"Nate reappeared suddenly. My ex. He wants custody of Amelia, and I need an expert in international family law."

"Jake will find you someone, Josie, but your problem has no easy answer. International law is tricky when it comes to child custody. Nate could just take Amelia and run."

"I know that. He has enough money to disappear anywhere. I can't believe I loved him," Josie said. "What was wrong with me?"

"Nothing. You were twenty years old. We all fall for at least one jerk. If we're lucky, we don't marry him. You made the right decision to break up with Nate."

"But now he's back. Too bad I didn't get the custody issue worked out first, while he was in jail." Josie couldn't believe she was having this surreal conversation.

"Josie, he could still have come back and stolen Amelia, no matter what he signed. At least this way you have some warning. If you're really worried, bring Amelia and stay with us until Nate goes home to Canada."

"If he goes home. Alyce, he's changed so much, it's like he's another man. The only things I recognize from the Nate I knew are his recklessness and his stubbornness. I don't know when he became an alcoholic. He wasn't a drunk when I dated him."

"People change," Alyce said. "Adults rarely change for the better. I had a crush on a guy in high school that was so bad I thought I'd die of love. He was the funniest boy in our class. A friend married him and then divorced him three years later. She got tired of his jokes and his irresponsibility. Whenever she suggested he grow up and go to work, he ran home to his mother, who spoiled him. He was still the same boy I loved, but my priorities changed. Yours did, too."

Josie was carefully navigating the traffic lanes around the construction at the turnoff for her house. "I can't believe Highway 40 is going to be closed for another year."

"The work is long overdue," Alyce said. "It will be good for the city. People who work downtown will move into those wonderful new loft apartments along Washington Avenue."

"I know. I shouldn't whine," Josie said. "But St. Louis has always been such a convenient city."

"Josie, it still is. What St. Louisans call 'traffic' makes people in other cities laugh."

"But I got used to the easy living." Josie pulled her car into Phelan Street. Her two-family flat looked handsome in the fall light. Her mother had planted ornamental purple cabbages in the garden and set pots of yellow mums on the porch.

"Mom better take in those mums tonight," Josie said. "There's supposed to be serious ice by morning."

Mrs. Mueller was raking the last fall leaves on her lawn. She wore a red jacket and an old-fashioned housedress. Her hair was so firmly sprayed into place, it could have repelled bullets.

"Oh, heck," Josie said. "Look at that red car."

"What's wrong with it?"

"I think that's Nate's rental. I bet Amelia let him in against my orders—while her grandmother was at church."

"You shouldn't confront him alone, Josie. Not if he's drinking. I'll go in with you," Alyce said.

The two women marched up the front walk in battle mode. Mrs. Mueller leaned on her rake, watching them. The old bat knows there's going to be trouble, Josie thought. She can smell it.

Josie opened her door and found Nate lounging on

her couch, talking to Amelia. Josie's daughter had a big, happy smile. It died when she saw her mother.

"We're catching up," Nate announced.

Josie glared at her daughter.

"I want to take my little girl skating at Steinberg Rink in Forest Park," Nate said. "It's a St. Louis tradition."

"Please, Mom," Amelia said.

Josie was reluctant to let her daughter go out with Nate, especially since he drank.

"Go to your room, Amelia, while I talk to your father."

"All right," Amelia said, dragging the words out. She flounced out of the room and slammed her door. Josie wondered if she'd have to listen to slamming doors until her child went off to college.

Nate patted the seat cushion beside him. "Sit down, Josie, and let's talk."

"I can't," Josie said. "I have to work. I want to talk to you, Nate, but you can't keep dropping in like this. Please give me a call and we can make an appointment to discuss things."

"Our daughter is not a thing," Nate said loftily. Josie thought she caught a whiff of alcohol on his breath. Alyce stood uncomfortably by the door, looking like she wanted to bolt outside.

Nate give Alyce a flirtatious smile. She gave him a stony look. "Is this the famous Alyce my little girl was telling me about? You've got a pretty face, darlin', but you need to do something about that fat ass."

Josie boiled with fury. How dare he insult a friend in her home? And talk about fat asses—Nate had a beer gut and a wide bottom.

"I'll take care of it now," Josie said. "Out!"

Nate looked around the room, as if she were ordering someone else to leave.

"I mean you, Nate," Josie said.

"But I only said the truth. Your friend does have a pretty face but a fat—"

Before Nate could finish, Josie grabbed him by his jacket collar and nearly ripped it off. He stood up, looking confused. Josie pushed him hard toward the door, using both hands.

"Out," she said. "Out of my home this minute."

She threw open the door and shoved Nate outside. He stumbled and fell on the porch, landing on all fours.

"I'll get my daughter," Nate cried, slowly standing up. "If it's the last thing I do."

"Keep this up and it will be," Josie shouted through the locked door.

Mrs. Mueller stared openmouthed at the spectacle. This show was better than she'd hoped. Josie's mother would be mortified that her daughter was once more the topic of neighborhood gossip.

Josie slammed her door and locked it.

"Josie, honey, let me in," Nate said. "I'm sorry."

"You're damn right you're sorry," Josie shouted through the door. "You're going to be sorrier. Go away or I'll call the cops."

Nate went quietly. Soon Josie heard the sound of a car starting. Nate drove off in a squeal of tires.

"Amazing how quickly you can get rid of a fat ass," Josie said.

Chapter 11

Nate's red rental car was still squealing down the street when Josie's phone rang. Alyce whispered, "You're busy. I'd better go."

Josie waved good-bye as Alyce let herself out the front door, then turned her attention to the phone.

"Ms. Marcus?" a woman asked. "I'm calling about your Visa account."

"On a Sunday?" Josie said, and swallowed hard.

"There's been some unusual activity and we wanted to alert you. You are more than two thousand dollars over your credit limit."

"I'm what?" Josie shrieked into the phone. "I haven't charged anything recently."

"You didn't order a new RAZR phone, a laptop, and a sixty-dollar hooded sweatshirt?"

"No!" Josie said. "When did this happen?"

"About an hour ago," the company said. "The purchases were made from your home phone. Are you in possession of your card?"

"Yes. No. Let me check."

Josie usually left her credit card on her dresser when she went mystery-shopping. She ran into her bedroom and saw the card still sitting there. If I fingerprint this card, Josie wondered, whose prints will I find on it?

"I have the card, but I didn't make those purchases," Josie said. "I wasn't home at the time."

"Someone may have obtained your account information illegally. Would you like us to prosecute?"

"No," Josie said. "I'll handle the situation."

Josie marched to Amelia's bedroom and opened the door, careful not to slam it into the broken plaster wall. She'd have to fix that hole later.

Amelia was sitting on her bed, sulking. Her closet door was open, and Josie could see her daughter's childhood games stacked on the upper shelves—Chutes and Ladders, Go Fish, and Candy Land. How many games of Candy Land had they played at the kitchen table? The sweet days of the Candy Cane Forest and Gum Drop Mountain were gone. Now Josie was mired in a molasses swamp, with no way out.

"Amelia Marcus, did you order a new laptop, a hoodie, and a RAZR cell phone and charge them to my credit card?" Josie asked.

"No!" Amelia's eyes shifted left, then right. Josie could watch the struggle on her daughter's face. Amelia would never make a good poker player. The kid practically had a flashing sign on her forehead that said, "I'm lying!"

"Then your father did," Josie said. "The calls were made from this phone with my card, so it had to be one of you. If it's him, I'll have him arrested for theft."

Amelia took a deep breath. "Daddy didn't do anything," she said. "But he wanted me to have the gifts you're returning. He said he'd give me money for them before the credit-card bill arrived."

"No, he won't," Josie said. "They're being returned the minute they arrive at this house."

"You can't. They're mine," Amelia said.

"They're mine," Josie said. "Unless you want to pay for them with your own money."

Amelia had three hundred and six dollars squirreled away from gifts from her grandmother—more money than Josie had managed to save this year. But the kid would never touch her precious cash stash, not even for the coveted hoodie.

Amelia's face took on the same stubborn look her grandmother Jane had perfected. "I'm going to run away and live with my father," Amelia said. "You don't want me here. You just want Mike."

Josie wondered if aliens had taken control of her daughter. Amelia had always been well-behaved—before her father showed up. Now she didn't recognize her own child.

"You're grounded for a month, young lady," Josie said. "No visits to Emma, no computer except for school assignments, no IM-ing your friends. On the way to school, I choose the radio station."

Josie wasn't sure that last punishment would have any effect. The Barrington girls talked about what they heard on The Point on the way to school, but they got their music these days from their computers. In high school, Josie's station had been The River, and she'd listened to Pearl Jam, Nirvana, and that great St. Louis band, the Urge. But she suspected the Internet had ruined radio's influence.

Amelia reacted as if she'd been severely punished. "You're mean. You're mean and a liar and I hate you. I want to live with Daddy and never see you again."

Welcome to tween hell, Josie thought. It's going to be a rough ride from now on.

It took all Josie's strength to keep from saying something hurtful. She knew what it was like to want something all the other kids had. Josie would have sold her young soul for a white fake fur coat, but Jane couldn't afford it and Josie had blown her spare cash on magazines. Now, with some years' distance, Josie knew she would have looked like a polar bear in that furry monstrosity. She was too short for that style. But when she was ten, Josie had yearned for the coat as much as Amelia wanted the pink hoodie.

Josie was grateful when she heard a knock on her front door. She peeked out the miniblinds, in case Nate had come back. Jane, in her pale lavender church coat, was on the doorstep, impatiently tapping one black heel.

Uh-oh, Josie thought. Trouble.

Josie opened the door and her mother barged in. "What's going on here?" Jane demanded. "I could hear you shouting halfway down the street. Do you have to let the whole neighborhood know our family business?"

"I'm disciplining my daughter," Josie said.

"Then do it a little more quietly," Jane said. "I'd like to take a nap."

"You'll have lots of peace and quiet when Nate steals your granddaughter and takes her to Canada," Josie said. "He was here while you were at church."

"I can't be everywhere at once," Jane said. "I'll go see Mrs. Mueller right now. We'll work out a schedule to protect Amelia." Though they had been friends for years, Jane always called the woman Mrs. Mueller.

Jane's back was rigid with anger as she tip-tapped her way to Mrs. M's house. If anyone would watch Josie's home, it would be Mrs. Mueller.

Josie shut the door and sighed. Could her life get any worse?

There was a pinging sound on the windows. The promised winter storm was growing worse. The sky was the color of old sheet metal and the temperature felt like it was dropping. The cars were still making it up the steep hill on Josie's street without fishtailing. That was a good sign. But she'd better get moving, or the roads would be impassable.

Josie shivered and turned up the heat, then went to her room to write the mystery-shopping report for Harry the Horrible. Her heart felt like lead. She knew this report would probably destroy her romance with Mike.

She gave Elsie's Elf House a nearly perfect score for the quality of its service, merchandise presentation, and friendly staff.

Naughty or Nice got the lowest marks possible. Josie also noted that the store was not selling franchise-approved merchandise. She gingerly examined the South Pole elf she'd bought that morning, as if it were diseased. It was an ordinary china elf ornament, the kind sold at craft stores. The tumescent South Pole had been glued on and the elf had been hand-painted. It was a crude job, in more ways than one. Josie wondered if Doreen made the thing in her home. So much for Christmas crafts.

Josie finished her report and faxed it off to Harry, wishing she could warn Mike. The fun would hit the fan tomorrow.

Outside, the ice was pinging harder on the porch and sidewalk, as if someone were firing a BB gun. Josie saw snowflakes in the mix, but they hadn't started to stick yet. Judging by the trail of footsteps on the sidewalk, Jane was back home again. Josie called her.

"Mom, I have to run an errand. Can I pick you up anything at the store?"

"Soup would be nice," her mother said. "This weather calls for chicken noodle soup."

Josie thought it called for a roaring fire, mulled wine, and a hot man.

"Do you want me to watch Amelia?" Jane said. "I can sleep on your couch as well as mine."

"I'll leave the phone by the couch if you need to call 911."

"Never mind. I have my pepper spray," Jane said. "That man comes near my granddaughter, and he'll regret it. I don't know why you didn't get Nate to sign away his rights ten years ago."

"He was in jail, Mom."

"Exactly the time a man wouldn't want to worry about supporting a new baby. You had a golden opportunity and you lost it." Josie heard the rest of her mother's unspoken sentence: "the way you lost so many others."

Jane knocked at her front door, wearing a red sweater with leaping brown reindeer. Josie waited until her mother was comfortably settled in with magazines, hot tea, and the TV clicker before she left.

"I have my cell on if there's a problem," Josie said.

"There will be no problems I can't handle," Jane said.

The sleet was quickly turning into snow. Josie picked her way gingerly to the car and drove slowly down the slippery streets. The supermarket was in the usual pre-storm panic, with frantic shoppers crashing carts into one another and pushing their way into checkout lines. Fights broke out as irritated shoppers discovered fourteen or fifteen items lurking in baskets in the "twelve items or less" line.

Josie would never understand why St. Louisans rushed to the store at the first hint of a snowstorm and stripped the shelves of milk, bread, and toilet paper. Okay, milk and bread made sense. But toilet paper? What were they expecting, a citywide attack of diarrhea?

Josie grabbed the last loaf of sandwich bread in the bakery section, picked up a gallon of milk, then stood in line at the deli department for a pound of sliced ham and chicken soup for her mother. She got through the checkout line in less than ten minutes and wheeled her cart to her car.

The snow was falling faster, nearly doubling in intensity in the half hour she'd been in the store. Josie scraped her windshield, cracking the sleet glaze and getting ice crystals inside her gloves. By the time the car was loaded and started, Josie was afraid she'd have to scrape the windshield again.

It was only three o'clock, but the sky was so dark, Josie turned on her headlights. Her small car skidded in the snow. Impatient drivers passed her, going too fast for the road conditions. Josie needed twice as much time to crawl home around the multiple fender benders.

By the time she pulled in front of her flat, the snow was serious. Her lawn was completely covered in a thick white coat. Mrs. Mueller was shoveling off her sidewalk and spreading rock salt on the concrete.

Stan the Man Next Door was shoveling Josie's sidewalk. Stan was hidden inside a hideous down parka that made him look like the Unabomber. Stan put down his shovel and helped Josie carry in her sacks of groceries. He even wiped his feet before stepping inside. His nose was red from the cold.

"Want to come in for some hot cocoa?" Josie asked.

"Thanks," Stan said, "but I'm having dinner at Mom's and I don't want to be late." He went back outside to finish her sidewalk.

Stan was kind, loyal, and hopelessly dull. He'd rather have dinner with his mother than cocoa with the woman he worshiped from afar. Josie wished she could love Stan back, but she seemed fatally attracted to men with serious flaws. Stan didn't make her heart beat faster the way Mike did.

She had a date with Mike tonight. Josie looked forward to spending the night at Mike's place and possibly getting snowed in with him. Jane had promised to sleep over and watch Amelia if that happened.

"Let it snow, let it snow, let it snow," Josie sang, as she unpacked the groceries.

Jane was huddled under a knit throw on the couch, watching television.

"You're going to get your wish," Jane said. "The TV says they've closed the airport already. It's early in the winter for a storm this bad. We're supposed to have more than a foot of snow by nightfall."

Josie added another sweater for warmth. She didn't want to turn up the thermostat on the ancient furnace. The heating bills were already outrageous.

The snow kept piling up as night approached. Josie figured there was nearly twelve inches on the ground already. She checked the clock. Another hour before she left for Mike's. She showered, shaved her legs, put on her best underwear and her new black wool pants.

She was deciding between the pink or the beige sweater when her phone rang.

"Josie?" Mike said. "I'm really sorry, but I can't see you tonight. There's trouble at Doreen's store, and Heather is involved."

"What's wrong?" Josie said, trying to sound concerned and hide her disappointment at the same time.

"Everything," Mike said. "Doreen left Heather alone at the store all day, and those nuts were still picketing outside. Plus, the place has cockroaches, and one of them wound up in the gingerbread."

Josie had to stop herself from saying *I know.*

"Maybe she needs to keep the kitchen cleaner," Josie said.

"It's not Doreen's fault," Mike said. "Elsie gave her the roaches."

"Elsie?"

"The Elf House lady. Heather says she saw Elsie turn a box of the bugs loose near the back door. Doreen thinks Elsie is trying to ruin her business."

Doreen's doing a terrific job of that all by herself, Josie wanted to say.

"Doreen also found mice in the storage room. Mice come inside when the weather turns cold, but Doreen doesn't believe that. She says her rival Elsie introduced the critters to her store."

"How?"

"There's a gap between the door and the threshold. Mice can squeeze through a space that small. But Doreen swears Elsie let the mice and roaches in that way. Doreen's business has been dropping off."

Dropping off? Josie thought. She never had any.

"Doreen is worried she may lose her franchise. The picketers won't go away, and the more TV time they get, the longer they stay and the louder they chant."

"I'm sorry, Mike." Josie tried to sound sincere.

"But that isn't the worst," Mike said. "When the storm intensified, some snow and ice slid off the roof and seriously injured a picketer. A church lady was nearly killed. She's in intensive care."

"Omigod," Josie said. "The snow is that heavy?"

"Well, it had some help. The police are talking attempted murder. The place is crawling with cops and they want to interview Heather, and I have to stay here for her."

"Of course you do," Josie said. "She's not a suspect, is she?"

"No," Mike said. "But the police did find the snow on the roof had been deliberately loosened, probably by a shovel. There are footprints in the vicinity. They're interviewing all the neighbors and they have a witness who saw something."

"They do?" Josie said.

"Yep. An old woman says she saw Santa Claus up on the roof loosening the snow. The cops are laughing their asses off."

Ho, ho, ho, Josie thought.

Chapter 12

"There's a suspect in the attempted murder at the Naughty or Nice Christmas shop," the TV anchor said, staring earnestly into the camera. The show cut to a commercial for tile cleaner, leaving the audience waiting.

Jane was dozing. Josie rushed over to the TV and turned up the volume, waking her mother.

"What are you doing?" Jane was huddled under Josie's knitted throw on the couch.

"That's the shop run by Mike's ex," Josie said. "I need to see this story."

Sixty seconds later, the anchor was back. He could barely keep from laughing. "Naughty or Nice is the store that is being picketed for selling allegedly obscene ornaments," he said.

The television showed picketers chanting and circling the shop, then flashed on the pornaments.

Josie groaned. Poor Mike. He was going to lose his investment, thanks to murder and malice at Christmas.

"Mildred Sprike, a fifty-eight-year-old church picketer, was seriously injured when snow and ice slid from the roof of the Naughty or Nice shop," the anchor said. His lips twitched. "Mrs. Sprike, mother of four, was picketing the store when a shelf of ice came loose and hit her on the head. Mrs. Sprike was taken by ambulance to Barnes-Jewish Hospital and remains in critical condition.

"A police spokesperson said Mrs. Sprike's injuries were no accident. The ice was deliberately loosened from the roof. In an exclusive interview with Channel Seven, a neighbor says she saw the culprit. Mrs. Edna Pickerel, age ninety-eight, said she witnessed the incident from her kitchen window."

An elderly woman in a fluffy blue sweater and flyaway white hair was interviewed in her kitchen. Josie estimated the Magic Chef stove was at least half a century old. The woman's head trembled and her rheumy eyes peered through thick glasses.

"It was Sanny Claus," the woman said. "Sanny Claus got up on that nasty shop's roof with a snow shovel and pushed the snow down on that church lady's head. Nearly killed her. I saw him do it."

"You really saw Santa?" the reporter asked. Josie could hear the smirk in his voice.

"I saw what I saw and Sanny Claus was on that roof," the woman insisted. "He wore a red suit, a long white beard, and black boots."

A graphic of Santa in a WANTED poster flashed on the screen.

The news anchor was giggling so hard he could barely talk. "Police have declined to make an arrest in the case," he said. "If they check the malls, they'll find Santa has an alibi for this afternoon." He ended with a snorting giggle.

"A woman is in intensive care at Christmas and that idiot thinks it's funny?" Jane asked. "Why is Channel Seven interviewing that poor old soul? You know she's senile, and so do they. No respect for her age. I swear, that station gets worse and worse."

But she didn't change the channel.

Josie settled into her big chair with hot cocoa to watch the weather report. She drifted off as a cold front was crossing Nebraska.

Josie woke up around eleven p.m., feeling more tired than she had before her nap. Her cocoa cup was in the sink, and her mother was gone, along with the chicken soup. The knit throw was folded neatly on the couch. Josie checked on Amelia. Her daughter was sleeping in her flannel pajamas. Thank you, Mom, Josie thought, as she tucked her daughter in for the night. She showered and headed for her own bed.

Monday morning dawned crisp and cold. The snow on the lawn was like a down comforter. The neighborhood streets were slushy, but open. Cars moved fearlessly down the road, most going a little too fast for the icy conditions.

At breakfast Amelia listened intently to the radio's list of school closings. She was disappointed when Barrington School wasn't called.

"Parkway District is closed," Amelia said. "We should be, too."

"It's seven thirty," Josie said. "If the school was closed, we'd know by now."

"Can't you call, just to make sure?" Amelia begged.

"No one answers the office phone until eight," Josie said. But she made the call and got a taped message: "The Barrington School for Boys and Girls will be open Monday. This is not a snow day. Unexcused absences will not be accepted."

"Sorry," Josie said. "It's school for you."

On the way, Amelia flipped the radio from station to station, still hoping her school was closing. Josie didn't remind her that she'd been barred from the radio controls. As the Honda pulled into the Barrington driveway, Amelia's last hope died. She spotted her friend Emma and waved, barely waiting for Josie to stop the car before Amelia hopped out, dragging her backpack. Josie was relieved to see her daughter go. She didn't want to face her today and get into another argument about Nate.

Josie hurried home on the traffic-clogged streets. She dodged an SUV that was going too fast. The big vehicle spun out on a patch of ice, narrowly missed Josie's Honda, and bashed into a tree. Josie checked to make sure the driver was unhurt. He waved her on as he called 911 on his cell phone.

She was relieved to park in front of her house. She noticed it was the only home on the block with no holiday decorations. Josie's pristine yard seemed cheerless and bare.

Inside, Josie made coffee and checked her e-mail. Her boss, Harry, acknowledged that he'd received her mystery-shopper report, but made no other comment. He also had no work for her. It was time to drag out the outdoor Christmas decorations, a task Josie was in no mood for. Her trips to the mall had soured her Christmas spirit.

Might as well wallow in my bad mood, Josie thought. She put on the Dixie Chicks' "Goodbye Earl" video and cranked up the sound, something she did only when she was alone. She sang along with the story of the wife basher who was done in by poisoned black-eyed peas. If only my problem could be solved as easily, Josie thought. She imagined a dead Nate rolled up in a tarp like a burrito.

Josie brushed the picture from her mind and hauled Jane's pride and joy out of the basement—a five-foot-tall toy soldier in red, white and yellow twinkle lights.

Josie had bought the outdoor decoration cheap at an after-Christmas sale and regretted it ever since. But Jane and Amelia insisted it belonged on their lawn, guarding the twinkle-light reindeer, the snowman, and the nearly life-size Nativity scene.

The garish display embarrassed Josie, but she told herself she was being a snob. She stripped the protective plastic wrap off the soldier in the kitchen and dragged him through the living room.

"Get out here, you worthless bitch!" a voice screamed. For a moment Josie thought she was back in the Dixie Chicks' trailer park.

"You ruined my store, you bitch," the woman cried, and Josie realized that was no video. It was her life.

A furious Doreen was on the porch, clutching a fistful of paper that was probably Josie's mystery-shopper report. Josie peeked out the blinds. Doreen was a fearsome sight in dead black, her hair flying every which way. She pounded on Josie's door until her sallow skin turned red.

"Get out here, so I can tear the hair out of your slutty head," Doreen screamed.

Where did Doreen get that report? Josie wondered. Her name wasn't on it. But Harry wouldn't hesitate to sell out his staff. He'd done it before. Thanks to Heather, Doreen knew where Josie lived. Now Mike's ex was on Josie's doorstep, demanding retribution.

Might as well face her—but not without a weapon. Josie hung on to her giant toy soldier as a flimsy shield. She flung open her front door. Doreen nearly smashed Josie's face with her fist.

"How dare you make up those lies?" Doreen shrieked. "You said there were roaches in my gingerbread. It's not true."

"It is true," Josie said. "I have the cake and the roach."

"You planted that roach in my gingerbread. Heather saw you."

"No, she didn't," Josie said. "I brought a witness when I mystery-shopped your store. She saw me bite into that roach. Your daughter charged me for insect-infested cake. I should report you to the health department."

"It's not me," Doreen said. "I don't have roaches. Elsie and her damned Elf House planted them in my store. She's out to ruin my business."

"She doesn't need to," Josie said. "You're doing a fine job all by yourself."

Josie looked up and saw Mrs. Mueller watching the show. She wished the older woman would help break up the fight, but she stood there like a lawn ornament.

Suddenly a broom came out of nowhere. A furious Jane whacked the witchy Doreen in the head.

"Don't you dare threaten my daughter," Jane said. "Get off my porch before I call the police. You and your juvenile delinquent Heather are both trouble. She was here the other night. She got drunk and threw beer bottles at my neighbor's fence. Drunk! Now you dare accuse Josie of lying? I'll tell everyone at the St. Philomena Sodality, and we'll boycott that nastiness you sell. Pornaments, indeed. They belong in a Hustler store, not in Maplewood. For shame! You're the mother of a young daughter. What kind of example are you?"

"Shut up, bitch," Doreen said.

"Don't you talk to my mother like that." Josie hit Doreen with the toy soldier. She heard a cracking noise, and hoped it was Doreen.

Doreen didn't move.

Jane brandished her broom. "Go on, get out of here. Out, before I sweep you away like the trash you are!" Jane thumped Doreen on the shoulders like a disobedient dog and shooed her out to her car.

"You'll be sorry, Josie Marcus, and so will that shitty plumber you date."

After Doreen started the engine and drove off, Josie hugged her mother.

"Thanks, Mom," she said. "You saved me."

Jane was fluffed up like an angry hen. "I can't believe that woman, selling filth in my neighborhood—and accusing you of lying. I had enough."

"I'm glad you did." Josie gave her mother another hug. Mrs. Mueller was barricaded in her house, probably telephoning the whole neighborhood with the latest Marcus disgrace.

"What have you done to my soldier?" Jane said.

Josie saw that his arm hung crooked and his shoulder was broken.

"I'm sorry, Mom," Josie said. "I'll get you a new one."

"He died in a good cause," Jane said.

For the rest of the day, Josie dragged out lawn ornaments and set them up in the front yard. She hung a pinecone wreath on the door and stockings on the fake fireplace. Then she went out to the car, retrieved the roach-infested cake, and put it in a plastic bag with a sign that said, POISON. DO NOT EAT.

She hoped Mike would call so they could go out tonight. Noon. No call. One o'clock, no call. Two o'clock passed without a word from Mike.

By the time she left to pick up Amelia at school, Mike still hadn't called. Was he mad at her because of that report? Well, she wasn't waiting around for her phone to ring, like a lovesick teenager. Josie turned on the outdoor lights so Amelia could see the full display on their lawn when she came home.

"Awesome," Amelia said, when they pulled up in front of the house. "We've got the brightest house on the block."

"Yes, we do," Josie said. She wished they didn't.

"There's the snowman, the giant candy cane, and the Nativity scene. But where's the toy soldier?" Amelia asked.

"He met with a little accident," Josie said.

"What happened?"

"He ran into Heather's mom. She tried to attack me."

"She's nutso-crazy," Amelia said.

"I'll find you another toy soldier," Josie said.

"Can we get a Christmas tree, Mom? A real one?"

"Do you really want to kill a tree for Christmas?" Josie asked.

"It's a sacrifice we should make," Amelia said.

Chapter 13

Josie crunched her way across the parking lot to Elsie's Elf House. She checked Naughty or Nice carefully, hoping she wouldn't see the awful Doreen peering out the windows. The last thing she needed was that crazy woman screaming at her.

Josie wanted a peaceful shopping moment before she picked up Amelia at school. She was going to buy Alyce's Christmas present. If that upset Doreen, too bad.

The picketers were still circling Doreen's store and chanting, despite the cold. Some carried the wounded woman's picture, with the slogan, NEARLY KILLED IN A CHRISTIAN CAUSE. Another said, MILDRED SPRIKE—CHRISTIAN MARTYR.

She's not dead yet, Josie thought. But the injured woman had a saintly look with her halo of light hair and high-necked blouse.

A sign in Elsie's window proclaimed: TRY OUR FAMOUS CHOCOLATE SNOWMAN—A SPECIAL YULETIDE TREAT.

The bells jingled merrily on Elsie's door. Josie breathed in the air, richly scented with pine and cinnamon.

"Get out of my way," said a woman. She rudely elbowed herself past Josie, hitting her arm with an empty plastic bottle.

"And Merry Christmas to you, too," Josie said.

It was only after the door slammed shut that Josie realized she'd been elbowed by Doreen.

The little woman in the elf hat was at Josie's side, looking concerned. "I'm terribly sorry," she said. "She's not a regular customer."

"I know. That's Doreen. She owns the shop next door," Josie said. "You're stuck with a real doozy for a neighbor."

The elf-hat woman sighed and said, "She's a very unhappy person. Do you know she came over here yesterday and accused me of letting roaches loose in her store? In front of my customers. Doreen screamed that I shoved the disgusting creatures under her back door. People were staring at me like I actually did it. One woman canceled her order for my snowman cake and walked out."

The elf woman had short red hair, a sharp pointed chin, and eyebrows that looked like triangles. Josie tried to see her ears through the hair, in case they were pointed, too.

"That Doreen is mentally ill," the elf woman said. "I told her if she spread that false story, I'd sue her for slander. She left. Today she tried to make amends by bringing me this poinsettia."

A bushy pot of pink-red flowers bloomed on the counter.

"Lovely color," Josie said.

"Doreen is trying," the elf woman said.

"Very trying," Josie said.

The woman laughed. "The peace offering didn't work. I was so distracted by a sudden rush of customers, we didn't get a chance to talk. Doreen saw all those people in my store, when her own shop was empty, and it made her angry all over again. She stomped out just as you came in. I'm sorry you caught her bad temper. I'm Elsie, by the way."

"I guessed that," Josie said. "Nice to meet you."

"May I give you one of my chocolate snowmen? On the house, to sweeten your day? They make them at Christmas All Year Round, but I think mine are better."

"Thanks, but I'll take a rain check," Josie said. Her jeans were a little snug. "Do you have a toy soldier lawn ornament? Mine was damaged."

"Yes, I do," Elsie said. "It's about five feet tall and made of twinkle lights. Let me show you." Elsie hauled the soldier out of the back room.

"It's perfect," Josie said. "He could be the brother of the one I lost."

"I can let you have him for fifty percent off," Elsie said.

"Deal," Josie said, "but I really came for something else."

"You've come back for that crème brûlée torch for your friend, haven't you? She really wanted it. I'm getting a steady run of customers. I have two crème brûlée torches left. This one even has a childproof switch, if your friend has children."

"A little boy," Josie said. "Justin is at the grab-and-chew stage. Alyce will appreciate that feature."

Josie mentally crossed one gift off her Christmas list, and carefully stowed the toy soldier in her car's backeat. Her mother and Amelia would be happy. Certainly happier than Josie was today. She'd spent a sleepless night wondering why Mike didn't call. Her mood swung between anger and hurt. Was he upset about her damning mystery-shopper report? Mike would understand, wouldn't he?

Last night Josie had tossed and turned until four in the morning before she finally decided to heck with him. I was just fine before I met Mike, she told herself. I'll be fine now. I'll survive. She almost made herself believe it.

She sang "I Will Survive," the anthem of furious females, as she drove. She had a voice like a scalded cat. After yowling a few verses, she nearly convinced herself she didn't care about Mike. She added Eliza Doolittle's angry tirade against Henry Higgins and felt better.

If they can live without you, ducky, so can I, Josie thought. Yeah. Right. So why was she still thinking about him?

When her cell phone rang and she saw Mike's number on the display, Josie pulled into a parking lot and scrambled to answer it, hoping she didn't sound too breathless.

"Mike!" she said.

"Hi, Josie." Mike's voice sounded flat. "I'm sorry I didn't call sooner. It seemed like all the plumbing in St. Louis went haywire yesterday."

"How's Heather?" Josie asked.

"Scared, but I stayed with her while the police questioned her. Her mother is still convinced Elsie set the roaches loose in her store."

"Are you?" Josie said.

"No way," Mike said. "Elsie's store is successful. Doreen's business is failing. She's just not cut out for retail."

"Do you know about my mystery report on Doreen's shop?" Josie asked.

"I haven't heard about anything else since headquarters called Doreen with the news yesterday. Her franchise is in danger of being canceled."

"I'm sorry about your investment," Josie said.

"Yeah, well, I knew better. I knew better from the moment I fell into bed with Doreen. But some things you just can't fix. You have to live with your mistakes."

"Doreen said I planted a dead roach in the ginger-bread I bought at her store," Josie said.

"She told me that, too. But I know you too well. You'd never lie on a report. You did what you had to do."

Josie couldn't tell if Mike was angry or resigned. "Anyway, Josie, I'd like to go out with you tonight, but I have to work."

"I understand," Josie said. "Besides, I have a date."

"With Nate?" Mike asked.

"I'd rather not say," Josie said.

She'd rather not say it was her monthly Girl's Night Out with Amelia. Once a month, Josie and her daughter went to the Barnes & Noble in Ladue. Amelia got ten dollars to spend on a book. Josie read a magazine and drank coffee in the café. Amelia might still be too angry to go out tonight, but Josie was hoping for the best.

"Gotta run," Mike said. "Catch you later. Enjoy your date."

He didn't sound upset that Josie might be going out with someone else. He also didn't say he loved her. Is our romance over, she wondered, or doesn't he care anymore? Josie's brain raced in circles, like a hamster on a wheel, until she was exhausted. She didn't know. She couldn't know. She didn't care. She didn't *want* to care. She set up the new lawn ornament, then picked up her daughter at the Barrington School.

Josie and Amelia rode home in a thorny silence until her daughter saw the toy soldier on the lawn.

"You found him," Amelia said.

"His brother, I think," Josie said.

"You can't tell the difference, except his colors are brighter," Amelia said.

"Glad you like him."

Josie had made a pot of beef stew, which she thought was perfect for the cold weather. Amelia carefully picked out the carrots.

"Are we going to the bookstore tonight?" she said.

"Sure," Josie said.

"Good. I need book five of The Spiderwick Chronicles."

She needs a book, Josie thought. How many moms get to hear their daughters say that?

After dinner, Amelia and Josie washed the dishes together, and then Josie put on her best blue sweater, jeans, and black boots. She studied her reflection in the mirror.

Not bad, she decided, for a mom with a nine-year-old.

Amelia looked older than nine. Her hair was getting longer and she had budding curves. She could almost pass for a teenager. She certainly acted like one.

The vast bookstore was crowded on a cold night. Josie headed for the café, but then stopped abruptly behind the greeting cards. Amelia ran into her back.

"Is that Mike?" Amelia asked in a voice that Josie was sure could be heard around the store.

"Shh," Josie said, dropping her voice to a whisper.

"Who's that woman at the table with Mike?" Amelia asked.

"Quiet," Josie pleaded.

Mike was sitting with a blonde. A beautiful thin blonde with perfect teeth, salon-styled hair, and a soft cashmere outfit. She was drinking bottled water. Mike was eating a cookie the size of a hubcap.

Josie tried to hide behind a bookshelf, but Amelia ran right up to the table and said, "Hi, Mike."

Mike stood up, as if Amelia were a grown woman. "Amelia, how are you?"

"Fine. Is this your new girlfriend?" Amelia asked.

Josie prayed that the greeting card display would fall on her, but it stayed in place.

"Mr. Wheeler would be very unhappy if that were true," Mike said. "Mrs. Wheeler and I were discussing business."

Right, Josie thought. Mrs. Wheeler looks like business to me. I'd put her on the cover of *Fortune* magazine.

"Are you here with your mother?" Mike asked.

"Yes," Amelia said. Please lie, Josie prayed for the first time in her life. Please don't tell the truth.

"She's hiding over there behind the greeting cards," Amelia said. "It's our date night."

Josie's shame was complete.

Chapter 14

"Josie," he moaned. "Josie, why don't you love me?"

Josie could hear the man's voice in her bedroom with the door closed. Nate. It had to be Nate. She tiptoed into the living room and peeked out the miniblinds.

Nate was on her front porch, weepy drunk. The skin on his face was so baggy, it looked like a red rubber mask. His clothes were rumpled and stained. He looked like he'd slept under a bridge.

Josie left the security chain on the door and opened it wide enough to say, "Nate! Please be quiet."

"Quiet?" Nate said. "You didn't used to care if I was quiet. Remember that time in my apartment when we were going at it and I yelled so loud the lady downstairs nearly called the police? She thought you were murdering me."

Josie's face burned at the memory.

"Nate, leave this instant or I will call the police," Josie said.

She looked up and saw Mrs. Mueller pretending to shovel Josie's sidewalk. The woman's right ear practically stuck out of her head like a satellite dish, she was eavesdropping so hard. The nosy old cat, Josie thought. She's listening to our conversation.

Nate raised his voice another notch. "There was a

time when you used to yell, too, Josie. Remember that night with the hundred candles? I've never forgotten it. Was that when we made Amelia?"

Mrs. Mueller dropped her snow shovel. It hit the cold concrete with a clang. Nate didn't notice.

But Josie blushed as Nate broadcast the intimate details of their romance to the neighborhood's biggest gossip.

"Nate, please," Josie begged. "Quiet, before the whole neighborhood hears you."

Where's Jane with her broom when I need her? Josie thought. The toy soldier was firmly planted in the lawn, too far out of reach to clobber Nate.

"Josie," Nate said, his voice soggy with alcohol, "I got a present for my li'l girl. A chocolate snowman from Elsie's Elf House." He held up a holiday bag. "Extra chock-lit sauce, just the way she likes it. Wanna give her some. Wanna give you some, too, but not chocolate." He wiggled his hips. "You used to think it was sweet, Josie. What happened?"

"Nate, we can't talk about this on my front porch."

"Then lemme in," Nate said, swaying slightly and slurring his words. "Lemme in so I can see my li'l girl."

"Go away," Josie said. "You don't want your daughter to see you like that."

"Like what?" Nate said, raising his voice again. "You mean happy? Don't you ever get happy anymore, Josie? You don't laugh, Josie. I love my li'l girl. I like to see her smile. I got a present for her. Lemme give Amelia her present." He belched.

"Sober up, Nate," Josie said. "Then you can see your daughter, and she'll be proud of you."

"What's wrong with me?" Nate asked, his voice suddenly angry. "What's wrong with poor old Nate?" He was crying again. Fat tears ran through the stubble on his unshaven cheeks.

"You're a drug dealer," Josie said.

"But I'm legal. I don't sell coke any more. Mari— Mari— Pot is legal in Canada for medicinal purposes. I'm not a dealer. I'm as good as Shoppers Drug Mart."

"I just bet you are," Josie said.

Nate rattled the storm door handle and howled. "Let me in. I have the right to see my daughter. I want to take her to Toronto, so she can see her grandfather. That's where she belongs. She's mine."

"My daughter is not going anywhere with a drunk," Josie said.

"I'm not drunk," Nate said. "I only had two beers."

The famous two beers, Josie thought. That's all any drunk ever has. The other four or six or ten beers must have been invisible. She slammed the door in his face and locked it. Nate rattled the handle for a few minutes, then sat down on the steps and cried.

Josie couldn't bear to watch this weeping wreck. She ran to her bedroom, shut her door, and called her mother. "Mom, I need help. Nate's drunk and camped out on the front porch. I have to pick up Amelia, but I don't want him following me to the Barrington School."

"That's the last thing Amelia needs—her father making a scene in front of those snobs." Jane disapproved of the Barrington School.

"I'll go pick her up," Jane said. "Nate won't recognize me after ten years."

"You haven't changed that much, Mom. Besides, Nate will see you coming outside. You'll have to step around him. He knows you live right upstairs. Amelia probably told him. She told him everything else."

"Then I'll go down the back steps to the garage and drive out the alley way," Jane said. "He'll never see me."

"How are you going to get Amelia inside without Nate seeing her?" Josie said.

"We'll take the back stairs to my flat and bake Christmas cookies. I've promised her a lesson."

"Thanks, Mom," Josie said. "I'm glad she inherited your cooking gene."

"You just keep Nate occupied, Josie, but don't stir him up."

Easier said than done, Josie thought. When she went back to the living room, Nate was pounding on the storm door. Josie was afraid he'd crack the glass.

"Where's my li'l girl?" he yelled. "I want my girl."

Josie could hear her mother clop-clopping down the stairs in her sensible shoes. "Nate," Josie said through the door, "your daughter is at school, where's she's supposed to be. Go home." Josie heard the garage door creak open.

"Will you give her the chocolate snowman?" Nate said.

"No," Josie said. "You can give it to her when you're sober."

She heard a loud thump. Nate must have sat down on the porch. "Why won't you give her my present, huh? Why do you hate me?" His voice was a crying whine.

"Nate, I don't hate you," Josie said. But I'm starting to, she thought.

"Why not?" he asked. "Why can't she have it?"

"Nate," Josie said. "Go sober up. Don't embarrass yourself."

"How am I embarrassing myself?" Nate said. "There's only one old biddy out here pretending to shovel the sidewalk. Any idiot can see she's faking it."

Josie put her head against the cold glass and wished she could sink through the floor into another place, far, far away. Mrs. Mueller had to have heard Nate, and Jane would get an earful.

"You want me dead, don't you?" Nate said. "Tha's what will make you happy. Nate dead. Dead Nate."

Josie heard her mother's car start up. Tires crunched on the salty slush in the back alley and the garage door clunked shut. She breathed a sigh of relief. Jane had gotten away unnoticed.

"Good-bye, Nate," Josie said.

"Okay, if I can't give the snowman to my li'l girl, I'll eat it myself," Nate said, his voice thick with self-pity. "You'll both be sorry." Nate raised his voice still louder. "Did you hear me? I'll make you sorry, Josie. I'll make you wish you were dead. I'm gonna take my little girl where you'll never find her. You owe me nine years."

As Josie closed the door, Nate was flopped on the porch steps, eating the gooey concoction. She watched him pull off thick pieces of cake with his fingers and dip them in the extra chocolate sauce.

"You're missing something good, Josie," Nate said, licking his fingers. He'd nearly polished off the whole cake. All that sweet goo was going to make him sick. Josie hoped he wouldn't throw up on her porch.

She was relieved to see that Mrs. Mueller had gone back inside. She wished Nate would go, too. Josie locked the door.

It was nearly an hour later when she heard Jane's garage door go up, then the sound of her daughter talking. "Can we make Christmas tree cookies, Grandma?" Amelia asked. Their voices trailed off as they climbed the stairs to Jane's second-floor flat.

Josie sat down on the couch for a minute, and she must have fallen asleep. She was startled awake when the phone rang. What time was it? She glanced in the kitchen. Seven o'clock, according to the wall clock.

"We've had dinner and baked Christmas cookies," Jane said. "Amelia will be bringing you sugar cookies and snickerdoodles. Is that man gone yet?"

"Let me check," Josie said. She put down the phone

and looked out the door. Nate was still huddled on the cold, dark porch. He looked like a bundle of rags. I'd better wake him up before he freezes to death, she thought.

Josie opened the front door. "Nate," she called. "Wake up."

Nate didn't respond.

"Nate, please wake up."

He ignored her. Josie tiptoed out on the porch. The wood felt cold and gritty with rock salt on her bare feet.

Nate didn't move. He was sprawled on the steps, leaning against the banister. Nate was breathing in a strange way, as if a heavy beast was in his chest.

He's passed out from the alcohol, Josie thought, as she shook him again. "Nate," she said. "Nate, please. You're scaring me."

Then she saw the vomit on his jacket. She shook him again, and Nate tumbled down the stairs and hit the sidewalk with his head.

Josie screamed. She heard her mother running down the stairs, saw all the lights pop on in Mrs. Mueller's house, then the flashing lights of the ambulance.

The last thing Josie remembered, as the paramedics took Nate away, was the sound of her daughter weeping.

Chapter 15

The emergency room hit Josie with the sharp stink of hospital disinfectant, sweat, and something indefinably nasty. Was it fear, blood, or restrooms that needed cleaning?

Josie couldn't tell. The misery in the waiting room left her dazed. A forlorn collection of people were huddled on the hard plastic chairs, like shipwreck survivors.

Josie tried to follow Nate's stretcher through the ER doors, but she was stopped by a stern nurse and steered toward the business section. Josie took a pale pink chair in a cramped cubicle. An African American woman with an elegant chignon began asking Josie questions. Her name tag said DIEDRE.

"The patient's name?" Diedre asked.

"Nathan—Nate—Weekler," Josie said.

"Who is the next of kin?"

"His father, I think," Josie said. "His name is Jack, or John Weekler. I believe Mr. Weekler Sr. lives in Toronto. I don't have his address or phone number. It might be in Nate's wallet or on his passport."

"We'll check," Diedre said. "Is Nate Weekler married?"

"I don't know," Josie said.

"Do you know if he has health insurance?" Diedre

had a high forehead and shiny dark brown skin. Her eyebrows were delicate arches. One went up with the question.

"Nate is Canadian," Josie said. "He lives in Toronto. Don't they have national health insurance?"

"Yes. But unless he has private supplemental insurance, the province will probably pay only a limited amount of his hospital bill," Diedre said. "He may be responsible for the remainder."

"Oh," Josie said. "I think he has some cash." I just don't know where he stores his drug money, she thought. Maybe she should have hung on to that ten thousand dollars for a rainy day. It was pouring now.

"What's your relationship to the patient?" Diedre asked.

Good question, Josie thought. "He's the father of my nine-year-old daughter, but he left the United States before she was born." She didn't add "in handcuffs." That would make Diedre's eyebrow go up even higher.

"Nate came back to see his daughter this week," Josie said. "He was drunk. I didn't want to let him in my home in his condition. I locked the door. Later, I found him collapsed on my porch. He'd been drinking, but I don't know if that caused his medical problem. He was eating a chocolate snowman cake. I brought the container with me."

Josie held up a plastic bag with the sticky cake remains. She'd already told the paramedics. They told her to bring it along, just in case.

Diedre made a face. The delicate arched brow went up a millimeter higher. "The doctor on duty will take that information."

"May I see Nate now?"

"No, the doctor will see you when the patient is stabilized."

Josie was ushered into the waiting room, still clutching the cake bag. The only chair open was next to a tired woman with two small children. The little boy was bouncing on a side table as if it were a trampoline. The baby pulled the woman's worn brown hair and cried. The mother tried to rock the child, but she didn't seem to have the energy. The bouncing boy was unstoppable.

An old man clutched his cane with two hands and stared straight ahead. A young dark-skinned woman held an ice pack to her eye and moaned. The muscular man next to her rubbed her back and told her everything would be okay.

The television blared a news program no one watched.

"Josie Marcus," called a doctor in green scrubs. He looked younger than Josie's thirty-one years but weary. He had green-gold eyes, dark brown hair, and dark circles under his eyes. When was the last time he had any sleep?

He escorted Josie to a small room in the ER. She gasped when she saw Nate. He had an IV line in his right hand and an oxygen line in his nose. A horrible machine covered his mouth and made an evil sucking sound.

"Is that a ventilator?" Josie said. Her voice shook.

"Yes," the doctor said. "The patient needs assistance breathing. We're waiting for the results of some lab work."

"Is he going to die?" Josie said.

Nate looked dead already. The red hue had fled his face, leaving his skin pale and lardlike. His thin hair clung like old rags to his scalp. His body was unnaturally still, except for the forced rise and fall of the ventilator.

"We don't know the prognosis yet," the doctor said. "We're still waiting for the test results. What can you tell us about the patient?"

"I haven't seen him in ten years," Josie said. "When I knew him, he was a helicopter pilot. I don't know what he does now. He seems to have a drinking problem. Today he turned up with a chocolate snowman cake from a little shop on Manchester. He wanted to give it to his daughter, but I refused. He was intoxicated again, and I was afraid to let him in my home. Nate ate the whole cake—or most of it—sitting on my porch in the cold. At first I thought he was asleep. Then I realized he was unconscious."

"Was the cake from Elsie's Elf House?" the doctor asked.

Josie's eyebrows rose in surprise. "Yes, how did you know?"

"We had a woman in here two hours earlier with similar symptoms. She'd eaten a big slice of chocolate snowman cake from that store. Her daughter said there was something wrong with it."

"Do you suspect poisoning?"

"We're still testing, but her daughter does. She insists her mother was healthy. She blames the cake. She called the shop a few minutes ago and Elsie pulled the remaining batch, just in case."

"Is the woman still alive?"

"So far. But her kidneys are shutting down. She's in a coma. We pumped her stomach and gave her activated charcoal to absorb a possible toxin. The tests will show if she's been poisoned."

"What kind of poison do you suspect?"

"We can't tell until we get the results. It may not even be poison. In Mr. Weekler's case, the alcohol could be causing his kidney and liver problems. And despite the daughter's protests, the other victim was sixty-seven years old and she had health problems."

The blood drained from Josie's face. What if Nate

had given that poisoned snowman cake to Amelia? Her daughter could be dead now. She grabbed a countertop to keep from falling.

"Are you okay?" the doctor asked, his brown eyes concerned. "You look pale."

"I'm fine. It's just that this is so horrible."

"Do you know who would want to try to kill Mr. Weekler?" the doctor said.

"No," Josie said. "He hasn't been in St. Louis for a decade. He has friends here, but I don't know if they knew Nate was in town."

What if the killer was one of Nate's drug buddies from the old days? she wondered. Didn't drug dealers shoot people rather than poison them?

"What's the name of the woman who might have been poisoned?" Josie asked.

"I'm not at liberty to say," the doctor said. "But it should be on the news later."

"May I stay with Nate in case he comes to?" Josie said.

"Sure," the doctor said. "As soon as he's settled in the ICU. But he needs complete rest. If he becomes agitated, the nurses will ask you to leave. They'll let you know when he's ready."

Josie stepped outside to call her mother on her cell phone. Jane had stayed home to watch Amelia while Josie followed the ambulance to the hospital.

"It doesn't look good, Mom," Josie said. "Nate's on a ventilator in the ICU."

"Poor Amelia. She's going to take this badly," Jane said. "She's still crying."

"I don't think Nate will be too happy, either," Josie said. "I have to find his father and let him know."

"I'll try to track him down," Jane said.

"Thanks, Mom. I'm going to stay with Nate a while, in

case he regains consciousness. I don't want him to wake up alone at a hospital in a strange country."

"You do that, dear. I'll make sure Amelia has dinner and goes to bed on time."

"Thanks, Mom." Josie hung up the phone, relieved. Jane could be irritating, but she came through when Josie needed her. How many single moms had a free sitter on call 24/7?

Josie stared at the TV in the lounge, but she had a hard time watching the program. Even a mindless game show was too much for her.

Finally a nurse told her she could go into the third-floor ICU. Nate's room was dark, except for a harsh light over the bed. The tubes, wires, and computer monitors made Nate look like a lab experiment. He remained perfectly still except for the mechanical rise and fall of his chest.

The nurse checked his IV line, then left.

Josie held Nate's left hand, the one that wasn't stuck with an IV needle, and said, "Nate, please get well. Your daughter needs you."

Nate didn't move. The room was strangely still, as if he were waiting for Josie to beg him to live for her. She couldn't do it. There were only the beep of the monitors and the inhuman hiss of the ventilator, which sounded as if it were sucking the life out of Nate.

Josie wondered if he would survive. He's only thirty-five, she thought. He looks like an exhausted old man.

She searched his face for signs of the young man she'd loved so wildly. She tried to remember their time together. She saw him as he'd looked the first time, at the Irish bar in St. Louis. She realized now that he'd been drinking all afternoon, but Nate had an amazing capacity for alcohol. He never looked drunk. She could tell, though, when he started slurring his words. Then he would propose some reckless plan, and they would run off to New York or Martinique.

So many of their dates had involved alcohol. I thought I was intoxicated by love. Maybe I was just drunk, Josie thought.

Their days together had passed in a whirl of champagne, margaritas, and beer, with Bloody Marys and mimosas for breakfast. She'd been in college then, and no one gave a second thought to drinking. It was what they did at that age. Sometimes Josie had been too hungover to go to classes. Jane had warned her that she was drinking too much, but Josie had ignored her mother. What did a dried-up old woman like Jane know? Her own husband had walked out on her, Josie had thought, with the casual cruelty of the young.

Josie had discovered she was pregnant about the same time she'd learned that Nate had been arrested. He'd been on his way back to the States. His friend Mitch had called Josie with the news. "I'm sorry, Josie," he'd said. "He was arrested as he was leaving Canada. He can't enter this country. They found some contraband in his plane."

"Contraband," Josie repeated dully.

"You know. Coke."

"What kind of coke?" Josie said.

"Drugs, sweetie. You knew how Nate made his money, didn't you? He was a dealer, and I'm not talking about Tupperware. Hello? Josie, are you there?"

She'd dropped the phone. Josie hadn't spoken to Mitch since.

For a while Josie thought that she might lose the baby, but the child survived. So did Josie. She'd learned a terrible truth: few women died of love, though some wished they could.

What had happened to Mitch? Josie hadn't seen him in years.

Jane had been angry when she discovered her daughter was pregnant and leaving college to be a mystery shopper. But once Jane saw Amelia, she forgave Josie, though she was not above reminding her daughter of her mistake.

Josie's cell phone went off and she hurried out of the room to the stairway to talk to her mother. "I found Nate's father," Jane said. "Jack can get a seat on a flight out of Toronto first thing in the morning and be in St. Louis before noon tomorrow. I'll pick him up at the airport."

Josie looked at the time on her phone—11:16.

When she returned to the room, there was a buzz of activity. Nate was thrashing around in the bed while two nurses held him down. A doctor brushed past Josie. Alarms and buzzers sounded.

"What's wrong?" Josie said.

"We think he may be waking up," the nurse said. "You'd better go."

"But—" Josie said.

"We have your number in the files. If he needs you, we'll let you know. You can't help him now."

The nurse practically pushed the bewildered Josie out the door. She drove home alone in the dark.

Chapter 16

Josie's phone rang. She woke up and fumbled for the phone by her bed. Glowing green numbers on her bedside clock gave the time as 3:08.

A call at this hour can't be good news, Josie thought.

The voice on the phone was crisp. "Ms. Marcus, this is Maddie in the ICU at Holy Redeemer Hospital."

"Nate!" Josie said. "Is he okay?"

"He's asking for you," the nurse said. "He's very agitated. He says he has to tell you something, for your ears only. I'm sorry to call you at this hour, but he insists."

"Will he make it until morning?" Josie asked.

"There's always hope," the nurse said, which told Josie there might not be.

"I'll be there in twenty minutes," Josie said.

Josie shivered in the early-morning cold. She pulled her robe tighter around her and called Jane. "I'm sorry to wake you, Mom. I know this is an awful time, but the hospital said Nate is asking for me."

"Oh, no," Jane said. "I hope he makes it until his poor father shows up."

"Me, too, but I have to see him now. Will you keep an eye on Amelia? She's asleep, but I don't want her to wake up alone in the morning."

"I'll be right downstairs."

Josie threw on a sweater and jeans and dragged a comb through her brown hair. She heard the patter of her mother's slippered feet on the back steps and opened the door. Jane was shivering in a thick royal blue robe. Fat round rollers stuck out of her silver hair like a pink plastic crown.

"Go," Queen Jane commanded. "Quit staring at me."

Josie went. The night was clear and cold. A single yellow light burned upstairs in Mrs. Mueller's house. Josie wondered if the old woman was watching. Living next door to the Marcus family must be like having her own private soap opera.

Maplewood had a small-town peacefulness in the early morning. The big old last-century houses had wide porches meant for hot summer days, not dreary winter nights. The bare tree branches rattled like old bones. Footsteps marred the perfect white blanket of snow on the wide lawns.

Josie couldn't stand the empty quiet. She turned on the "all news, all day" radio station and caught the end of a newscast. The announcer said, "And a sixty-seven-year-old woman died of kidney failure just before midnight at Holy Redeemer Hospital in Maplewood. The victim was Mrs. Sheila Whuttner, the Big Loser contestant on radio station KPVC."

The announcer had trouble hiding his glee at this bad luck for a rival station.

"Mrs. Whuttner publicly pledged that she would lose fifty pounds by Christmas to win fifty thousand dollars. At her last weigh-in Friday morning, Mrs. Whuttner had lost forty-eight pounds. Mrs. Whuttner's daughter, Lorraine, said her mother died after eating a chocolate snowman cake from Elsie's Elf House. Hospital sources say an autopsy has yet to confirm a connection between the cake and Mrs. Whuttner's death. The owner of Elsie's Elf House could not be reached for comment. KPVC's manager said the station regrets the death of Mrs. Whuttner and the Big Loser contest is canceled. Even though Mrs. Whuttner was within two pounds of her goal at her last weigh-in, the prize money will not be awarded."

That was cold, Josie thought. The poor woman was canceled, along with the contest. Big Loser indeed.

Josie swung into the hospital drive at three thirty, parked her car under a bright light in the nearly empty lot, and hurried in the night entrance. There was no one in the lobby but a uniformed guard, who took her name, made a call, and issued her a badge for the ICU.

Maddie was at the ICU nurses' station. She was a fireplug with blunt-cut gray hair and a no-nonsense air.

"How is Nate?" Josie said.

"He's had a restless night," Maddie said. "He wants to talk to you. He's awake and off the ventilator. You can go in now."

Josie was shocked by Nate's appearance. His face was sunken and covered with a fine sheen of sweat.

"Nate," Josie said. "Are you okay?"

"Hell, no." His voice was a hoarse whisper. He managed a ghost of a smile. "Whoever thought I'd be done in by a chocolate cake?"

"The nurse said you wanted to talk to me," Josie said.

"Throat hurts from that ventilator thing." He swallowed. Josie offered him ice chips from a foam cup. Nate waved them away. "There's a key in my leather jacket. It's for my storage unit by the airport. Company name's on the key ring. What's in there is for you. And don't give me any shit about drugs, Josie. You need that cash and so does my daughter. For once in your life, do it the easy way."

Josie opened his closet door and felt in the zippered pockets until she found a brass key. It had a yellow plastic UR-Storage tag with an address on Airport Road.

"Got it?" Nate asked. Josie nodded and dropped the key in her purse.

"Good." Nate seemed to relax. "I also have a life insurance policy. I left it with my father. Should come to about a hundred thousand U.S. You're the beneficiary, but the money is for Amelia. Put it in trust. Make sure she goes to college. Don't let her get knocked up like her mother."

"Amelia has more sense than her mother," Josie said.

"And her father," Nate said. His eyelids were at half mast and his voice was a mumble. He was drifting off. "Tell her I love her."

"She already knows that," Josie said.

"I'm sorry, Josie," Nate said, and squeezed her hand.

But before Josie could learn what he was sorry about, Nate drifted away on soft waves of sleep. Josie held his hand until she followed him into soothing blackness.

About five thirty in the morning, they were awakened by a too-cheerful phlebotomist. The thin dark-skinned woman had a big smile and a rattling cart. "I'm Angela. I'm here to take your blood," she said.

"Is there any left?" Nate asked. "You got it all yesterday."

Angela laughed at the feeble joke.

Josie turned her head while the nurse filled two tubes with rich red blood. By the time Angela packed up her gear and rattled her cart to the next room, Nate had drifted off again.

Josie was awakened half an hour later by a cleaning woman, who noisily emptied the wastebasket and moved a mop around on the tile floor, pushing the needle caps and bandage wrappers under Nate's bed. He slept through the racket.

Breakfast arrived at seven thirty. Nate woke up and managed a smile for the young woman carrying the tray. "Why don't you get yourself something, Josie?" His words were slurred.

"Maybe some coffee," she said.

Josie took the elevator to the hospital cafeteria on the first floor. Her face felt oily and her clothes were rumpled from sleeping upright in the chair by Nate's bed. She bought a cup of watery coffee, then called her mother in the cell phone area.

"How's Nate?" Jane asked.

"He's eating breakfast now. How's Amelia?"

"She's fine," Jane said. "She's right here, eating breakfast, too." Jane's voice was too cheerful.

"She's not fine, but you can't talk," Josie said.

"That's right," Jane said.

"Is she still crying?"

"Right again," Jane said. "We're leaving for school shortly. I'll pick up Jack Weekler at the airport about noon and he can stay in my guest room. Amelia wants to make a Charlie Brown Christmas tree out of that tree by the back stairs, and decorate it with suet and seed for the birds."

"Sounds like a good idea," Josie said. "Is Amelia studying birds in school?"

"She's supposed to look for a Eurasian tree sparrow," Jane said. "The Audubon Society says there's a flock of them nearby in Dogtown. Little brown birds. Amelia's showed me a picture. Look like plain old chippies to me."

Josie hung up and went back to Nate's room. His untouched tray was filled with unopened containers of juice, apple sauce, gelatin, and a dry muffin.

"Aren't you going to eat?" Josie asked.

"Not hungry," Nate mumbled and closed his eyes. "Can you get me a drink?"

"Do you want juice or water?"

"Beer," Nate said.

"Not unless the doctor approves it," Josie said.

"Not even for a hundred thousand dollars?" Nate said, in a sad attempt at banter.

"Not for a million," Josie said. "Your daughter is crying her eyes out because you're sick. She wants you to get well."

"Everyone wants something I can't give them," Nate mumbled, and slipped back into sleep. His hands scrabbled across the covers like crabs on a beach. The sight chilled Josie. She didn't like the dark bruises under his eyes or the yellow tinge to his skin.

Soon Nate was snoring, his breathing full of stops, starts, and snorts. Waiting for him to resume snoring was nerve-racking.

This is not good, Josie thought. Nate really might die. She tried to push the ugly thought away, but it seemed to squat on her chest. I wished him dead the other day. I wanted him out of my life. Now I'm about to get what I wanted.

Josie dozed off again. She vaguely remembered two or three doctors coming in, looking concerned. A nurse with squeaky shoes took Nate's vital signs and checked his IV.

I need to call Mom, Josie thought. She took out her cell phone and went into the stairwell to make the call.

"I'm on my way to the airport to pick up Nate's father," Jane said. "Please tell me that boy is still alive."

"Nothing's changed, Mom, but he doesn't look good. What couldn't you tell me about Amelia?"

"She wants to see her father in the hospital."

"Children aren't allowed," Josie said.

"She's nine," Jane said. "She's old enough to say good-bye."

"I think he's dying," Josie said.

"All the more reason she needs to see her father," Jane said. "And he needs to see her. You've made a hash of this by lying. Amelia will never forgive you if you deny her this opportunity. You can't protect your daughter from the unpleasant facts of life."

"I'll think about it, Mom," Josie said.

"No! You'll listen to me for once, Josie Marcus, and do it. I'll bring Amelia after school. I'll prepare her first." Jane hung up before Josie could answer.

Josie went back to the ICU unit. She could see through the glass that Nate was asleep. His room door was closed.

Josie opened the door slowly and bumped into a shaggy-haired man in a white lab coat. He was standing in front of the closet, with his hand in Nate's bomber jacket.

"May I help you?" Josie asked.

Then she stared at the doctor. "Mitch!" she said.

"I didn't think you'd recognize me after all these years," he said, a smarmy smile on his face. "I've put on a few pounds." He patted his gut like a beloved pet. "And my hair is grayer."

Those "few pounds" looked like fifty to Josie. His black hair was now iron gray. But his slablike forehead and jutting jaw were the same. He still had odd, crooked teeth, like tombstones in an old cemetery. His sneer was unchanged.

"I recognized you immediately, Mitch, as soon as I saw your hand where it shouldn't be," Josie said.

"You never let me forget that one mistake, Josie. I made a pass at you, but it was a compliment."

"I was dating your best friend!" Josie said.

"You were doing more than dating, sweetheart. It's too late to act all pure and innocent. The evidence is about nine years old now, I think."

"How dare you!" Josie said, and started to punch him in the mouth.

Mitch grabbed her arm. "Quiet," he said. "We don't want to wake Nate, do we?" He squeezed Josie's arm until she cried out in pain.

"Where is it?" Mitch asked, pulling her closer. She could smell cigarettes and cheap shaving lotion.

"Where's what?" Josie said.

"Don't play dumb. The key. I want the key to the storage unit."

"I don't have it," Josie said.

Mitch bent her arm back until Josie was afraid he'd dislocate it. "You're lying. I want that money. It's half mine. That's why Nate came back. To give me my share. The rest goes to his lawyer."

Just when Josie thought she couldn't take any more pain, she heard the rattling of a cart, and the big, scuffed door opened. It was the cheerful phlebotomist.

"I'm here for more blood," Angela said, with that wide smile.

"Gotta go," Mitch said. "But I'll be back, Josie. I won't forget. Don't you forget, either." Then he disappeared down the hall.

Chapter 17

Josie waited until she heard the *ding* of the elevator. The doors whooshed open and then shut again. She hoped that meant the frightening Mitch was gone. She stuck her head out of Nate's door, saw the hall was empty, and ran straight to the ICU nurses' station.

A young red-haired nurse working on some notes looked up. "May I help you?"

"I found a strange man in Nate's room when I came back from the cafeteria," Josie said. "He wore a white lab coat, but I didn't see any hospital ID. He was going through Nate's jacket." She didn't add that the man had threatened her.

"What's his description? I'll call security," the nurse said.

Josie gave her the details, without much hope that anyone would catch Mitch. A gray-haired man in a white lab coat would be invisible in a hospital.

Nate was still sleeping when Josie returned to his room. He seemed to be growing smaller, as if his life were slowly leaking away. Who would have thought my handsome young pilot would end like this? she thought. Nate looked old and exhausted. His skin had an unhealthy yellow tinge.

"Nate," she whispered. "Fight. Your daughter needs you."

Nate didn't move. Josie squeezed his hand, and wished she wasn't so useless. There was nothing she could do but wait. She settled into the uncomfortable turquoise chair next to the bed. Her arm ached where Mitch had manhandled her. Why didn't I give Mitch the key to the storage locker? she asked herself. I don't want that money.

Because Nate doesn't want Mitch to have it. But what am I going to do with a storage locker full of cash? There are worse problems to have, Josie decided. She held Nate's hand and eventually drifted off to sleep.

"There you are," a man said. His loud voice startled her awake. Josie had been asleep—and drooling. Lovely.

She blinked and saw Nate standing at the room door. He was thin again, and muscular. His hair was thick and gray, but it was her Nate, hands in the pockets of his bomber jacket, confident smile on his face.

"Nate?" Josie said.

"Jack Weekler," the man said. He had a slight British accent. He shook Josie's hand. "And you must be Nate's . . . erm." His voice trailed off.

Nate's erm, Josie thought. That describes me as well as anything.

"I'm Josie Marcus," she said, standing and shaking his hand. "I'm sorry we have to meet in a hospital. My mother, Jane, called you in Toronto."

"Fine woman. She was kind enough to pick me up at the airport. Jane is parking the car. She told me to go on up and see my son. How is he?"

"I'm not sure," Josie said. "He was talking a little while ago, but he sleeps a lot. I'm not a relative, so I can't get a complete report from the doctors."

Jack studied the pale, still form of his son. "Doesn't look good, does he? Was he on a bender?"

"He'd been drinking a little," Josie said.

"A little? You don't have to lie to me, Josie. If Nate was drinking, it was a lot."

"Okay, he was drunk," Josie said. "But I'm not sure this was caused by alcohol. Nate might have been poisoned."

"Poisoned! The only poison Nate ever took was in a beer bottle. He's nearly destroyed his liver with drink. The doctors warned him to sober up."

"I don't think he took poison on purpose," Josie said. "It may have been accidental. They suspect it was in some chocolate cake."

"Nate doesn't eat cake," his father said. The man's voice grew louder with every sentence.

Nate opened one bleary eye and said, "Hi, Pop. Why are you bellowing in my room?"

"I came to see you, you idiot," his father said. "What kind of mess are you in now?"

"I think I've been killed by a cake," Nate said. "I knew there was a reason I drank. Can't trust food."

"You're not dead yet," Jack said. "What can I do for you?"

"Quit staring at me like a sick basset hound. Make sure my daughter, Amelia, gets my life insurance."

"I was going to do that anyway," Jack said.

"Then shut up so I can sleep," said his son, and closed his eyes.

"Have you eaten yet, Mr. Weekler?" Josie asked.

"Jack, please. I feel old enough already. I had some food on the plane. I'm not really hungry. Maybe later. I'll go talk to the head nurse and see what I can find out."

Jack had been gone about five minutes when Josie's mother came in, cheeks bright pink from the cold, every hair in place. Jane took off her coat, and Josie saw that her mother was wearing her new rust-colored pantsuit. It made her look slim and stylish.

"You wouldn't believe the hospital parking lot," Jane said. "Every space was taken. People were double-parking in the driveway. I finally found a place by a Dumpster and hiked here. How's Nate?"

"About the same," Josie said. "How's Jack?"

"He's cute," Jane said.

Cute? Her mother was calling a man "cute"?

"Why are you looking at me like that?" Jane said.

"Because you sound like your granddaughter. You really think Jack is cute?"

Jane shrugged. "He's a good-looking man with nice manners. These are trying circumstances, Josie, but he's behaving well. He's offered to take me out to dinner tonight."

"Are you going?" Josie asked.

"I'm thinking about it. But a woman shouldn't be too available."

"Oh, for heaven's sake, Mother."

"Call me old-fashioned, Josie, but sometimes the old ways work," Jane said.

"What old ways?" Jack asked. His trip to the nurses' station had aged him by ten years.

"What's wrong?" asked Jane.

"Let's step into the family waiting room down the hall," Jack said.

The little room was furnished with comfortable pale pink couches, a basket of apples, a pile of magazines, and a TV that played mindless shows at high volume. The set had no OFF switch.

Jack reached up and yanked the TV's plug.

"Thank you," Josie said. "Now I can hear myself think. You look like you got bad news."

"I did. They think it's poison, possibly antifreeze. They're testing the cake carton you brought in, Josie. My son's liver and kidneys are damaged. His ammonia levels are up, which is a bad sign. They're going to try dialysis, but they're not holding out much hope."

"I'm sorry," Josie and Jane said together.

"They said a woman already died of antifreeze poisoning. At least that's what the autopsy found. Nate ate the same thing she did. That damned cake."

"Why would anyone try to kill Nate?" Josie asked.

"Nate ran with a bad crowd for a while, Josie. He's kept money hidden away for years. I don't know where, but I suspect it's a lot. They may be trying to get it. But I don't think they'd poison a cake to get my Nate. They'd be better off pouring antifreeze in his beer—or shooting him."

"Nate wasn't a regular at Elsie's Elf House," Josie said. "I think he only went there once, to buy a treat for Amelia."

Josie watched the horror register on Jane's face. Her granddaughter had been nearly poisoned.

"It must have been random, like those horrible Tylenol killings years ago," Jane said. "Remember when that man killed those innocent people so he could murder his wife and make it look random? Otherwise, I'm sure no one would want to kill Nate."

Except me, Josie thought. A few days ago I would have given anything to make that man disappear.

Her unspoken words seemed to hang in the air. Jane finally broke the awkward silence. "We should go back and see Nate. What time is it?"

Josie checked her cell phone clock. "Two thirty-two," she said.

"I'd better get Amelia at school," Jane said.

"Mom, I don't want Amelia here at the hospital," Josie said.

"It's her right, Josie, and don't argue with me."

"Please let her come. It may help Nate," his father said.

Josie couldn't refuse his request, but she was worried. Amelia was so young. Would the sight of her dying father scar her for life? But if I don't let her see Nate, she's already scarred. A parent can't win, Josie thought.

After a long time, Jane returned with Amelia. Josie blinked in surprise. Her daughter looked so grown-up she could have been eighteen. Amelia must have stopped at home first and changed into her good coat. Under it she wore a navy sweater and pants. She was nearly as tall as Jane, and Amelia's rich brown hair fell almost to her shoulders. There was no doubt that Amelia was Nate's daughter.

Jack gave a little gasp and said, "You're beautiful, my girl."

"Thank you. You must be my grandfather," Amelia said gravely, and gave him a shy kiss on the cheek.

Then she ran for the hospital bed. "Daddy!" she said. "I'm sorry you're sick."

"Me, too, sweetheart," Nate said.

"When are you going to get out of here?" Amelia asked.

"In a few days," he said.

"Are you going to marry Mom?" Amelia asked.

"Amelia!" Josie said, her cheeks red with embarrassment.

"No, honey," Nate said. "If I did that, she'd inherit all my debts and all my troubles. The law would be watching her every move, and so would some of my bad friends. I love your mother, and she loved me—at least the man she thought I was. I should have married her before you were born, but I did something selfish and wrong."

"Did you really sell drugs?" Amelia asked.

"Yes. I'm ashamed to say I did."

"But why, Daddy?" Their daughter was an innocent accusing angel. Josie wanted to weep.

Nate looked like he was in terrible pain. Josie was about to ask Amelia to stop, but Nate said, "Because I wanted easy money. It was wrong. It was stupid. I learned a hard lesson, Amelia: There's no such thing as easy money. It cost me too much. It cost me my life. It cost me time with you."

Bright tears slid from Amelia's eyes. "You're going to leave me, now that you've come back."

"No, Amelia, I'll always be with you. You have my hair. You have my eyebrows." He traced their arch with a shaky finger.

"You have my nose." His index finger slid lightly down her freckled nose.

"Look in the mirror and you'll always see me. I'll be there with you. You won't be alone. I suspect you also have your mother's grit and stubbornness. And her temper. I bet you're pretty pissed at her right now."

Amelia nodded.

"But you must promise me. No matter what, you mustn't be mad at your mother. She did the right thing."

"But—" Amelia said.

"No daughter of mine should associate with a drug dealer, even if he is her father. You will stay away from drugs, and you will try to understand that your mother did the right thing."

Nate held out his little finger and crooked it. "Pinkie swear," he said. "That's the most sacred oath of all."

Josie felt her eyes tear up. Nate used to say that to her.

Amelia locked little fingers with him. "Pinkie swear," she said.

"And you are going to college," he said.

"Absolutely," Amelia said, as if she'd never considered any alternative. That's why Josie wanted her daughter to go to the Barrington School. Almost all the students went to college. "My grades are good enough for a scholarship."

"Promise me you'll keep them that way?" Nate said.

They locked fingers again.

A nurse came in with a strong-looking man in purple scrubs. "It's time for dialysis, Mr. Weekler," she said. "Chet will take you on down."

Amelia looked like she was going to cry again, but her father held her.

"Don't cry, sweetheart," he said. "We didn't have much time together. But it was quality time."

Chapter 18

Nate's room looked like a medical battlefield. The floor was littered with torn-open alcohol-wipe packets and plastic needle covers. The sheets on his empty bed were twisted, and his thin pillow was flattened. The bed looked hard and uncomfortable, a rack for pain.

As Nate's stretcher disappeared down the hall, Jane wiped her eyes. Amelia sobbed in her mother's arms, all accusations against Josie forgotten. Now Amelia looked much younger than nine. She was a hurting little girl. Josie clung to her, and wished she could take away her daughter's pain. Her own eyes were wet with tears.

"Come, dear," Jane said, putting her arm around Amelia. "Let's go home. We can't do anything here. Mr. Weekler, do you want to join us? You can rest up in my guest room."

"I think I'll stay here for now," Jack said. "I'm worried about my boy. Josie, do you want to go home for a bit? Jane says you've been here since the wee hours."

"No, thanks," Josie said. She was worried, too.

Josie went back to the family waiting room. It was empty. The perpetually blaring TV was still blank-screened. No one had plugged it back in. She poured herself a cup of free coffee, grown thick as old roofing tar on the burner, and steeled herself to call her awful boss. Harry the Horrible always had some insult.

"Sorry, Josie, no work for you." Harry seemed to delight in delivering bad news. "Things are slow for mystery shoppers. Everyone assumes retail service is crap until January. I'm sure work will pick up after the holidays."

Josie snapped her phone shut. She wasn't sure at all. She couldn't work now, not with Nate dying. But what if Harry was deliberately cutting her out of jobs? She didn't trust him.

Won't happen, she told herself. The stores ask for you personally. They like you.

A more insidious voice told her, "There's always the money in the storage locker."

You can't use it, Josie thought, and automatically straightened her spine. You haven't needed a man's money yet, and you aren't starting now. You can make it on your own.

Her cell phone rang. Josie checked the caller ID display. "Mike," she said, hoping her smile carried on her voice. "How are you?"

"Not so good," he said. "It looks like Doreen's store will close. The cops are all over her parking lot. Homicide detectives are searching the Elf House after that woman was poisoned. The police and crime-scene vehicles are keeping any customers away from the stores. You can't have a holly, jolly Christmas when customers are dying."

"I'm sorry," Josie said.

"I'm glad Heather's going to be out of that store," Mike said. "But I wish I hadn't sunk twenty thousand dollars in it."

"Maybe Doreen can recoup some of your money when she sells the building," Josie said. "It's in a prime location."

"I don't think the location is so prime anymore," Mike said. "You haven't seen today's *City Gazette.*"

"There's a paper here in the waiting room." Josie picked a wrinkled newspaper out of the wastebasket and checked out the front-page headline. DEATH TAKES A HOLIDAY ON THE BAD-NEWS BLOCK, it screamed above two photos. One showed the church picketers circling Naughty or Nice. The other pictured police clustered at the entrance of Elsie's Elf House. A boxed quote in the center of the story said, "Her death is a judgment from God."

"Oh, boy," Josie said. "'Death Takes a Holiday' is a poor headline choice after an innocent woman died. 'A Judgment from God' won't sell real estate, either."

"Who wants a property where God kills the customers?" Mike asked.

"Do they have any suspects besides God?" Josie said.

"Nothing. I unclogged a drain for a friend in the department. He says the police have supposedly gone through the credit-card sales at Elsie's yesterday and cleared the people who paid that way. All innocent pillars of the community. No history of mental illness. No ties to organized crime or connections to the victim. I didn't realize Sheila Whuttner was in that Big Loser radio station contest."

"Did you know her?" Josie asked.

"I dated her daughter a few years ago," Mike said. "I didn't get along with her—or her mother."

"Maybe the station killed Sheila to save the money," Josie said.

"Nope, her death brought them a boatload of bad publicity. Take a look at page 3A."

Josie opened her newspaper and found, DYING FOR CHOCOLATE. She winced at the headline. An interview with the victim's daughter said, "My mother deserved that money. She'd lost another five pounds since her weigh-in and celebrated with a piece of chocolate cake, and it killed her. The station should pay her the fifty thousand dollars."

"Guess who inherits all her widowed mother's money?" Josie said. "I bet it's the daughter. What about Nate? He ate the poisoned chocolate, too. He's in Holy Redeemer hospital. He may die."

"That's awful. Are you with him? Why didn't you call me?" Mike said

"You've been so busy," Josie said.

"Nate wasn't suicidal, was he?" Mike said.

"No," Josie said. "But he was a drug dealer."

"Do you really think drug dealers poison people with chocolate sauce?" Mike said.

"No, no, it was a crazy idea. Any word on who pushed the snow off the roof and nearly killed that poor church lady?"

"The neighbor, Edna, still insists Santa did it, but she looks a little gaga. Doreen blames Elsie, but her theory is just as crazy.

"Please let me come over and sit with you," Mike said. "You shouldn't be alone."

"I appreciate the offer, but Nate's father is here from Canada. It could be awkward."

"When will Nate be out of the hospital?"

"I don't think he's going to make it," Josie said.

"I'm sorry." Mike sounded like he meant it.

"Me, too. It's rough on Amelia."

"And you," Mike said.

There was an awkward pause. "Mike, I haven't loved Nate for a long time. Our romance has been over for years. That obnoxious drunk you saw at my home was not the Nate I loved."

"I know that, Josie. People change, and not always for the better. Especially Doreen. She gets meaner."

Josie heard a loud beep in the background. "Oops. I have to go back to work. If you need me, I'm here for you."

What about the blonde at the bookstore? Josie wondered. Where are you with her?

"Thanks," was all she said.

Josie returned to the empty ICU room. Nate's father was pacing up and down in the small space. Josie could feel the tension radiating from the man. The room wasn't big enough to contain it.

"There's bad coffee in the waiting room, if you want some," Josie said.

"Thanks," Jack said. "Coffee will only make me more jittery. This is all my fault. My actions created a reckless, drunken son. I was everything Nate didn't want to be."

Sober? Josie wondered. But she let him talk, hoping he'd stop that infernal pacing.

He stopped and leaned against the wall, much to Josie's relief.

"I wanted to be a commercial pilot," he said. "It was my dream. But instead of waiting for the job I loved, I took a job that was safe and available—an administrative assistant to a director in the Ministry of Finance. That's a fancy name for a secretary. I had a boring job with a pension. I piloted a desk."

Josie couldn't imagine a man who looked like her dashing Nate settling for a safe job.

"The job paid very little. I pinched every penny until my wife ran off with a free-spending lawyer she met at an office party. Then I had another excuse to stay at my desk. I had a son to support. I wasn't going to risk my pension. The truth is, I was comfortable in my rut. Now it's too late to change.

"My son swore he'd never turn out like me. He loved flying as much as I did. Nate got his pilot's license, and made a little money. Then he started selling drugs and made a lot more. He was throwing money around like mad. He bought a plane and a helicopter, expensive clothes, a Porsche and a Harley. I was afraid he was attracting the wrong kind of attention. Anyone with half a brain would know a pilot didn't make that much money. I warned Nate, but he didn't believe anything bad could happen to him. When he was arrested and sent to jail, it broke him.

"I mortgaged everything to find him the best lawyer. Eventually, he got my son out of prison. But Nate wasn't the same man anymore. He couldn't stop drinking. I saved everything and lost it all. Nate squandered his gifts."

"Nate's a grown man," Josie said. "He's responsible for his actions."

"So am I," Jack said.

"You shouldn't blame yourself," she said. "Children need stability. I'm sorry Nate and I didn't work out. I wish Nate didn't sell drugs. I wish he'd stayed sober."

"You aren't the only one," Jack said.

"Nate would have made a wonderful father. I could tell by the way he talked to Amelia. I wish I'd stayed in touch with him."

"Why? So Nate could drag you and Amelia down, too? You don't want to mix with the crowd he hung around with, Josie. Nate was a lot of fun, but he wasn't good for the long haul. He—"

Before Jack could continue, they heard the rattle of the stretcher outside the room. Nate was back. He looked worn. Two orderlies lifted him back into bed. A nurse fussed with the sheets.

"How are you feeling, Nate?" Josie asked softly.

He didn't respond. Nate's features looked sunken and his skin was waxy yellow.

He's dying, she thought. I'm watching Nate die. She shivered in the hospital room and wished there was a way to turn up the heat.

Jack put his arm around Josie and whispered, "He doesn't look good, does he?"

"No," Josie said, her voice heavy with tears.

"Let's stay here with him, in case he wakes up and wants us."

Josie and Jack sat in companionable silence, watching Nate sleep. For some reason, Jack's remark made Josie feel like she was doing something useful. The room grew darker as night fell, but no one turned on the light.

Why would someone try to poison the customers at Elsie's Elf House? Josie wondered. She'd met Elsie. The woman didn't seem like a killer. She was too cute and friendly and yes, elflike. Maybe Doreen did it, to ruin Elsie's business. Except it ruined hers, too. And Doreen didn't exactly run over there every hour to say hello to her business rival. Maybe she sent her lumpish daughter.

With a big plastic jug of antifreeze to pour in the sauce? That would be a little obvious. What was Heather going to do—disguise it with holly?

Josie tried to make the pieces of this Christmas puzzle work, but nothing fit. She dozed a bit, and was awakened by her mother announcing, "I'm here to take you up on that offer of dinner, Jack."

Josie jerked upright and found a little puddle of drool on the arm of the chair.

Jane was wearing another new pantsuit, this one black with silver buttons. It set off her freshly washed hair. Jane's makeup was perfect.

"I'm not hungry," Jack said.

"Well, I am," Jane said. "And you have to eat sometime. You won't help that boy of yours if you get sick, too. If nothing else, you can watch me eat."

Jack shrugged and obediently put on his coat.

Josie was stunned by the spectacle of her mother going after a man. So much for the old ways, Josie thought. Mom did everything but tackle the guy.

"Are you coming with us, Josie?" Jack asked. Jane seemed to have forgotten her daughter.

"Thanks, but I'll stay here," Josie said. "I'll call Mom on her cell if there's any change."

Jane hauled her catch of the day off to dinner. Josie resettled herself in the uncomfortable bedside chair and wondered why hospital chairs were always turquoise. Was there a special Medical Warehouse of Blue-Green Backbreaker Chairs?

When the room was quiet again, Josie held Nate's hand and said, "Thank you for what you said to our daughter. It will make a big difference—to her and to me. We appreciate the insurance money, too. I'll invest it and make sure Amelia goes to college."

She waited, hoping for a flicker of an eyelid. Nothing. She could have been talking to a wax figure.

"I'm sorry we didn't have more time together, Nate, but we created someone exceptional. Our daughter is the best of both of us. She won't make our mistakes."

Josie wondered if every parent believed that. She hoped it was true.

Nate gave no sign he heard her. Josie felt bone tired, as if she'd been digging ditches instead of sitting in a hospital room. She shifted her weight, trying to ease her aching back. Nate grabbed her hand, but she couldn't tell if it was on purpose or a reflex.

In the dark room, it seemed to Josie that the outline of the Nate she once knew showed through the wrecked man in the bed. She saw Nate's cheekbones in the flab on his face. She could almost believe her Nate was back.

In her mind's eye, she saw Nate the way he was on one of their first dates. She was young and carefree again, crunching through the dry leaves. She and Nate were tossing handfuls of leaves at one another and laughing.

Jane was there, too, disapproving. "You'll regret this, Josie. You're heading for trouble."

"I'm young and I want to have fun," Josie told her. "What's wrong with that?" Her voice got louder and she was screaming at her mother. Then Josie realized the scream was actually an alarm on the monitor above Nate's bed.

Nate's arms were flailing, and his body was jerking like a puppet with broken strings. Josie thought he was trying to get up, and then realized he must be having some sort of seizure.

A nurse came running into the room. "You'll have to leave," she said, and shoved Josie out the door as a team of medical professionals pushed past her. She heard someone call "code blue" and another person demanding oxygen.

"Nate," Josie said. "Nate, come back."

But she knew he was already gone.

Chapter 19

"I hate you! I hate you!" Amelia screamed at her mother.

Josie felt as if those words were hacked into her heart with a rusty knife. There was no soothing way to tell Amelia her father was dead.

She'd already called Jane and Jack and waited for them at the hospital. That was a nightmare. Now she had to break the news to her daughter.

"You got what you wanted," Amelia added, twisting the knife. "I hope you're happy." She ran to her room and slammed the door.

And stayed there.

Josie made Amelia's favorite dinner of mac and cheese that night, but her daughter refused to eat it. Amelia's hospital clothes were tossed on the floor. She was wearing jeans and her beloved pink hoodie. She must have dug it out of the back of Josie's closet, but Josie didn't have the heart to say anything. Amelia stayed in bed, fully dressed and curled up in a fetal position, weeping. Her computer was off, and so was the television. She wasn't listening to her iPod.

Josie decided to leave her alone. She felt as if she'd bungled her mission, but there didn't seem to be any way to make it better. Josie left Amelia's door open a crack and checked on her every half hour.

Amelia sobbed herself to sleep about ten thirty that night. Josie tucked a blanket around her daughter and saw the tear tracks on her face. She was so tired, her bones ached, but Josie couldn't sleep. She couldn't cry, either. She moved restlessly from room to room, a lost soul who blamed herself for the disaster that had hurt her daughter.

About midnight, Josie heard something bumping down her mother's stairs. She peered out the front door and saw Jack leaving her mother's home with his suitcase. A cab was waiting out front. Josie guessed Nate's father was not going to sleep in Jane's guest room.

Jane followed Jack downstairs and stood at her door, staring after him. She didn't wave or say good-bye.

"Want to come in for coffee?" Josie asked her mother.

"Coffee?" Jane said. "I want a drink. Do you have any wine?"

"I think I have a bottle of white in the fridge. Come in and get warm," Josie said.

She put on coffee for herself and poured her mother a glass of cold Chardonnay. "What's with Jack?" Josie asked.

"He won't forgive me because I dragged him out to dinner and his boy died while we were gone." Jane gulped down half the glass.

"That's not your fault," Josie said.

"That's not what he says. He's moving to a hotel by the airport. He barely spoke to me."

"How's he going to get around?" Josie asked.

"Take a cab. Rent a car. I don't really care." But Josie could tell her mother cared very much. Her hand trembled as she knocked back the rest of the glass. "How's Amelia?"

"Not so good," Josie said, pouring Jane another half a glass. "She blames me for her father's death. Says I got what I wanted."

"Ouch," Jane said.

"Yes, it hurts," Josie said. She could barely hold back her tears. "Amelia skipped her favorite dinner tonight. Want some mac and cheese?"

"No, thanks," Jane said, a little too quickly. She took another gulp of wine.

Josie put out a bag of pretzels. She didn't want Mrs. Mueller to see her mother staggering across the porch. The old biddy must have noticed Jack leaving in the cab. The entire neighborhood would know by morning.

"Don't worry, Josie," her mother said, crunching a pretzel. "She'll come around. Kids make dramatic statements, but they don't mean them. At least I hope they don't."

There was a long pause while Josie remembered the angry words she'd hurled at her mother years ago. "Hate" had definitely been one of them.

"Amelia's a good girl," Jane said. "She needs to mourn her father."

"I'm not sending her to school tomorrow," Josie said.

"That's probably wise," Jane said.

It was three a.m. before Jane crossed the porch to her door. Her walk was surprisingly steady. Mrs. Mueller's lights were off.

Josie did not sleep the rest of the night. Nate's return had caused some seismic shift in her little family. She no longer knew her own daughter. She couldn't predict what Amelia would say or do. She'd tried to protect her daughter from Nate's drug-dealing past and instead caused Amelia more pain. It would have been better if she'd faced who and what Nate was.

Well, too late now. *I ran away like a coward, Josie*

reminded herself. Now she spent the dark hours of the new day in an unproductive game of what-if.

What if she'd discovered she was pregnant before Nate left for Canada?

What if Nate hadn't been arrested in Canada for drug dealing?

What if she'd married Nate?

What if we'd lived in a cottage with a picket fence and roses?

She angrily hurled a couch pillow across the living room. I fell in love with a drunk and a drug dealer. I'm not fit to judge bananas at the supermarket.

The sky was lightening to pale gray when Josie put her head down on the pillow for a moment's rest. The phone woke her at 9:03.

"How is Amelia?" Jane asked.

"Huh?" Josie said. "Omigod. I've been asleep, Mom."

She dropped the phone and rushed in to see Amelia. Her daughter was sound asleep, still wearing the pink hoodie. Josie realized she'd better call the school and say that Amelia would be out for a few days due to a death in the family.

The school secretary was crisp with Josie. "I'm sorry for your loss, Ms. Marcus, but we prefer that you notify us by e-mail before eight o'clock in case of an absence."

Josie hung up the phone, wondering if the secretary would have been so snippy if Josie was a major donor taking her child skiing in Vail.

Josie made herself some coffee and heard the water running in Amelia's bathroom. She poured her daughter a glass of milk and popped two pieces of bread in the toaster. She waited for Amelia to come out to the kitchen. When she didn't appear, Josie put the jar of grape jelly on a tray with the toast and milk and a napkin and carried it to Amelia's room. Her daughter pointedly ignored her, her chin stuck out like a bulldog's. She'd inherited that from her grandmother.

"You can be mad at me all you want, Amelia," Josie said. "But you have to eat sometime."

Amelia treated her mother to more stubborn silence. Josie set the tray on Amelia's desk and left. She felt like a complete failure. She cleaned the kitchen and dusted and vacuumed the living room.

Amelia skipped lunch and dinner. Now Josie was worried.

"Let her alone," her mother counseled, but Josie was afraid her daughter's grief would make her sick.

When Amelia declined breakfast again the next morning, Josie called Jane. "Do you know where Jack is staying?" Josie asked.

"I don't know and I don't care," Jane said.

"Well, I care about my daughter," Josie said.

It took real effort for her to hang up the phone gently. Josie started calling every airport hotel she could find on the Internet. She finally reached Jack at the Marriott.

"I'm sorry I behaved the way I did," Jack said. "It was childish. Your mother is a good woman and I regret hurting her feelings."

"She'll survive," Josie said. "But I'm really worried about your granddaughter. She's refusing to eat. She hasn't had a bite since yesterday. I wonder if you would come over to talk to her."

"Of course. We'll go out to lunch. What does she like to eat?"

"McDonald's is good enough," Josie said.

"Not for my granddaughter," he said.

"How about a big, thick sandwich at the Posh Nosh?" Josie said. "It's nearby in Clayton and not as expensive as the name sounds."

"Good," he said. "I could eat a horse, as you say."

"No horses, but the Posh Nosh does have buffalo pastrami and buffalo corned beef. I think the deli calls it bison."

"What about my granddaughter? Does she eat bison?"

"I think she prefers salami and Swiss on sourdough. But she'll probably have a Canada Dry ginger ale in your honor."

"My son tried to drink Canada dry for years," Jack said.

There was an awkward silence. Josie didn't know what to say.

"Yes, well, I'd better drive to your home and see my granddaughter," Jack said. "Would you give me the directions again?"

Josie did, careful to steer him around the maze of highway construction.

"One more favor," Josie said. "Would you talk her into changing out of that pink hoodie her father gave her? She won't take it off."

"I'll do my best," he said.

Josie hung up, feeling a little better. She was giving up some of her control over her daughter, but she no longer felt she could cope with the problems Nate had caused.

Josie knocked on Amelia's door. "Your grandfather is coming to see you," she said. The girl was still curled up in bed, pale and unmoving, wearing the rumpled hoodie.

Amelia made no response. Josie decided to leave her alone. She reheated a cup of coffee and was gratified to hear sounds of running water coming from Amelia's bathroom.

Jack made it to Josie's home in less than half an hour. Once again, Josie was struck by how much he looked like Nate. It hurt her to see him. She could almost imagine Nate was alive again. She brushed away those thoughts and the tears that went with them, and opened the door.

"Thanks for being here," she said.

"How is my granddaughter?" Jack said. "May I see her?"

"I'm right here," Amelia said. She was still too pale, but washed and dressed, with her dark hair neatly pulled back by a headband. She was still wearing the precious hoodie, which was getting a bit gray around the edges.

"You look nice," her grandfather said. "You've made an effort with your appearance. I'd like to ask one more favor, please?"

"What?" Amelia's voice was suddenly frosty with suspicion.

"That hoodie is lovely, but not as fresh as it should be. Would you change into something a little cleaner? Your mother will wash it while we're gone."

Amelia's jaw started to thrust forward with that bulldog stubbornness. Jack saw it, too.

"I hear the Posh Nosh has good buffalo pastrami," he said. "If we're going to lunch at some place posh, we should dress the part."

"I don't trust her," Amelia said stubbornly.

"I do," Jack said. "Your father trusted your mother. Nate said Josie did the right thing to keep you away from him when he was dealing. No matter what you see on the television, there is nothing romantic about what my son did. He sold drugs that killed people."

"No!" Amelia said. "Daddy wouldn't do anything bad."

"You can still love him, Amelia, even though he had his faults. Now, will you please change so we can go for a bite to eat, just the two of us?"

Amelia stood there, and for a moment Josie was

afraid she would refuse. Then she turned around and walked toward her room.

Josie let out the breath she didn't realize she was holding. "I think she's going to be all right," she said.

"I'll do my best to talk to her," Jack said.

Amelia reappeared, wearing a blue-and-white striped shirt. "That's my girl," her grandfather said. "You look posh indeed."

Josie felt a momentary panic when she saw her daughter get in the car with her grandfather. What if Jack drove off and didn't return? What if he took Amelia to Canada?

And not claim his son's body for burial? I don't think so, Josie told herself.

But just in case, she made a note of the rental car's license plate.

Chapter 20

"You're going to throw Daddy away?" Amelia said.

Josie heard fresh tears in her daughter's voice. Amelia had hardly stopped crying since Nate died five days ago. Amelia's eyelids were rimmed with pink and her nose was red. She didn't want to go to school, and Josie didn't have the heart to insist. Amelia needed to mourn in privacy.

"No, no, sweetheart," Jack said. He leaned forward in his chair. "I'm going to *scatter* your daddy's ashes. There's a big difference. Scattering a man's ashes is respectful."

"But then Daddy won't have a grave." Amelia looked even more upset.

"I can't stick my son in a box in the dark ground," Jack said. "He hated being cooped up like a chicken in—" His words skidded to a stop. He couldn't bring himself to say "prison."

"Amelia, it wouldn't be right," her grandfather continued. "Pilots need freedom. They belong in the sky."

"But how will I remember him?" Amelia asked.

"Look in the mirror and you'll always have your father with you," Josie said. "That's what he told you. You look just like him. Remember?"

Amelia nodded. Her lower lip trembled. More tears were threatening to burst loose.

Jack, Josie, and Amelia were planning Nate's memorial service in Josie's worn living room. Jack sat as far away from Jane as he could get without going outside. Jane was like a chastened child, huddled in a frumpy brown sweater. She said nothing, wore no makeup, and made no effort to flirt. She must blame herself, too, Josie decided.

Josie felt numb, as if she were in the middle of some horrible reality show. Jack looked so much like a middle-aged version of her Nate, it hurt Josie to watch him. She was starting to realize what she and her daughter had lost.

"We'll have two memorial services," Jack said. "Your father will be doubly honored. One will be here in the States for Nate's friends and family. The other will be in Toronto, his home. The crematorium in St. Louis has a chapel we can use."

Josie had seen that chapel. It was cold as a walk-in freezer.

"Are we going to have problems with the press?" she asked. "What if they show up?"

The media had almost hourly updates about what they dubbed the Death by Chocolate poisonings. Were the victims killed by a crazed murderer? Were more people supposed to die before the antifreeze-laced chocolate sauce was discovered? Did the radio station want its Big Loser dead?

Nobody knew, but everyone had a theory.

The police still had no solid leads. Nate's drug-dealing past did not make the news, and for that Josie was thankful.

"The service will be invitation only," Jack said. "We won't have time to send them out, but we can call Nate's friends and make a list of names. That way, we can keep the vultures out of the chapel. Besides, it's supposed to snow again tomorrow and the temperature will drop below zero. They'll freeze their a—" He looked at Amelia and finished, "Arms off."

Amelia managed a tentative smile, the first since her father died.

Tuesday, the morning of Nate's funeral, dawned clear and cold. Almost as cold as Canada, Josie decided, though she'd never been there. Lined up at the wrought-iron cemetery gates were TV satellite trucks and reporters' cars, waiting for the last rites of the latest victim.

Josie took a small satisfaction in seeing the TV reporters shiver as they did their stand-ups by the icy iron gates. She could see their breath in the cold air. Good. Maybe they'd leave quicker.

Inside the cemetery, the weeping stone angels and gray granite slabs were softened with fresh snow. She read the tombstones closest to the cemetery lane: BELOVED HUSBAND, BELOVED FATHER, and BELOVED SON were glazed with ice and frosted with snow, like grim candy confections.

I don't see one with BELOVED LOVER, Josie thought. But Nate was loved—by his father, by his daughter, and by me.

Josie's gray Honda skidded on the icy cemetery lane, and she steered into the slide, praying she didn't hit a gravestone.

"Slow down," her mother commanded, "before we all join him."

Josie pumped the brakes and slowly brought the car under control. She could see the little marble chapel ahead, white and cold as an ice cube. Josie parked near it. Alyce, Josie's best friend, pulled up in her SUV and waited for them to climb out of the car.

"I'm so sorry," Alyce said. She hugged Josie and then Amelia. She smelled of cinnamon and face powder.

Her white skin was nearly translucent. Somehow Alyce managed her odd floaty walk even on a salt-sprinkled sidewalk.

"Where's Nate's father?" Alyce asked.

"Inside," Josie said. "He wanted some time alone."

The chapel wasn't as grim as Josie had feared. Wreaths with red velvet bows hung on the doors, swags of evergreen draped the windows, and candles shone on the nondenominational altar. Solemn organ music played, but Josie couldn't identify the composer. She wondered if there was a special CD for memorial services: *Death's Greatest Hits*.

Josie was pleased that her favorite framed photo of young Nate in his leather bomber jacket was on the altar. Nate looked the way he had when Josie first knew him, smiling and confident. Next to the photo was a spray of red roses and a small silver filigree box containing Nate's ashes.

My love is reduced to ashes, Josie thought, then decided she was being a drama queen, and marched up the aisle to the front pew.

We must look like a flock of crows, she thought, as the women settled into their seats. Josie wore black for Nate's memorial service. Alyce sat on Josie's left, also in black. Occasionally, she reached over to pat Josie's hand. Amelia, on Josie's right, wore a navy pantsuit and a wide-brimmed hat with a black ribbon. Josie called it her "Madeline" hat, because it looked like the style worn by the storybook French schoolgirl.

Jane also wore black. She sat in the back of the chapel. She'd volunteered to check off the guests' names. Also, she was as far away from Jack as possible.

Mike had offered to be at the service with Josie, but she thought that would cause Jack more pain. Mike seemed hurt by her refusal. Again, he didn't tell Josie he loved her. Those words seemed lost. Josie wondered if he was seeing the bookstore blonde.

Some of Nate's friends were at the chapel. They were a decade older, and it showed on most of them. Sandy, once a wild red-haired beauty, was now a plus-sized matron with short brown hair. She had three children and sold real estate in West County. She was probably the most successful of the old crowd.

Elliott was the smartest of the old group. Josie had thought he'd be a full professor by now, but Elliott was still a bartender taking night-school classes. His hair had gone completely gray, and he'd developed a bitter streak.

Josie saw no sign of the awful Mitch. She was relieved. He hadn't been invited to the service, but that wouldn't have stopped Mitch.

Mrs. Mueller, wearing a black hat that looked like a squashed velvet wastebasket, took a seat right behind Josie and Amelia. Josie knew her nosy neighbor hadn't been invited, but Jane was too awed by her friend to evict her.

Behind Mrs. M was a handful of men in battered topcoats and gray suits. Josie wondered if they were homicide detectives. Unfortunately, she knew their look.

Josie couldn't believe Nate's death was a random murder by an unknown stranger. There had to be a reason. Nate had died of a heart attack, but the autopsy confirmed that antifreeze had killed him. Did Mitch follow his former friend to Josie's house and pour antifreeze into Nate's chocolate sauce?

Josie knew that was a crazy idea. She hadn't seen Mitch in years. But Mitch had the only reason for wanting Nate dead, and it was powerful: He wanted Nate's storage locker full of money.

Josie heard the chapel doors open and prayed it wasn't

Mitch. She looked around cautiously and saw another friend of Nate's. Harvey looked hungover. He'd always looked hungover, but now it showed. His face seemed to be melting. Harvey had the pouchy basketball-shaped gut that went with liver damage. His gray-brown hair was wild and his black sweater was stained.

The funeral music stopped and Nate's father stepped up to the dark wood podium. The microphone gave a haunted-house creak as he pulled it toward him. There was a screech of feedback.

"My son," Jack said. The two words echoed off the cold stone.

"My son," he repeated, "is Nathan Weekler. I never thought I'd outlive him. Nate was too alive." His voice faltered.

Jack took a deep breath and continued, "My son made mistakes in his life. But he knew how to live and he knew how to love. He gave me the finest gift of all— my granddaughter, Amelia."

Amelia started crying again. Josie felt all the eyes in the chapel turn toward her daughter. Alyce reached over and patted Josie's hand.

"Nate wanted to be a pilot from the time he was younger than Amelia. It didn't matter how many toy cars and red wagons we gave him—Nate always made whatever it was into an airplane. He broke his arm when he was six trying to fly a cardboard box off the front steps."

Josie smiled through her tears. She was glad Amelia heard these stories about her father's boyhood.

"The happiest day of my son's life was when he got his pilot's license," Jack said.

"Nate was a man who had everything: a woman he loved, a beautiful daughter, and a chance to fly. Not many men get those opportunities. His time with us was too short, but he had a life we can celebrate."

"Here, here!" Harvey said and stood up. He lurched to the front of the room. "Wanna say a few words about Nate."

Don't give him the microphone, Josie prayed, but Jack sat down in the front row like a man who'd put down a great burden. Harvey gripped the podium as if he were on a ship in a stormy sea. Josie suspected Harvey was one of Nate's dealer buddies, but she could never prove it. She'd pulled herself away from that world.

"Nate," Harvey said, and bowed to the filigree casket. "You made an ash of yourself. An ash. Get it?" His words were slurred.

Josie shut her eyes. Please, she begged, don't talk about what you did in the old days, Harvey. Not with Nate's daughter here.

"Nate and I got drunk a lot," Harvey said. "I still get drunk. In fact, I'm drunk now." He grinned, as if he'd said something clever, reached into his suit coat pocket and pulled out a flask. Harvey raised his flask in a toast. "Here's looking up your old address, Nate." He took a long drink. The mourners shifted restlessly.

"I can't believe Nate was done in by a snowman cake." He sang three words, "Frosty the Deadman—"

"Mom," Amelia whispered. "Is that man drunk?"

"Yes," Josie whispered back.

"Can I say something about Daddy when he finishes?" Josie nodded, afraid to speak.

"Nate and I drank a lot, like I said," Harvey said. "But we were beer drinkers. Never any of that anti— that anti— that antifreeze. Nate liked beer. I like beer."

Harvey stopped, as if he was suddenly lost. It took a long moment for him to collect his scattered thoughts.

"But despite our differences, we respected each other. Respect. That was us. Let me sing Nate's favorite song. I taught it to him, and I hope to hell it isn't true."

His voice wavered as he sang out of tune:

"In heaven there is no beer / That's why we drink it here—"

That's when Josie heard the militant clatter of high heels on the stone floor. Jane marched to the front of the church and turned off the microphone. "Thank you very much," she said crisply.

"But, little lady—"

"It's Mrs. Marcus to you, sir. And I said sit."

Harvey sat, like a large, shaggy dog. Josie wanted to applaud her mother.

Amelia stood up and went to the podium. Jack turned the microphone back on and bent it down to Amelia's height.

My daughter seems so grown-up, Josie thought. Amelia looked fragile and pale.

"Nate Weekler was my father," she said. "I didn't have him very long. He didn't live with us. But he told me he loved me, he was proud of me, and he would always be with me. He made me promise that I would finish college. I will keep my promise.

"My friend Zoe at school, her father lives with her all the time. He's never said anything like that to her in nine whole years. Zoe's father is gone a lot on business. I had more from my father in one day than most girls have in their whole life. Thank you, Daddy."

Thank you, Amelia, Josie thought. When her daughter returned to her seat, Josie hugged her and whispered, "You did good. I'm proud of you. Your father is, too."

"Anyone else?" Jack asked.

Mercifully, the group stayed quiet.

"Let us have a moment of silence for my son," Jack said.

Josie stared at her black gloves, and thanked Nate

and her daughter. They had both eased her burden of guilt.

The funeral music played again, and the people began filing out.

As she approached the door, two men in gray suits flanked Josie and said, "Josie Marcus? We'd like to talk to you about the murder of Nathan Weekler."

"What?" Josie asked in a daze. She could see Mrs. Mueller waiting by the door, smiling triumphantly.

Alyce stepped between Josie and the homicide detectives. "Not without counsel present. That's me, gentlemen."

Chapter 21

"Are you a lawyer?" the young detective asked. His rumpled gray suit looked like he'd borrowed it from his father.

With his peach-fuzz skin and round, innocent face, he seems too young to be a police officer, Josie thought. Or maybe I'm getting old. Isn't that a sign of age when the cops look young?

"I'm representing Ms. Marcus," Alyce said.

Josie's friend looked every inch a lawyer in her severe black pantsuit. She'd neatly sidestepped the young man's question. Alyce had audited law school—especially Jake's early-morning classes—and had taken tests for her husband in the big auditorium courses.

"May I see your credentials, gentlemen?" Alyce asked.

"It's 'detective,' " the older suit said. "We're with the Rock Road force."

"I thought the hospital was in Maplewood," Alyce said.

"The hospital is on the border," Detective Baby Face said. "We caught the squeal."

You've caught too many TV shows, Josie thought.

St. Louis County was divided into more than ninety municipalities, some the size of matchbooks. Rock Road

Village was one of those. Josie was surprised it was big enough to have its own detectives. Rock Road was a notorious speed trap.

"We'd like Ms. Marcus to accompany us to the Rock Road station," the older detective said. His gray suit was the same shade as his hair. He gave his name, but his worn face registered in Josie's addled brain as Detective Gray.

"Is this a custodial interview?" Alyce asked. "Are you planning to charge her?"

"Uh," Baby Face said. "We just want to ask a few questions."

"Good. Then let's get them over with now." Alyce plopped down in a pew by the chapel doors and dragged the dazed, silent Josie after her. That left the two detectives standing. Baby Face rested his rump on the pew back. Detective Gray stayed ramrod straight.

He's the tough one, Josie decided.

"Mom?" Amelia asked. Her frightened face was shadowed by the big-brimmed hat.

"Your mother is fine, honey," Alyce said. "Go with your grandmother. This will only take a few minutes. I'll drive Josie home."

She practically pushed Amelia out the door with Jane. That left Josie and Alyce sitting together in the chilly chapel. Alyce said, "Detectives, please state your business."

"We found antifreeze jugs in Ms. Marcus's trash," Detective Gray said.

"I—"

"Don't say a word, Josie," Alyce said. "Did you get a search warrant for those jugs, detectives?"

"Didn't need one," Detective Gray said. "The Dumpster was in a public alley. We found the jugs in a trash bag containing junk mail addressed to Ms. Marcus."

"Anyone could have planted those antifreeze jugs, along with the junk mail, in an unlocked Dumpster," Alyce said.

"They didn't," Detective Gray said. "Unless they added her daughter's schoolwork. Amelia. That's her name, right?"

Josie nodded.

"What was Mr. Weekler's demeanor when you last saw him at your house, Ms. Marcus?" Detective Gray asked.

"He was drunk," Josie said. "He wanted inside, but I wouldn't open the door."

"Mr. Weekler had a problem with alcohol abuse," Alyce said. "Drunks die all the time from the things they do to their bodies, especially in cold weather."

"Mr. Weekler died of antifreeze poisoning," Baby Face said. "The autopsy found oxalate crystals in the victim's urine."

"What kind of antifreeze?" Alyce asked.

"We can't determine the brand from our tests," Detective Gray said.

"I mean, was it traditional ethylene glycol or the newer, organic coolant—the safe antifreeze?"

Josie was impressed. She didn't know that much about antifreeze.

"No antifreeze is safe to drink," Detective Gray said.

"You didn't answer my question," Alyce said.

"We didn't test for the brand. That's beyond our capabilities. However, Ms. Marcus's fingerprints were all over the empty antifreeze jugs."

"How do you know?" Alyce said. "She didn't give you her prints."

"The hospital gave us the snowman cake box from the Elf House," Detective Baby Face said. "We eliminated Mr. Weekler's prints, the shop owner's, and the admitting clerk's prints. The fourth set had to be hers. Ms. Marcus poured antifreeze into the chocolate sauce and killed Mr. Weekler."

"She didn't," Alyce said. "You're looking at a major lawsuit if you say she did. According to the news, a woman also died of antifreeze poisoning. She was a contestant on a radio station. Ms. Marcus didn't know the woman."

"Credit-card receipts show Ms. Marcus was at the Elf House the day the poisoned chocolate was discovered," Baby Face said. "She could have used the death of the woman as a cover for the murder of Mr. Weekler. Like those Tylenol product-tampering murders that killed eight people."

"Ms. Marcus brought the cake box to the hospital voluntarily," Alyce said. "She wanted the box tested to save Mr. Weekler's life. If she was trying to kill him, she would have thrown the box away and destroyed any evidence."

"What was your relationship to Mr. Weekler, Ms. Marcus?" Detective Gray asked.

Josie looked at Alyce. "You can answer that," Alyce said.

"Mr. Weekler was the father of my nine-year-old daughter. He—" Alyce gave Josie's hand a warning squeeze and Josie shut up.

"Did you have a fight with the victim about the custody of your daughter shortly before his death? Did he want to take Amelia back to Canada?" Gray asked.

"Don't answer that," Alyce said. "Where did you get that information, detective?"

"It's common knowledge in the neighborhood," Baby Face said.

Josie knew where that information came from— common Mrs. Mueller.

"Why was Mr. Weekler sitting on your steps with a chocolate snowman cake?" Detective Gray asked.

Alyce nodded at Josie. "He wanted to give the cake to my daughter. I would not let him in the house until he sobered up."

"But he died," Detective Gray said. "And your custody issue died with him."

"That isn't a question, detective," Alyce said. "Do you have anything else you'd like to ask?"

"Are you dating a plumber named Mike?" Detective Gray asked.

"Yes," Josie said.

"And this Mike had an altercation with Mr. Weekler shortly before he died? I believe he escorted Mr. Weekler out of your home."

Alyce stood up. "This interview is over. Of course my client had antifreeze jugs in her trash. So does every driver in St. Louis this time of year. As for the fingerprints—if they were her fingerprints—on the cake box, so what? Ms. Marcus mystery-shopped that store. She can show you the instructions from her employer. You don't have anything, detectives. Josie, let's go."

Josie followed Alyce outside.

"Don't say a word until we're in the car," Alyce said in a low voice. Josie collapsed into the plush seats of Alyce's SUV, and her friend drove through a gloomy landscape of cold granite and snow-covered graves under a lead sky.

"You were amazing," Josie said. "They were going to arrest me."

"They couldn't arrest you," Alyce said. "What do they have? Fingerprints on some antifreeze jugs left in an open Dumpster. Big deal. Fingerprints on a cake box you voluntarily brought to the hospital. So what? They have no witnesses."

"But plenty of motive," Josie said. "I wanted Nate out of my life, Alyce. I spent his memorial service wondering who would benefit from his death. It's me. I have the best motive."

"Don't even say that in an empty room," Alyce said. "You're safe for now. Once the police arrest you, the 'speedy trial' rule kicks in. No sane prosecutor will go to trial with that rubbish, and I mean that literally."

"Thanks," Josie said. "I'd better call Mom. She's at O'Connell's Pub for Nate's wake."

"Do you want me to take you there?" Alyce said, as she turned out of the cemetery and onto the main road.

"No," Josie said. "O'Connell's has too many painful memories. It's where Nate and I first met. I can't go back there for his wake."

"Why don't you stop at my house for coffee?" Alyce said. "I'm baking for the subdivision cookie exchange. Ten batches. I'll make some for you, too."

"That's too much work," Josie said.

"No, it's not," Alyce said. "I'm letting out my inner Cookie Monster. You can lick the bowl. Little Justin is not supposed to eat raw cookie dough, but it's safe for adults."

"Definitely worth any salmonella risk," Josie said. "Will there be chocolate chip cookies?"

"Yes, and gingerbread men, cherry tuiles, royal icing trees with silver ball ornaments."

"You've got a deal," Josie said, as she speed-dialed Jane.

"Hello? Mom, I can't hear you. It sounds like you're in a bar. Oh, you *are* in a bar, right. The police are gone. I'm fine. Alyce handled them. No, there's no problem. Sorry, I won't be at the wake, Mom. I can't go back to O'Connell's.

"How's Amelia? Should I swing by and pick her up?

Well, as long as she's with her grandfather, she's fine. I'm going to Alyce's house. See you in a couple of hours. What?"

Josie fumbled the phone and nearly dropped it. The blood drained from her face.

"Mitch! He's there now? He said to tell me hello? Stay away from that man, Mom. He's one of Nate's drug-dealing friends. Keep Amelia away from him, too."

Josie ended her call and folded her phone shut. Her arm still hurt where Mitch had twisted it at the hospital.

"Everything okay?" Alyce asked. "I couldn't help overhearing."

"No. It's not good at all. I surprised one of Nate's drug-dealing buddies in his room at the hospital. Mitch was looking for the key to Nate's storage locker. It's supposed to be full of cash. Nate wanted me to have the money."

"Did you give Mitch the key?" Alyce asked.

"Of course not. I pretended I didn't know what Mitch was talking about."

"How much money is in there?"

"Thousands. But I'm not keeping it," Josie said.

"Should we go get Amelia?"

"She's safe with her grandfather. Besides, Mitch can't make a scene with everyone around."

"I hope not." Alyce headed west, toward her home in the Estates at Wood Winds. They were out of the cemetery, driving past strip malls and fast-food franchises.

"The detectives would hound me forever if they knew about Nate's drug money stash," Josie said. "I think that's the real reason Nate came back."

"If I were you, Josie, I'd clean out that storage locker fast," Alyce said. "The police aren't stupid. Don't underestimate them. Especially the older guy."

"He did seem smarter than his sidekick," Josie said.

"I'm impressed by the way you handled those detectives, Alyce. How do you know so much about antifreeze?"

"It's a hot topic in my subdivision," Alyce said. "The Wood Winds homeowners association tried to outlaw traditional antifreeze, because ethylene glycol has a sweet taste that can attract pets and children. As little as a teaspoon can kill a cat. Two tablespoons can kill a toddler.

"The homeowners were up in arms over the proposed ban and voted the board out for even suggesting it. This subdivision is crawling with lawyers, and half of them threatened to sue. Some parents care more about their cars than their kids. Jake takes no chances. He uses Sierra, the so-called safer antifreeze."

"I know antifreeze can be dangerous," Josie said. "I kept it locked away when Amelia was little. *Stop!*"

Alyce hit the brakes and the SUV screeched to a halt. Her already pale skin looked like it had been dusted with flour. "What's wrong?"

"Forget the cookies. We need to get Amelia," Josie said. "Right now. I can't leave her alone with Mitch. O'Connell's is close to too many major routes. Mitch could grab my daughter and run."

"Now you're talking," Alyce said.

Chapter 22

Alyce made a U-turn to a chorus of angry horns and raised middle fingers. She gave the drivers a ladylike wave.

"We'll be at O'Connell's in twenty minutes," she said. "Sooner if I hit enough green lights. Anyone else we have to watch out for besides this Mitch?"

"Yes, Harvey, the drunk who sang 'Frosty the Deadman' at the memorial service."

"He was a piece of work," Alyce said. "Was he like that when you were dating Nate?"

"Is that your tactful way of asking if Harvey was always an insensitive drunk? He was always over the top. But I was twenty years old—a really stupid twenty. You look at your friends differently when you don't have children."

"I sure wouldn't want Justin pulling some of the stunts Jake and I did when we were single," Alyce said. She sailed through a red light to furious honks.

"Please, Alyce," Josie said. "Don't get a ticket on my behalf."

"My husband is a lawyer," Alyce said. "A ticket is nothing when a child's safety is at risk. Josie, how are you going to get rid of this Mitch guy? I don't think he'll be scared of you."

"Maybe if I got a tattoo," Josie said.

"Or sent Mike to threaten him," Alyce said.

"No, I do my own dirty work," Josie said.

"You look really scary to me," Alyce said. "What do you weigh—a hundred and ten pounds?"

"One twenty," Josie said.

"And you have a black belt in karate."

"I have a black belt from Donna Karan, but it was on sale. I can make my way around any mall in the city, but I don't think that will impress him."

"Josie, he's going to stick to you like white on rice for that money. How much is in there—thousands?"

"At least. Maybe hundreds of thousands. Possibly as much as half a million. I've never been there, and have no idea. But he wants it bad. I'm going to tell Mitch that Nate gave me some incriminating information and if he doesn't leave me alone, I'll turn him in to the police."

"I saw that *Miami Vice* episode. Everybody got killed except Crockett and Tubbs. Josie, even if you have some useful information—and you don't—it's at least ten years old. The statute of limitations could have run out by now. You don't want the money, right?"

"No. It's dirty money."

"But you could find clean uses for it."

"It's bad karma, Alyce. I really believe that. I don't want it, and I don't want the murder and the pain associated with it."

"Then give Mitch the money."

"But Nate didn't want him to have it."

"Nate's dead, Josie. And you're going to be, too, if you don't let go of something you don't want. Nate wouldn't want anything to happen to you or his daughter. Get rid of Mitch. He's dangerous."

"You're right," Josie said.

She pulled the storage-locker key out of her purse,

wrote down the address and unit number, wiped the key clean with a tissue, and stuck it in her coat pocket. She put the address and unit number in her other pocket.

Josie sighed. Nate meant well, but this gift was more trouble he'd brought into their lives.

"Are you okay?" Alyce asked.

"I guess," Josie said. "Nate was so wonderful in the hospital. It was like the man I loved was back. But he was a devil when he drank. I wished that drunk Nate dead, but I also lost my Nate."

"Josie, your Nate was gone long ago, if he ever existed."

"I know, I know. He was selling drugs when I was dating him, and I was too dumb to know that. God knows what else he was doing. I'm better off away from him, and so is our daughter."

Alyce turned into the pub's crowded parking lot. "What's the plan?"

"Circle the lot. I'll be out as soon as I get Amelia."

Josie stood at the doorway inside the dimly lit bar. Her black outfit seemed to melt into the shadows. Jack was laughing, playing darts and drinking with his son's friends. Jane was nowhere to be seen. Amelia was sitting with Mitch, sharing a basket of crispy fries. The table next to them was piled with thick-bottomed beer steins and empty food platters.

Great, Josie thought. How am I going to get Amelia away from Mitch?

She picked up an empty, lipsticked beer stein and marched over to Mitch's table.

"Amelia, we have to go. Right now." She held out her hand.

"Mom?" Amelia looked confused. "Is something wrong? I was just talking. Mr. Mitch knew Daddy."

Mitch smiled, showing those crooked-tombstone

teeth. His eyes were flat and yellow, like a goat's. "Aw, don't be mad, Josie. I was telling my little friend a few *key* facts about her daddy." He hooked one huge hand around Amelia's arm. A Rolex watch glowed on his wrist. Josie could tell it was a fake by the jerky movement of the second hand.

"Amelia," Josie said. "We have to leave."

Mitch gripped Amelia's arm tighter. "We've had an interesting conversation. I didn't realize you still live in your mom's house in Maplewood. I could drop in anytime and surprise you. And your daughter. I've got lots of stories about her daddy."

The yellow goat's eyes narrowed. "Give me the key, Josie."

Josie threw the tissue-wrapped key on the table and it slid across the top. Mitch let go of Amelia's arm to reach for it. Josie slammed his wrist with the heavy beer stein. His fake watch crystal cracked.

"Oops," Josie said. "It slipped. I'm so sorry." Insincerity dripped from her voice like acid.

"Ow," Mitch said. "Shit. That was a Rolex."

Josie threw a twenty on the table. "It was a fake, Mitch, just like you. This should buy you a new one. If you want a real Rolex, I'd head out to that storage locker soon. You've got twenty-four hours before I call the police and they impound the cash."

Josie bent down and whispered in his hairy ear, "If I catch you talking to my daughter again, there won't be enough of you left to bury in an envelope."

"I won't forget this," Mitch snarled, rubbing his wrist and removing the shattered watch.

"I hope not. Amelia, tell your grandfather good-bye."

Amelia and Josie both hugged Grandpa Jack. Jane emerged from the restroom. "Mom, I'm taking Amelia home. You can drive my car, okay?"

Josie and her daughter headed for the door. She passed Harvey throwing darts.

"Josie!" Harvey cried, loud enough so the whole bar could hear him. He came over and gave her a hug and said, "You aren't mad at me, are you?" The stench of beer on his breath nearly knocked her over.

"Harvey," Josie said, "why would I be mad at you? Listen, keep an eye on Mitch. He has the key to Nate's storage locker. I think he's going out there very soon, probably sometime today."

"You kidding me? I've been looking for that place for ten years. I'll give you a cut of the cash."

"No need," Josie said. "Nate left us well provided."

"How can I thank you?" Harvey asked.

"Your surprise will be thanks enough," Josie said, and virtually pushed Amelia out the door. "Quick! There's Alyce."

Alyce had the SUV's engine running. Josie nearly threw Amelia into the backseat. She noticed her daughter was carrying a blue velvet box, but there was no time to ask about it. Josie jumped in the front, then slammed and locked the door as if the devil were after her.

"Drive off," Josie said. "Hurry!"

"Where to?" Alyce asked.

"Home," Josie said. "I mean, my home. Maplewood."

"Josie, are you and Amelia going to be okay, or do you want to stay with Jake and me?"

"We'll be fine," Josie said. "Mitch has an errand that should keep him busy the rest of today and most of tomorrow. I know you have to bake those cookies, but do you have time to swing by the Galleria?"

"Are we having a shopping emergency?" Alyce said.

"I need to go to the California Pizza Kitchen," Josie said.

"Yay!" Amelia said. "Pizza for dinner!"

"Somehow I can't see you in a hurry for a chopped salad, Josie," Alyce said. "Don't worry about the cookies. Come over tomorrow if you want."

"I'll call the restaurant now for our order," Josie said. "What would you like, Alyce?"

"Nothing, thanks. I'll take a rain check."

"I want a pepperoni-and-mushroom pizza," Amelia said.

"You have your mother's same love of healthy food," Alyce said.

Amelia looked puzzled.

Josie placed her phone order while Alyce threaded the traffic-clogged streets to the mall. Josie studied the traffic behind them, making sure Mitch or Harvey wasn't following them. She saw only matronly minivans and sedate SUVs.

Alyce turned into the Galleria mall parking lot and stopped in front of the California Pizza Kitchen entrance. Josie jumped out.

"I'll circle around until you're out again," Alyce said.

Amelia started to follow her, but Josie said, "Stay with Alyce, please. I'll only be a minute."

Josie headed for the pay phone just inside the mall's lobby doors. She dialed information and asked for the St. Louis Regional CrimeStoppers number. Then she dialed it.

When a woman answered, Josie interrupted her. "I only have a minute. I don't want a reward and I can't give my name. Some dealers have been keeping large amounts of cash and drugs in a storage locker by the airport. One is dead and the other two are after his money. Here's the address."

She read the information, then said, "Hurry. It will be cleaned out in the next twenty-four hours."

Josie hung up, feeling frightened, triumphant, and

ashamed. She'd never reported anyone to the police before. She was turning into Mrs. Mueller. But Mitch had threatened her daughter. She'd cut his heart out with a dull knife before she'd let him hurt Amelia.

Josie raced into the restaurant, paid for her order, and ran out again, waving down Alyce. The whole transaction took maybe ten minutes.

"Look what Grandpa gave me," Amelia said, when Josie settled into the front seat with the pizza box.

She held out a small crystal heart that looked like Waterford.

"It's beautiful, honey," Josie said.

"It's Daddy," Amelia said. "Grandpa said I could have some of him."

Josie saw the gray-white ash and bone chips through the glass and felt queasy. This was a spoonful of Nate.

"That was very—" Very what? She searched for the right word. Sad? Morbid? Freaking weird?

"Grandpa said this way I could always have my daddy with me. I'm thinking of burying him in the backyard, by the roses, so he'll have his own grave."

"Just like a pet cat," Josie said softly.

"What?" Amelia said.

"It's such a pretty crystal heart," Alyce said. "Maybe you'll want to keep it in your room. That way you'll have your father close to you. When you grow up and move away, you can take him with you."

Josie didn't know which was worse. Having a spoonful of her drunken ex buried in the backyard was creepy. But so was keeping a fancy ashtray of dear Daddy on her daughter's dresser.

"Do you really think Daddy's heart is inside this box?" Amelia asked.

"If that's what your grandfather told you," Josie said.

"It is," she said. "When I visit my grandpa in the summer, we're going to take the rest of Daddy to his favorite place."

"That's nice," Josie said. The ghoulish conversation made the hair stand up on the back of her neck. She was relieved when Alyce turned down their street. "Here we are."

"Thank you, Alyce," Josie said. "I'll see you tomorrow about ten, unless Harry calls and wants me to work."

Josie carried the pizza box, careful to avoid getting grease on her black coat. Amelia held her velvet heart box as if it might leap from her hands. They cast black shadows on the white snow.

What a picture we make, Josie thought. We should call this *Daddy's Coming Home*. But I don't think Norman Rockwell ever painted a scene like this.

Chapter 23

Did I love Nate or a man who never existed? Josie asked herself.

She stared at her glass of red wine, as if the answer were hidden in its depths.

"Well, if you can't tell me anything useful, I've had enough of you," Josie said, and gulped it down.

She was curled up on the couch in her darkened living room, watching the winter shadows fall. She'd barely moved since she'd come home three hours ago. Josie felt too drained and exhausted. She didn't bother changing out of her black pantsuit. The memorial service, the detectives' interview, the tense encounter with the scary Mitch, and the cold, gray cemetery had made for a grim day.

Josie shivered and pulled the knitted throw around her. She poured herself another glass of red wine, then opened the tiny box of Godiva dark chocolate pearls and ate one.

Health food, she thought. Red wine and dark chocolate. Both good for the heart. Not that my heart is good for anything. It hurts, and all the wine and chocolate in the world won't help.

"Did you say something, Mom?" Amelia came into the living room with a square of pizza in one hand and the Waterford crystal heart in the other.

"Honey, you're going to get grease on your grandpa's present," Josie said.

"It's okay, Mom. I wiped my hands," Amelia said. "Why are you sitting in the dark?"

"I was just talking to myself," Josie said.

"You're nutso-crazy," Amelia said.

"Only if I answer back," Josie said.

Amelia had changed into the pink hoodie her father had bought her. Josie had washed it by hand so that it wouldn't be damaged. Amelia wore her present while she ate pizza in the kitchen, with the crystal heart on the table. Dinner with Daddy, Josie thought.

It had been a hard afternoon for her daughter. Amelia would nibble on a slice of pizza, then cry, then call her friend Emma, then go back to the kitchen and start the cycle again.

Josie wanted to take the crystal heart away. But she knew it would cause a terrible scene. Her daughter needed to mourn her lost father, and if her grandfather's creepy gift gave her comfort, so be it. Besides, Josie didn't have the energy to fight with Amelia.

A tear cascaded down Josie's cheek, and she didn't bother wiping it away. More tears came, hot and hurting. She didn't know if she was mourning the real Nate or her idealized lover. Josie sat in the dark room and tried to examine her own heart, which wasn't crystal clear at all.

How could I have been so dumb? she asked herself. I've been wrong about every man I've ever dated. Now that I've seen Nate's friends—the mean Mitch and the drunken Harvey—I must have worked hard to keep my eyes shut to any clues about Nate. I never really *looked* at the man I fell in love with.

Little memories came trickling back, scenes long forgotten. Like the night at a rowdy Riverfront bar. A friend of Nate's had sat down next to him and said, "I feel really tense, dude. I need to relax."

"I think I have something," Nate had said, and the two men disappeared outside. They were gone maybe ten minutes, but both came back smiling. Nate seemed to have had lots of tense friends in those days.

And one stupid girlfriend, Josie thought.

Now she knew what that scene meant. Nate was selling drugs, probably out of his car trunk. Weed or coke? Josie had no idea. She never caught the pungent odor of pot on his clothes. He never used drugs around Josie or offered her any.

But he spent thousands on their romantic trips, dinners, and extravagant presents, all in cash. Where did the money come from? Josie never asked.

I assumed his family was rich, she thought. Assumed. She remembered her fourth-grade teacher, Mrs. Taylor, repeating, "When you assume, Josie, you make an ass out of U and me."

I *am* an ass, Josie thought. Maybe I should quit dating. I'm no judge of men. I'd probably think a serial killer was a nice, quiet guy and wonder what he used to grow such beautiful roses in his yard.

She took another sip of wine and was surprised to find the second glass was empty already. She was getting drunk, but it wasn't pleasant.

Enough, she decided. The last thing Amelia needed was a drunken mother. This pity party is over. Josie put down the empty wineglass, corked the bottle, and stood up. Her phone rang.

It was Harry the Horrible. Josie imagined him at his desk, tufts of hair growing everywhere, including his nose, neck, and knuckles. Everywhere except on his scalp. He looked like a troll that lived under a bridge.

"Hey, Josie," he said. "I've got some work for you

tomorrow afternoon. You want to mystery-shop the Vandeventer Department Stores?"

"Sure," Josie said.

"You have to buy a sweater."

"I need one," Josie said.

"Too bad. You have to buy it in West County and return it at the South County store. And you'd better hurry, Josie. I'm guessing the Vandeventer stores will close any day now."

"Then why are they hiring a mystery shopper?" Josie asked.

"How the hell do I know?" Harry said. "I just take their money. This time I made sure I got it up front. I'll fax you the paperwork."

"Thanks, Harry," she said.

Josie saw the lights pop on at Mrs. Mueller's house. Oh, no, she thought. I forgot about the police. I'd better warn Mike about the detectives.

He answered his cell phone on the first ring. "Josie," he said, his voice cozy-warm. "How are you? How did the memorial service go?"

"It's over," she said. "It was short and sad."

"How are you?" he asked.

"I'm okay," she said.

"You don't sound okay," Mike said. "Do you want me to come over?"

So you can see me drunk and weeping for another man? No thanks. "I'd love to see you, but I'm tired, Mike. Can I have a rain check?"

"If that's how you feel." Mike sounded hurt.

"I'm sorry," Josie said. "It was an exhausting day. That's why I called you. The police were asking about you."

"I know, Josie. They've already been here. They seem to think I murdered Nate."

"Oh, no. I'm too late. I meant to call you, but things got busy and I forgot."

"You forgot? These guys want to throw my ass in jail and you forgot?"

"Calm down, Mike. What did they ask you?"

"Two detectives, a young one and an old one, interviewed me about Nate's death. They asked if I was dating you. They said I had an 'altercation' with Nate shortly before he died. All I did was drive him to his hotel. You went with me."

"I told them that, Mike. They think I'm a suspect, too. I'm sure they got a colorful account from my neighbor, Mrs. Mueller."

"What was I supposed to do? Let Nate drive drunk and kill himself or, worse, some innocent person?"

"Of course not. I'm sorry. Mrs. Mueller is such a pain in the keister."

"Why do the cops take that old biddy seriously?"

"Because she's a church lady and a neighborhood fixture."

"I know exactly what kind of fixture she is," Mike said. "White porcelain."

"Mike, I'm sorry. If I had any say-so, we'd have moved away from her years ago. Mom adores her, but I can't stand the old bat."

"It's not your fault, Josie. She's an evil gossip."

"Mike, I'm really sorry," Josie said. "But things got out of hand today." She started to tell him about Amelia and Mitch, but he cut her off.

"Hey, I'm not looking for an apology."

"How's Heather?" Josie asked, hoping to change the subject.

"Delighted that her mother's store is closing soon. Doreen has been whining and complaining constantly. They're both driving me crazy."

"Sounds like you need a break. How about dinner at my place tomorrow?"

"I'll call you," Mike said, and hung up without giving her a definite answer.

Terrific, Josie thought. Nosy Mrs. Mueller is going to cost me the only decent man I've dated in ages. Unless there's something wrong with Mike, too. He does have that weird daughter and witchy ex.

Is our romance over? Josie wondered, and felt the tears well up again. He used to tell me he loved me every time he called. Sometimes he'd call just to say that.

The hell with it. I've lived without a man before. Maybe I can invent a better one. She pushed away her sad, angry thoughts and went out to the kitchen. Amelia was sleeping with her head on the kitchen table, one hand cradling the crystal heart. Josie carefully pried it out of her daughter's hand so she wouldn't drop it, and then gently woke up Amelia.

It was ten o'clock by the time Josie got Amelia in bed, with the precious Waterford heart in an honored place on the dresser. Then Josie heated some chicken noodle soup. She took the soup and buttered toast into her bedroom and turned on the television.

A red BREAKING NEWS banner trailed along the bottom of the screen. A chirpy blond reporter, posed in front of what looked like a garage, said, "The dead man was identified as Preston 'Mitch' Paylor, of South St. Louis. He was shot three times when he fired on police and federal agents at a UR-Storage facility near Lambert-St. Louis Airport. Another man was shot once in the leg and taken to the hospital. Police and DEA recovered more than four hundred thousand dollars in cash and drugs with a street value of nearly a million dollars from the storage unit."

Right, Josie thought. Moldy pot and cocaine nearly a

decade old were worth a million bucks? I don't think so. Didn't illegal drugs have a shelf life?

Mitch's mug shot flashed on the screen. His mouth was closed to hide those ugly yellow teeth. He must have been crazy to try to fight the cops, Josie thought. He'd paid too high a price for that money.

Josie expected to feel bad at the news of Mitch's death, but she was relieved. She wouldn't have to worry anymore about that man threatening her daughter.

Amelia was safe.

There's one less lowlife in the world tonight, Josie thought. I'm not a powerless little single mom. I can call down death on my enemies.

She smiled for the first time since Nate died.

Chapter 24

Josie felt like a postmodern woman. Yesterday she set up a man to die. Today she helped Alyce bake cookies. I am a woman of many talents, she thought. I can take the heat and stay in the kitchen.

"What do you want me to do now?" Josie asked her friend.

Alyce's kitchen was about the size of Josie's flat, but paneled in linenfold oak, like a rich person's library. Even the fridge had a paneled-oak door. The effect was handsome, but Josie wasn't sure about walls that had to be waxed and dusted.

"You can warm the apple cider in that saucepan on the stove," Alyce said. "When it simmers—that means just before it breaks into a boil—pour the cider over the currants to plump them up. They're in that blue bowl."

"Those stingy-looking raisins?" Josie asked.

"Most currants are raisins," Alyce said. "I like the ones made from the Zante grapes. They're small and tart. It will take about ten minutes to plump them up."

Josie put the pan of cider on medium heat. Alyce had pulled out the heavy artillery for her cookie-baking session, including her Martha Stewart and Williams-Sonoma cookbooks. For Josie, they might as well have been quantum physics textbooks, but Alyce reveled in complicated feats of cookery.

So far this morning, they'd baked six different kinds of cookies, including colorful candy-stripe cookie sticks, cherry tuiles, Earl Grey cookies made with real ground-up tea leaves, and black-and-white cookies. Now they were working on yet another Martha Stewart recipe for apple currant cookies. Josie thought it was ungodly difficult.

"What's wrong with bringing chocolate chip cookies to the cookie exchange party?" Josie asked. "I like them."

"Everyone likes them," Alyce said.

"And they're easy to make," Josie said. "Even I can bake a good chocolate chip cookie."

"That's why I can't bring them. They're too easy. We have to bring cookies that show some culinary skill. They have to look like little works of art on the serving plates."

"So this isn't really a cookie exchange, it's a bake-off," Josie said.

"It's a show-off," Alyce said. "Remember Shirley, who lived in my subdivision for about three months?"

"Shirley with the orange hair and the gold tennis shoes?"

"That's the one. She begged for an invitation to the Wood Winds cookie exchange. Her husband was a big-deal broker and she wanted to be accepted here. She knew the cookie exchange was one of the ways into Wood Winds society. We're one of the last groups of full-time homemakers in the area, and we still follow the old ways.

"Shirley brought slice-and-bake sugar cookies with walnut halves stuck in them. They were broken walnuts, too, probably from the generic bin. She never lived down the scandal. The neighbors cut her dead and canceled her kid's play dates. She and her husband sold the house at a loss and moved a month later."

"So you're making show cookies," Josie said, "even though everyone would rather eat chocolate chips?"

"That's pretty much it," Alyce said. She had lined up unsalted butter, flour, baking soda, cinnamon, and brown sugar on the counter like a culinary army. The nutmeg grater looked like a tiny spaceship. Josie watched her friend deftly sift the flour, baking soda, and spices together into a smooth white-brown mound.

"Josie," Alyce said. "That man who was killed in the shoot-out at the storage locker late yesterday. The TV said his name was Mitch. Was he the Mitch who threatened Amelia?"

"Yes," Josie said.

"The guy who got shot in the leg was named Harvey. Was he the drunk who sang 'Frosty the Deadman' at Nate's memorial service?"

"That's him," Josie said.

"Remind me not to tick you off," Alyce said. "You got rid of two guys in less than twelve hours."

"I didn't do anything to them," Josie said.

"You tipped off the police, didn't you?" Alyce said. "That's why you had the sudden urge for pizza. There's a pay phone at the California Pizza Kitchen entrance of the Galleria, one of the few left. Most of the pay phones at the hospitals and the airport are gone."

"You must think I'm awful," Josie said.

"Honey, if some creep threatened my son, I wouldn't wait for the cops. I'd kill him myself."

Alyce used some weird paddle device on her mixer to beat the cookie dough into submission. "You did the right thing—and you left the shooting to the professionals," Alyce said. "Are you worried this Harvey creep will rat you out?"

Josie swallowed her laughter. Alyce's "rat you out" sounded hilarious amid her Williams-Sonoma perfection. "No. Harvey will probably suffer a severe attack of amnesia. I'm betting that he'll claim Mitch invited him to the storage unit to help him move furniture or something. Besides, there's nothing to connect me—no fingerprints, no DNA, fibers, or hair. I've never been to that storage unit, and I wiped the key before I gave it to Mitch. That money is at least ten years old and Nate is dead."

"Do you think Mitch or Harvey killed Nate?" Alyce said.

"With poisoned chocolate? Too chancy. Nate rarely ate sweets. Besides, he bought that chocolate snowman for Amelia."

"Omigod," Alyce said. "If you'd let Nate give her that cake, she'd be—"

"Dead," Josie finished. "The thought still gives me nightmares. Thank goodness Nate was drunk and I didn't let him in the house. These currants look about as plump as they're going to get."

"Good. Drain the cider down the sink and put the currants in the bowl with the rolled oats. Now you can shred one of those apples with the box grater. It's in the third cabinet on the right, second shelf."

Josie opened the cabinet and pulled out a round yellow plastic device with an odd metal oval in the middle.

"What's this?" she asked. "An ice hockey mask?"

"It's a mango pitter," Alyce said. "Those big seeds are hard to remove."

"They make my life miserable," Josie said.

"Come on," Alyce said. "I bet a mango has never crossed your threshold."

"Maplewood is the mango capital of the Midwest," Josie said. "Ah, this looks like a box grater." She pulled out a squarish metal item covered with sharp steel warts.

Alyce handed her the bowl of dough. "Start shredding the apple into this," she said. "Be careful to avoid the seeds and core."

Alyce cored three more apples, then sliced them into thin rings. "Josie, who do you think killed Nate? He had a lot of unusual friends."

"Mitch wanted that storage-unit key," Josie said. "But he wouldn't kill Nate for it. He'd make sure Nate stayed alive until he found it. Harvey had his faults, but I don't think he's mean enough to kill. Besides, he's too drunk and disorganized."

"Then who wanted Nate dead?" Alyce said. "Who benefits?"

"I do," Josie said. "Or rather, my daughter does. My name is on a hundred-thousand-dollar life insurance policy, but it's really for our daughter. Nate wanted the money held in trust for Amelia's education."

"Is that in writing?" Alyce said.

"No," Josie said. "But I'll honor his wishes."

"I'm sure you will," Alyce said. "I'm more worried about what the police will think."

"Oh, my good neighbor Mrs. Mueller put the icing on that particular cake. She told the cops Nate was talking about taking Amelia back to Canada."

"Is that true?"

"Unfortunately, yes. And we were probably talking loud enough that she heard us. But I wouldn't have killed him over that. He would have never gotten his hands on Amelia."

"That old battle-ax is nothing but trouble." Alyce sliced an apple into thin, fine circles.

"Tell me about it," Josie said. "She also sicced the police on Mike as a possible murder suspect. Here's

Mike's big crime: He drove a drunken Nate back to his hotel. I followed in Nate's rental car, and we took him upstairs to his room. Nate was well enough to drive his car the next day and create all kinds of havoc, but Mrs. M couldn't wait to tell the police that Mike and Nate had an 'altercation.' "

"So she has two men fighting over you," Alyce said. "I know you or Mike didn't kill Nate, but we're overlooking something major. What about the other woman who died of antifreeze poisoning? She was in that weight-loss contest on the radio. Maybe she was the real target, and Nate just died by accident. What do you know about her?"

"Nothing," Josie said, helping herself to an apple slice. "The news stories said she was fifty pounds overweight, on a diet, and lived in Maplewood. I think she was a widow with a grown daughter. My mom or Mrs. Mueller might have known her. Between the two of them, they know just about everyone in the neighborhood."

"She's worth checking out," Alyce said. "Did you ever wonder if Nate committed suicide when you wouldn't take him back?"

"Alyce, I'm not the sort of femme fatale that men kill themselves for," Josie said.

"Well, Nate was drunk," Alyce said.

"Thanks a lot," Josie said.

"I didn't mean that," Alyce said. "But alcohol can impair judgment. How does Mike's awful ex fit into this? Maybe Doreen killed Nate to get even with Mike. She wanted Mike blamed for the murder."

"Mike is her child-support gravy train," Josie said. "If he goes to prison, she doesn't get any more money for her nasty daughter, Heather. From what I can tell, Doreen is spending Mike's money on herself, not on Heather. If the accidental poisoning happened at Doreen's, that might make sense. Her shop was badly run, and Doreen and Heather were a surly pair. But Elsie was little, cute, and careful."

"Then why was Nate killed by poisoned chocolate from Elsie's Elf House?" Alyce asked.

"Maybe we should go there and see what we can find out," Josie said. "But we should make it soon, before both places close."

"Good," Alyce said. "This cookie batch should be baked in twenty minutes. We can stop by the Elf House and then go mystery-shopping."

"But what about the rest of your cookies?" Josie said. "You still have four more Martha Stewart batches."

"It's more important to keep you and Mike out of trouble," Alyce said. "Martha Stewart would understand. She's been in prison."

Chapter 25

The three Christmas stores were huddled together like refugees in the dirty city snow. Their blinking lights were too bright. Their colors were too bold. Their forced cheerfulness made Josie want to run.

I have to do this, she told herself. I have too much at stake—my freedom and my future with Mike.

"It's hard to believe two people died because of that kitsch," Alyce said.

"Almost three," Josie said. "Don't forget that poor woman who was nearly killed by Santa. Is she still in a coma?"

"Don't know," Alyce said. "The media seem to have lost interest in her."

Naughty or Nice, Doreen's building with the steeply pitched roof and wooden icicles, was plastered with big red GOING OUT OF BUSINESS signs. The Santa butt in the chimney was starting to deflate.

"What happened to Santa's rear end?" Alyce asked. "It's sadly diminished."

"Looks like Santa lost his ass on this venture," Josie said.

"Maybe it's half off," Alyce said.

The stalwart flock of churchgoers still circled the sad

little building with their signs, chanting slogans. Mrs. Claus winked lewdly at them.

"Those protesters are staying till the bitter end," Josie said.

"Which is soon, I hope. I'm glad that store is closing," Alyce said.

"You and a lot of other people," Josie said. "Doreen's pornographic Christmas ornaments were nasty. I do feel sorry for Elsie. I liked her and her Elf House."

Elsie's fake Tudor cottage was also festooned with screaming GOING OUT OF BUSINESS! signs.

The two tiny shops were overshadowed by the huge and successful Christmas All Year Round, a big red box with a twenty-foot Santa waving from the roof. His mechanical "Ho, ho, ho" sounded mocking.

Intertwined with the hearty "hos" were the tinny sounds of competing Christmas songs from the dying stores. Madonna sang a whorish version of "Santa Baby" at Naughty or Nice. A syrupy "Little Drummer Boy" oozed out of Elsie's Elf House.

"I hope the drummer boy gets shot in the next battle," Josie said.

"Aren't you full of Christmas cheer," Alyce said.

"I know. I should be ashamed," Josie said. "But I've heard too many bad versions of that song. The only song more annoying is 'It's a Small World.' Might as well see Elsie before her store closes."

"You need to see the video where Bing Crosby and David Bowie sing 'Little Drummer Boy,' " Alyce said. "I promise you'll like the song again."

Josie pulled her car into a parking spot behind the Elf House.

"There's no problem finding a space," Alyce said.

Elsie's lot was empty except for a rusty brown Toyota

parked in the back. The bell on the door jingled merrily. The shelves were packed with Christmas ornaments and decorations, all sporting red discount stickers.

Elsie was one sad little elf. Her costume was wrinkled, her hat was askew, and her nose was as red as Rudolph's. She greeted them with a mouselike sneeze. "Sorry, ladies. I have a cold."

"And I'm sorry your store is closing," Josie said. "I liked it."

"I thought we were going to make it," Elsie said. "Early December sales were actually ahead of my projected business plan. Unfortunately, I didn't take into account the deaths of two customers."

"Any idea how they were poisoned?" Josie said. She decided she'd learn more if she didn't mention she knew Nate.

"I haven't the foggiest. I told the police that." Elsie gave another elfin sneeze. "Why would I want to kill my own store? If it didn't sound paranoid, I'd say that b— I mean that Doreen person next door did it. But her store is closing, too, so nobody benefited from those terrible deaths."

"Any details from the police?" Alyce said.

"Nothing except that it was ethylene glycol poisoning, which is regular old antifreeze. Lorraine Whuttner, the dead woman's daughter, raised such a fuss over the cake her mother ate that the cops came here and confiscated the sauce so no one else was killed. Thank the Lord for that. But I think the daughter is going to sue me, and I don't have a cent."

"Surely she can see that," Josie said.

"She's out for blood," Elsie said. "She was counting on half of her mother's fifty-thousand-dollar prize money."

"Ouch," Alyce said.

"Doreen's store wasn't closing at the time of the murders," Josie said. "Your Elf House was so successful, your customers were parking in her lot. Maybe Doreen thought if she put you out of business, her store would do better."

"Look, she's a witch," Elsie said, "but even I can't accuse the woman of killing my customers. She tried to make peace with me. She even gave me this poinsettia."

The peace offering was still blooming on the counter.

"Pretty color," Alyce said.

"They are pretty," Elsie said. "But Doreen doesn't belong in retail. She doesn't like people and doesn't have the personality for sales. I'm just sorry Mike was one of her investors."

"You know Mike?" Josie asked.

"Know him? Honey, I used to date him. He dropped me for Doreen."

Josie looked at Elsie. Her face was chapped and swollen from her cold, but she was a pretty woman and a lot more pleasant than Doreen.

"You're kidding," Josie said.

"When he knocked Doreen up, Mike did the right thing and supported the kid," Elsie said. "I admire him for that. He told me he was sorry about Doreen and wanted to go back with me, but I told him no. I knew once Doreen had her hooks in that man, she'd never let go. She'd be worse than a vindictive ex-wife.

"Then there's the daughter, Heather. That kid is heading for juvie, but her doting daddy believes she can do no wrong. Can I ask you something? Are you dating Mike?"

"Yes," Josie said.

"Well, let me give you a little advice, honey. He's a sweet man, but sometimes Mike shows poor judgment when it comes to women."

"Uh, you mean me?" Josie said.

"No, I'm talking about the night he got drunk and fell into bed with Doreen. There are some things you can't fix, and Doreen is one of them. Mike's a smart guy, until he has a few beers. Then he can get real stupid. He also has commitment issues. If you see him with another woman, turn a blind eye. He doesn't like it if he thinks you're possessive. He'll tell you it's just business."

Uh-oh. Josie remembered the night Mike was with the blonde at the bookstore, supposedly talking about kitchens. He'd been cool toward Josie ever since. Maybe that woman was the reason.

Elsie had another sneezing fit. "Sorry," she said. "I saw him with Doreen in a bar and asked him about her. He said he was working on her plumbing. He sure was. Too bad he forgot the condom."

Alyce's eyes widened in surprise, but Elsie kept talking.

"You want to hear the sad part? I wanted a kid with Mike. He said he wasn't ready for marriage. I told him I didn't want to get married. I hope I'm not shocking you, ladies, but sometimes a man gets in the way if you're not the marrying kind, and I'm definitely not."

"I understand," Josie said. Boy, did she.

"Mike said he didn't want a kid, and it didn't matter whether he was married or unmarried. I should have gone ahead and gotten pregnant. Instead, I respected his wishes, and turned my energies toward planning for this store. It took more than a decade to get it going, and one day to kill it. Now I don't have anything."

"I'm so sorry," Josie said.

"Not as sorry as I am," Elsie said. "My biological clock is ticking away. All I have to show for it is two dead customers and a looming lawsuit. I keep racking my brains to figure out who would kill those poor people, but I come up blank. I can't sleep at night, it's upset me so much. It's so sad. I didn't even know them and they're dead because of me."

Elsie wiped away a tear.

"It wasn't your fault," Josie said. "We want this solved as much as you do. Here's my cell phone number. Call me if you think of anything."

"Promise," Elsie said, and sneezed again.

On the walk to the car, Alyce said, "I think Doreen is the killer. She did it to ruin her enemy, Elsie. She poured antifreeze in that chocolate sauce."

"Right," Josie said. "Doreen, who doesn't speak to Elsie, waltzed over to the Elf House with a jug of antifreeze and poured it into the chocolate sauce. Somehow Elsie didn't notice. And how did one of the dead customers just happen to be Nate? He's the last person who would buy a snowman cake."

"Maybe Doreen saw him over at the store and wanted to get back at Mike by framing him for Nate's murder," Alyce said. "Unless Elsie knew Nate."

"No, she said she didn't know the two dead customers. I believe her. Don't you think Doreen framing Mike for Nate's death is a little convoluted?"

"Do you believe what Elsie said about Mike?" Alyce asked.

"Kinda sorta," Josie said. "Mike's been cool to me since I saw him with that blonde at the bookstore. They were supposed to be planning her kitchen."

"Maybe they were," Alyce said. "That bookstore is not a romantic spot."

"That's why it's a safe place for a first date—or to meet a married woman," Josie said. "I think I blew it, Alyce. I didn't call Mike about the cops interviewing me until late yesterday. By then they'd already seen him. I forgot to call him. Forgot! What's wrong with me?"

"Nothing. You were worried about your daughter."

"But Mike didn't give me a chance to tell him that."

"He will when he calms down," Alyce said. "If he doesn't, he's not worth marrying."

"I don't think we're going to marry," Josie said. "I've got my doubts about a man who would sleep with Doreen."

"Josie, didn't you ever make any bad romantic choices?"

"Way too many, Alyce. That's why I don't want to make one more."

Chapter 26

The men's department of the West County Vandeventer store had manly dark paneling. The display shelves looked like they'd been beaten with chains—and so did the mannequins. One fellow with waves of yellow plaster hair had a chipped nose.

Gray trails were worn into the navy carpet. Two dusty holiday wreaths did nothing to spread Christmas cheer.

"It's sad to see the Vandeventer stores in this shape," Alyce said.

"They used to be so elegant," Josie said. "When I was a kid, my mom took me downtown every Christmas to see the Vandeventer display windows. No wonder this chain is in trouble. The merchandise is tossed on the tables like a rummage sale."

Three clerks leaned against a wall, laughing and talking. A fourth shouted into a cell phone, "I'm not coming to Christmas dinner at Aunt Karen's. She's a hundred years old."

"My questionnaire asks if I was greeted by the sales staff when I entered the department," Josie said, "and if I was shown the item I wanted. It wants to know if the department is neat and clean and the items properly presented. The staff is supposed to be folding stock. Instead, they're holding a party. I'm going to have to give them a bad report. I hate doing that, especially at Christmas."

"Won't they lose their jobs?" Alyce said.

"My boss says the chain will probably close after the holidays, so they'll lose them anyway," Josie said.

"Where are their supervisors?" Alyce said. "I don't see a single manager on duty. They should be out here helping, too."

Josie yanked on the sleeve of a medium blue sweater and pulled it out of a jumble. It was cashmere, marked down to seventy dollars. "What do you think of this as a Christmas present for Mike? It's the same color as his eyes."

"A sweater?" Alyce said. "His mother can give him sweaters. Men hate clothes as gifts. It's not very romantic."

"Things aren't romantic for us right now," Josie said. "At least I'll give him something warm."

"I have a better suggestion," Alyce said.

Josie looked at her watch. "It's getting late. I'm going to have to break up the party over there. I'm getting cobwebs waiting for the staff to wait on me."

Josie walked over to a man mountain with haystack hair and a FRED name tag.

"Excuse me," she said.

Fred ignored her.

"Excuse me." Josie stepped into the middle of the party. "I'd like to buy this sweater." She held it up, retail exhibit A.

"Sorry, dudes," Fred said, apologizing to his friends for the unexpected customer interruption. He ambled over to the cash register, mumbling to himself. He was charmless enough to be Heather's older brother. Fred rang up the sweater and shoved it into a bag.

"Merry Christmas," Josie said.

Fred ignored her.

Josie and Alyce walked outside to the empty parking lot.

"Anyone who thinks shopping for a living is glamorous has never worked this job," Josie said. "Now we have to drive twenty-five miles to South County and return the same sweater. I'd better call Mom and ask her to pick up Amelia at school."

"You're lucky your mom is available at a moment's notice," Alyce said.

"Mom can be cranky, but she really pitches in when I need her."

Josie speed-dialed Jane on her cell. "Mom, I have to drive to South County. Can you pick up Amelia? Thanks. I was just telling Alyce how lucky I was to have you for a mom.

"I have a question: What do you know about that poor woman who was poisoned by antifreeze, Sheila Whuttner? She lived in Maplewood."

Josie repeated what her mother told her for Alyce's benefit.

"I figured you'd know her. Mrs. Whuttner was active in the St. Philomena Women's Society. Retired from the phone company a year ago. She used to live in Dogtown. Really? That's around the corner from Mike's home. She moved to Maplewood and remarried a widower who went to our church. Was it a happy marriage? They were cuddling like teenagers and Mrs. Mueller was shocked by their behavior? Sounds happy to me.

"Your network is amazing, Mom. What about her daughter, Lorraine? No, I don't think she lives in Maplewood. Right. Well, if anyone will know, it's Mrs. Mueller. She's our own private Neighborhood Watch program. No, Mom, I wasn't making fun of her. I know she's your friend."

Josie hung up the phone. "Let's return that sweater."

"How's Amelia?" Alyce said.

"She's having a hard time," Josie said. "She misses her father and she's mad at me for lying. But her grandfather had a talk with her and I think he helped."

"Death is tough for kids," Alyce said.

"It's not easy for grown-ups, either," Josie said.

The visit to the second Vandeventer store in South County went smoothly. The store was so empty Josie's and Alyce's voices echoed in the vast space. No shoppers disturbed the neatly displayed stock. The return line had no customers. The staff rushed to their stations to help. Josie and Alyce were out in less than ten minutes.

"That was better," Josie said, sighing with relief. "I can give this store a good report."

On the walk to the car, her cell phone rang. Josie checked the display. "I have to take this. It's Mike."

Alyce hung back discreetly while Josie talked. Mike sounded distracted. "Uh, hi, Josie. Sorry I haven't called. The cops have been here again, asking me about my antifreeze. I wished I'd listened to Heather. She wanted me to switch to the so-called safer antifreeze, because of my dog, Chudleigh. But I didn't want the hassle of flushing my radiator. Besides, Chudleigh won't drink antifreeze unless it comes in a can marked Alpo. He's too smart, but I'm not. I should have done what my daughter asked. The police have a credit-card receipt proving I bought enough antifreeze to kill all the dogs in Dogtown."

"When?" Josie asked.

"Two days before the Elf House poisoning."

"I'm sorry, Mike."

"Not as sorry as I am. I'll probably have to get a lawyer. I've been meaning to call, but I've been busy."

"Been working on that kitchen?" Josie said.

"Kitchen?" Mike sounded puzzled. "What kitchen? Oh, yeah, the kitchen."

"Did you know that the lady who was poisoned the same day as Nate used to be your neighbor?"

"Who?" Mike said.

"Sheila Whuttner."

"I guess so," Mike said. "The neighborhood is full of indestructible ladies. Most of them are friends with my mom."

"What about Heather? Are you getting her into an AA program for her drinking?"

"No," Mike said. "She was just being a kid."

"Mike, she's fourteen and she was drunk and angry. That's a bad combination."

"Well, I'll watch her. If I see anything wrong, I'll take her to a counselor," Mike said.

Josie was sure Mike would never see any faults in his daughter.

"Gotta go," Mike said. "That's my other cell phone. See you." He hung up.

Josie stared at her cell phone and nearly wept. Mike didn't have two cell phones. Or maybe he did. Some men kept another phone for their new lovers. Maybe he was doing more with that blonde than remodeling her kitchen.

"What's wrong?" Alyce asked.

"I think Mike just gave me the brush-off," Josie said. "He's still mad because Mrs. Mueller reported him to the police. They've questioned him twice."

"That woman is a menace," Alyce said. "What are you going to do about Mike?"

"What can I do?" Josie said. "I can't beg the guy to love me."

"No, but I bet if you found the killer, things would go back to the way they were."

"I wish, Alyce, but I don't think it will work that way. We've got serious problems. I love Mike, but I can't stand his daughter, and she's a troublemaker. Amelia comes first in my life. I made that choice ten years ago.

"Besides, what good would it do for me to look for the killer? I don't have the police resources, their training, or their investigative technique. I can't flash a badge and make people talk to me."

"But people don't talk just because a police officer flashes a badge," Alyce said. "Sometimes they clam up. The police don't have your mother and Mrs. Mueller, two of the best detectives in Maplewood. The police are bound by the law and rules of evidence. Your investigation isn't. Mrs. Mueller has ways of getting information out of people that would get the police sued. You have your own advantages. All you have to do is find the killer."

"That's all?" Josie asked. "How can I do that? We don't even know why Nate and Sheila Whuttner died."

"Then we'll have to find out. Who has the best reason to kill Nate?"

"The police think I do, because Nate was threatening to kidnap Amelia and take her to Canada. Mrs. Mueller heard him yell it to the whole block. Plus, I'll get a hundred thousand in insurance money, though Nate wanted it to be used for Amelia's education, and that's fine with me. But it still looks like a motive when I have sixty-three dollars in the bank.

"Then there's Mike. He bought antifreeze right before the poisonings, and they think he wanted to eliminate Nate as a rival, but that's ridiculous. Nate and I were over years ago. Nate had some scummy friends from his drug-dealing days, but I can't see them poisoning him."

"So we don't know who wanted to kill Nate or why," Alyce said. "But you and Mike are off my suspect list."

"What about Mrs. Whuttner?" Josie said. "Mom says she was happily married. It doesn't sound like her new husband wanted her dead."

"Let's check out the daughter, Lorraine," Alyce said. "I'll get her address from directory assistance."

Alyce fiddled with her cell phone for a few minutes and then said, "Lorraine lives in an apartment about ten minutes from here. I have some extra time. Jake doesn't come home until nine, and the nanny works late. Should I call Lorraine?"

"No, let's surprise her," Josie said.

Lorraine lived in Whispering Willows Apartments. The complex was nowhere near as pretty as its name. It was a brick shoe box surrounded by acres of gray asphalt.

Josie and Alyce knocked on Lorraine's door. Then they pounded—hard. No one answered.

"I wonder if she can hear our knocking over the next-door neighbor's television," Josie said.

"There isn't much whispering going on at this place," Alyce said, "unless you count the traffic from the highway."

The door next to Lorraine's apartment opened suddenly. A bag of wrinkles in a flowered housecoat said, "She isn't home." A cigarette dangled out of the old woman's mouth. Josie was fascinated by the network of lines on her face and the way her red lipstick crept into the crevices.

"Do you mean Lorraine?" Josie asked.

"Lorraine isn't good enough for her, though that's the name her mother gave her," the old woman said. "She wants everyone to call her Lori. Thinks it's more lah-de-dah. She says 'Lorraine' sounds like a truck-stop waitress, though why there's anything wrong with making an honest living is beyond me. You from the police?"

"Have the police been to see you?" Josie asked.

"Hell, no, and they ought to. The things I could tell them. What are you, lawyers or something?"

"Ah," Alyce said, anxious to tell the truth.

"Alyce represents me," Josie said, which was as close to the truth as she wanted to get.

"You aren't working for the lawyer she hired to sue that poor Elf House lady, are you? I could tell them a thing or two."

"Definitely not," Josie said. "And we'd love to hear what you have to say."

"Well, step right in. My name is Myrtle, and that's not a lah-de-dah name, either. I've got plenty to tell you."

Myrtle shooed them in like a flock of chickens. Josie had to fight to keep from wrinkling her nose. Myrtle's tiny apartment smelled like an ashtray, with top notes of tomato soup. The living room was barely big enough for a faded maroon couch, a black Naugahyde recliner, and an ancient Philco television. The TV's rabbit-ear antenna was topped by aluminum-foil flags for better reception. Josie hadn't seen one of those since she was a kid. The white lampshades were yellowed by cigarette smoke.

Myrtle walked over and turned off the loud TV.

"Is Lorraine—I mean, Lori—at work?" Josie asked.

"Work? Don't make me laugh. She's seeing her lawyer. She aims to win that lawsuit against the radio station and get her mother's prize money. That's all she cared about, the money."

"Do you think she poisoned her mother?" Josie asked.

"I'm no fan of little Miss Lori, but there's no way she could have killed her mother. Lori was up in Chicago the day her mom got sick, so she couldn't have put the poison in that chocolate. Ted, Sheila's new husband, called Lori with the bad news. She came tearing back to

St. Louis in four hours and rushed into the hospital, crying and screaming that her mother had been in perfect health.

"It wasn't true. Sheila only had six months left to live, if she was lucky. The woman told me so herself. Sheila had a bad heart. I'll tell you who has the bad heart—her worthless daughter. That girl is man crazy. Runs after anything in pants. Now that she's coming into some money, she may be able to keep them longer."

"Do you think Lori was trying to hurry along her mother's death?" Josie said.

"Honey, I'd love to see that girl behind prison bars, but I don't see how she could have. Why take the risk? Lori was going to inherit everything anyway. When her mother decided to marry Ted after a decade of widowhood, Lori carried on like she was robbed.

"Sheila caved and signed a prenup. Lori gets her mother's money and the house in Maplewood. Prices are rising in that area, you know. Maplewood real estate is suddenly hot. Sheila's little two-bedroom brick is worth about three hundred thousand now, and Lori can't wait to sell it. I'm surprised she hasn't put Ted out on the street already. Lori claimed she couldn't work, but there was nothing wrong with her except she was bone-lazy. Her mother paid her an allowance and Lori wasn't too disabled to cash those checks."

"Whose idea was the radio station diet contest?" Josie asked.

"Lori's. Her mother always wanted to be thin, and Lori talked her into it because of the big prize. When it looked like Sheila had a chance at winning, Lori watched that poor woman the way a snake watches a rabbit. Nagged her night and day. Made her eat that diet food. Tasted like cardboard in my opinion. Watched her like a prisoner.

"Sheila finally reached her goal weight plus a little less. Lori went off to Chicago to celebrate. Probably spent her mother's winnings before she even got them. Sheila sneaked off for some chocolate cake while her daughter was out of town. It killed her, poor thing."

"Is Lori heavyset?" Josie asked.

"Skinny as a snake, with a mop of dyed blond hair and a port wine stain on her face. Ugly inside and out, that one. She claimed that birthmark kept her from working, but it was her own nasty personality. Believe me, if Lori had walked into the Elf House, that Elsie would have remembered her.

"Well, ladies, it's been nice talking to you, but it's time for my program."

"You've been very helpful," Josie said.

"You call me if you need anything more," Myrtle said. "I'm glad Lori's leaving the complex at the end of the month. She had the nerve to complain that my TV was too loud. Can you believe that?"

Myrtle turned up the television sound to rap-concert level.

Chapter 27

"Josie, open your fridge. There's a little surprise in it," Jane said.

"Let me get my coat off, Mom. I just got in the door," Josie said.

She threw her coat on a kitchen chair, hunched her shoulder to hold the receiver, and opened the fridge. The milk, meat, cheese, and a lone tomato were piled in a corner. The fridge light was filtered through enough beer and wine coolers to stock a bar.

"Wow, Mom, that's what I called a full refrigerator. There's barely room for the milk. What's going on?"

"I want to give a little Christmas party for the neighbors," Jane said. "I got the beer and wine coolers on sale."

"Isn't it a little soon after Nate's death for a party, Mom?"

"It's just a gesture to mend fences," Jane said. "A little food, a little music. You and Nate had those terrible fights on our porch. Having the police and ambulance here didn't help."

"I'm sorry about the fights, Mom. Our good neighbor Mrs. Mueller reported the details to the police—and the rest of the block. The detectives questioned Mike and me the day of Nate's memorial service. We have her to thank for that."

"Josie, I'm trying to calm things down and restore your reputation."

"My rep is gone, Mom, and I'm too old to care. But I am grateful for the wine coolers. If I start drinking now, I should be calm enough by the party to say hello to Mrs. Mueller without punching her out."

"Josie Marcus!"

"I was joking, Mom. When is this shindig?"

"Next Saturday. It's going to be at your place. Some of our neighbors are too old to climb the stairs to my flat."

"Mom, when am I going to have time to clean my home?"

"Amelia and I will handle that. She's helping me bake now. She'll be downstairs in about ten minutes."

"How's she doing?"

"As well as can be expected, considering." Jane's voice was crisp as new lettuce.

"So who's invited, besides the usual suspects? Mike, I hope."

"Yes, and he can bring that daughter of his, too."

"I'll put up with Heather for Mike's sake. But Doreen is not invited, Mom."

"Of course not, dear. I wouldn't think of it. But your friend Alyce can come, especially if she brings a dish. She's a wonderful cook."

"I'll tell her the price of admission," Josie said. "Mom, it's almost seven. I need to pick up something at the store. Can you keep Amelia for an hour?"

"Of course."

"Wait! There's a knock at the front door. I'll be right back."

Josie peeked out and saw a meek little man holding a plain white envelope. He sported a dyed black comb-over and a white down jacket that made him look like a snowman. The guy seemed harmless. She opened the door and said, "Yes?"

"Josie Marcus?" the man asked.

"That's me."

He handed her the envelope. "Consider yourself served." He said it so fast it sounded like one word. He ran off.

Served? She was being sued? Who would do that?

Josie opened the envelope with shaking fingers and read through the legalese. She was supposed to appear in civil court on February 19. Josie and Suttin Services, her mystery shopping company, were being sued by Doreen for damages to her business, Naughty or Nice. Doreen wanted five hundred thousand dollars for Josie's inaccurate, libelous, and biased report.

"Over my dead body," Josie screamed. She'd better call Harry.

She found the phone dangling from its cord in the kitchen. "Josie?" her mother said. "What's wrong?"

"Doreen is suing me for my mystery-shopper report."

"Can she do that?" Jane asked.

"She can and she did. Will she get anywhere? I doubt it. I had Alyce for a witness and I've kept the cake slice with the cockroach. I have to call Harry, Mom. Then I'll leave for my errand and be right back. I promise."

Josie hung up on her mother and called Harry. Her awful boss sounded disgustingly cheerful. "Oh, yeah, the lawsuit. I wouldn't worry about it, Josie. She can't win. Our lawyers will handle it."

And if they can't, I'm out of work, Josie thought. Which would suit you fine. "Harry, I have a witness," she said. "And I have the gingerbread cake with the roach in it."

"Save it for the lawyers, Josie. See you in court."

"Wait, Harry. Is there any work for me?"

"I don't think it would be a good idea under the circumstances," he said. "But don't worry. It will all be over in February—one way or the other. Merry Christmas."

He hung up.

Merry Christmas, indeed, she thought. How am I going to pay the bills when I'm out of work for almost two months? Well, it won't do any good to stand in the kitchen and fume. Josie threw on her coat again and ran for her car. One crisis at a time, she told herself.

It was six thirty when she arrived at the Naughty or Nice shop lot. The store was locked and dark. There was no sign of Doreen's ancient VW Bug. The picketers were gone.

Josie parked behind the store, where her car couldn't be seen from Manchester Road. The Dumpster was surrounded by a high fence, but the fence gate wasn't locked. It creaked loudly when Josie opened it.

The old Dumpster was dripping rust trails and leaking something slimy. Josie threw back the heavy lid and peeked in. There were only four trash bags in the bottom, and she was too short to reach them. The stink was ferocious. She took off her coat, pulled over a heavy plastic bucket for a ladder, held her breath, and jumped in the Dumpster.

Terrific, she thought. Dumpster diving at my age. If only Mom could see me now. I wonder how this will help my reputation?

Josie threw the four bags over the edge of the Dumpster, then crawled back out and began opening them. The first was filled with typing paper and old foam coffee cups. Some of the liquid dripped on her jeans. Josie swore and was glad Amelia wasn't there to hear her.

The second bag had enough foam packing peanuts to feed an army of foam squirrels.

The third, and smelliest, bag had the remains of several lunches and old coffee grounds. The last one had broken ornaments, an elf whose South Pole had snapped off, bits of glitter, and broken china. Josie had hoped to find a container of antifreeze so she could nail Doreen. She'd love to sic the cops on that woman, especially after Doreen had filed a lawsuit.

Josie closed the bags and dropped them back into the Dumpster, then put on her coat. She thought she caught the faint perfume of trash on her hands. She was back home by 7:10, showered by 7:20.

Josie called her mother after she'd dried her hair. Jane promised to send Amelia down. "She made supper, too, Josie."

"I can't wait," Josie said. She set the table.

Amelia tapped on the back door. She was carrying a warm ovenproof dish, wrapped in towels and sealed with duct tape. Josie's mother was taking no chances with her only grandchild.

"Smells good," Josie said.

"I made it myself," Amelia said. "Tuna noodle casserole with potato chips on top."

"Just the way I like it," Josie said.

"And no vegetables," Amelia said. "Except mushroom soup."

Josie, in a bid for healthy eating, had once added veggies to Amelia's beloved mac and cheese. Amelia approached Josie's dinners warily after that experiment.

"There are brownies for dessert," Amelia added. "That's the foil package on top."

Josie praised her daughter's cooking, taking two helpings of tuna casserole. "You're as good a cook as your grandmother. I'm glad you didn't inherit my cooking skills."

"Me, too," Amelia said. She looked pleased by the compliment. There was no mention of her father. Amelia was more subdued than usual, but she seemed to be coping with her grief.

They finished washing up by eight o'clock. Amelia went to her room to IM her friends and do her homework.

Josie called Alyce. "Are you busy?" she asked.

"I can talk until Jake gets home," Alyce said.

"Mom's giving a party for everyone, and you're invited."

"Good. What shall I bring? A roasted garlic and herb dip?"

"Yum," Josie said. She gave her friend the party time and details, then told her about Doreen's lawsuit.

"She didn't!" Alyce said. "You still have the cake with the roach, right?"

"Yes," Josie said. "It's in the freezer."

"Oh," Alyce said. "Remind me not to have dinner at your house."

"It's all wrapped up and has POISON, DO NOT EAT on it, so Amelia won't touch it. Besides, my daughter is a better cook than I am."

Josie waited for Alyce to say, "That's not difficult," but she didn't take that cheap shot.

"I've got another problem," Josie said. "Harry won't give me any assignments until after the court date."

"He can't do that, can he? You can't be punished for doing your job."

"I don't know if he can," Josie said. "But he did."

"Josie, can you fax me your contract? I want to read it. If it says what I think it does, I want to read *him* the riot act."

"I'll fax it from Kinko's in about half an hour," Josie said. "Oh, one more thing. I searched Doreen's trash at the store. I was looking for antifreeze bottles."

"You what?" Alyce said. "Are you crazy?"

"Crazy enough to climb into a slimy Dumpster," Josie said. "But I'm convinced that Doreen is behind the deaths at the Elf House. She hated Elsie, she wanted to close down her rival's store, and she didn't care who got in her way."

"Josie, if she's suing you, you need to stay away from her," Alyce said. "Besides, if Doreen did poison two people she would have disposed of those antifreeze bottles long ago."

"I'm not sure anymore. But I have to find who killed Nate, if only for my peace of mind—and Mike's. He's going to be a suspect until the real killer is caught."

"Josie, take the advice of your non-lawyer, please. Stay away from that woman. Promise?"

"Gotta go," Josie said, and hung up quickly, before she promised anything.

Josie found Amelia standing at the kitchen door. "Something wrong?" Josie asked.

"Thought I'd have a brownie before bedtime," Amelia said.

"You're entitled," Josie said. "You baked them. There's milk in the fridge, if you can find it. Your grandmother parked a couple of cases of wine coolers and beer there. I have to fax a paper to Alyce. I'll be back in half an hour. Will you be okay on your own?"

"Sure," Amelia said.

Josie dug her contract with Suttin Services out of the filing cabinet in the corner of her bedroom she grandly called her office.

She stood at the door buttoning her coat and said, "If anything goes wrong, your grandmother is right upstairs."

"Mom, you could go to Kinko's and be back by the

time you give me instructions on how to be careful," Amelia said. "I'm not a baby anymore. I'm nine years old."

"Good-bye, sweetie," Josie said, and ran for the door. The bitter cold was like a slap in the face. She hurried to her car, watching her breath in the frosty air. She faxed the contract to Alyce and was back by eight thirty.

The front door was closed, but not bolted. She didn't hear the TV. "Amelia?" Josie called. "Are you all right?"

No answer.

Josie ran to her daughter's room. The bed was still made, and the computer was off.

"Amelia!" Josie called.

She checked both bathrooms. They were empty. Josie found the note propped up against the sugar bowl on the kitchen table: *Gone to find Daddy's killer.*

"Amelia!" Josie cried in the empty house. There was no one home to hear her.

Chapter 28

"Amelia!" Josie shouted.

Her frantic cry was ripped from her chest. Their home seemed frighteningly empty.

Amelia's coat and boots were missing, along with her backpack. Josie checked her daughter's bedroom closet. Amelia had gone on her quest for her father's killer wearing her precious hot-pink hoodie.

"Amelia!" Josie screamed again, and held back tears of fright. She ran outside and called again. "Amelia, where are you?"

No answer.

Josie pounded on her mother's door until a rumpled, sleepy Jane finally answered. "What's wrong, Josie?" she asked, barely disguising a yawn.

"I can't find Amelia. She left this note." Josie practically shoved it in her mother's face.

Jane read it, fingers trembling. "Dear Lord. She says she's going to find her daddy's killer. Who is that? She isn't going after one of Nate's dangerous friends, is she?"

"I don't know," Josie said. Her heart twisted. "She didn't say where she was going. But her boots and backpack are gone."

"Who do you think the killer is?" Jane asked. "Did she hear you say something?"

"I might have mentioned that Doreen and her daughter had something to do with Nate's death. But Amelia hates Heather. She'd never go to her apartment."

"Go next door and ask Mrs. Mueller," Jane said. "Maybe she saw something."

Josie thought the old woman watched everyone but never saw anything useful. Still, this was no time to argue. Josie beat on Mrs. Mueller's door until the old woman came out, wearing a pink chenille robe and matching rollers. Maybe she got messages from aliens on those rollers, Josie thought. Mrs. Mueller glared at Josie. "Why are you knocking on my door?"

"Did you see Amelia leave the house recently?"

Mrs. M sighed dramatically. "She left home about ten minutes after you did. She was wearing her backpack. Really, Josie Marcus, you aren't fit to be a mother."

She's probably right, Josie thought, but I'm not wasting time arguing with the old battle-ax. "Where did you see her go?" she asked. "Where was she going?"

"Toward Manchester Road," Mrs. M said.

She could be anywhere by now, Josie thought. She managed a thank-you, then ran back home across the soggy grass, not caring if she tore muddy footprints in Mrs. M's precious lawn. Her mother's so-called friend hadn't offered to help find Amelia.

Josie was tormented by nightmare visions of sexual predators, serial killers, and cruel boys in cars with the speakers tuned to earsplitting levels so no one would hear her daughter's cries for help.

"Amelia!" she screamed again, as if she could ward off those visions.

Stan the Man Next Door turned on his porch light and came outside wearing an old man's baggy brown cardigan. "Is something wrong?" he asked.

"It's Amelia," Josie said. "She took off on her own. She was last seen walking toward Manchester Road."

"I'll help you look for her," Stan said. "I can search around the Galleria and the shopping center's parking lot. Do you think she'd walk all the way there?"

"I don't know," Josie said. Were the buses running this late? Or, God forbid, did Amelia hitchhike? She could have caught the MetroLink on Manchester Road and gone downtown, or to the airport, or— Josie's heart froze. Her daughter could be anywhere in the metro area.

"Thanks," Josie said. "I'll go the other way on Manchester Road, toward the city." They exchanged cell phone numbers to stay in touch.

Jane was shivering on her front porch, but now she was awake and alert. "Well?" she asked.

"Amelia was last seen headed toward Manchester," Josie said. "I'll get my car and start looking for her."

"I will, too," Jane said.

"No, I need you to stay here, in case Amelia calls or comes home," Josie said. "Stan is going to help."

Jane reluctantly agreed. "I'll get coffee started," she said. "Should we call Nate's father at his hotel?" Jack was still cool toward Jane.

"No," Josie said. "Let him sleep for now. I'll call Mike." Even though things were iffy between them, Mike would help in an emergency like this. He picked up his phone after two rings, and Josie told him Amelia had disappeared. She edited out her own suspicions of Heather and Doreen.

"Where do you think Amelia is?" Mike asked.

"If I knew, I wouldn't be looking for her," Josie snapped.

"Josie," Mike said, "yelling at me won't help. I know

you're worried. But I need some idea of where to search."

"I'm sorry," Josie said. "I didn't mean to snap your head off. I'm upset. Terrible things can happen to a little girl on her own. Amelia was last seen heading toward Manchester. Stan is going to take the area around the Galleria, including those huge parking lots. I'll do the streets between Manchester and Clayton, then check out the Highway 40 construction site. Can you look around Dogtown and the DeMun neighborhoods for me?"

"I'll be glad to. But those are really far away, Josie. She's not likely to walk there," Mike said. "I'll check the residential part of Clayton, too, just in case."

Amelia wasn't likely to walk off without telling her mother, either. Except she did. Josie shuddered at the thought of her daughter wandering in the dark depths of the night.

"Josie, are you still there?" Mike asked. "What about Amelia's friends? Have you checked with them?"

"She might have gone to Emma's house," Josie said. "Emma's mother would have called me, I'm sure, but I'll call just in case."

"And I'll start searching. It's nearly ten o'clock. I'll check in with you at eleven, but I hope we have news before that. Josie?"

"Yes?" she said.

"Don't worry," Mike said. "It's going to be all right. She's a smart little girl."

"Do you really believe that?" Josie asked.

"Of course," he said.

Josie called Amelia's best friend. Emma was already in bed. Josie wished her own daughter was safe and warm at home. "Sorry, Ms. Marcus, I haven't even IM'ed her since about five tonight," Emma said. "Is she sick or something?"

"No," Josie said, not willing to admit her daughter had disappeared. "Thanks, Emma. You've been a big help."

Stan the Man Next Door had already left on his search. Josie started up her trusty gray Honda. The car was rusty and dented, but it was dependable. She drove slowly through the slushy side streets. Maplewood had a small-town stillness at night, but now that quiet seemed ominous. The big old houses looked like eyeless skulls. The bare tree branches were skeletal fingers, reaching out for her daughter. The Christmas lights in the yards spread false cheer on the snow.

Josie had been driving about ten minutes when she saw a small figure bundled in a dark coat and her heart leaped. She drove faster. As she got closer, Josie realized that was no child, but the thin, bent figure of an old woman. Josie was so disappointed she almost wept.

Josie saw groups of tweens and teens at the burger joints and clothing stores, but none was Amelia. Where were their parents? she wondered. Why didn't they make sure their kids were safe at home?

And where was her daughter? Josie couldn't lose her. She tried to drive faster, but her car slid on a patch of slushy ice. Slow, she reminded herself. Speeding up won't help find Amelia faster.

Josie kept driving up and down the empty streets, praying that her daughter was safe. In her mind she replayed scenes from the nightly news: desperate parents begging kidnappers to please let their child come home unharmed. She imagined weeping family members huddled around shallow graves in desolate woods. She saw yellow crime-scene tape fluttering in the dirty snow, and solemn officials wheeling away a black body bag with a small mound zipped inside.

Where was Amelia? Why didn't I let her have a cell phone? Josie asked herself. She could be texting me a message now. If someone kidnapped her, she could be trying to contact me.

Josie's cell rang at ten p.m. She jumped, then pulled the car over. She was too shaky to drive and talk to Jane.

"Mom?" Josie said. "What's wrong?"

"Did you drink any of those wine coolers for the party?" Jane asked.

"No," Josie said. "Why?"

"I opened your fridge looking for some milk for my coffee, and saw that six bottles were gone. Did Amelia take them?"

"I can't imagine why," Josie said. But now Josie could think of many reasons. Her crafty daughter was up to something. She knew it. But what? Amelia had never showed any interest in alcoholic drinks. She didn't like the taste. So why would she take the wine coolers?

Josie called Mike and Stan, but neither one had seen anything.

"I'm sorry, Josie," Mike said. "I'm over by DeMun now. Nobody's outside, except a guy walking his dog. He hasn't seen anyone. I'll keep looking."

"Me, too," Josie said. "I'm about to finish the Maplewood area. Then I'll head over to Forest Park."

Josie kept driving. The temperature was dropping, and the slush on the streets was starting to freeze. Twice her car skidded, but she brought it under control. Josie couldn't drive into the Highway 40 construction area, but she got close enough to check for signs of people moving around. Nothing. The big yellow earthmovers looked like prehistoric beasts. The concrete bridge pillars seemed to belong to a lost civilization.

She drove into the city's majestic Forest Park, nearly thirteen hundred acres of twisting paths and more lagoons and lakes than any mother wanted to think about.

At ten minutes to midnight, Josie's phone rang. She pulled over in the park and grabbed it.

"Josie," her mother said, "any sign of Amelia?"

"Of course not," Josie said.

"Then I'm calling the police and have them issue an AMBER Alert for a missing child."

"No!" Josie screamed.

"Why not?" Jane said. "My granddaughter is missing. We need to face facts. This is when we call in the police."

"Mom, the police have to confirm there's been an abduction, and there has to be a serious risk of injury."

"Bah! What are they going to do, arrest a worried grandmother?"

"And what do we do when her grandfather finds out and decides to take your granddaughter back to Canada because I'm an unfit mother? He's already angry at us. Amelia told me that her grandpa said she could live with him all year round and she'd love winter in Toronto. If he takes her, we don't have money to fight the legal battles or hire the detectives to find her."

"And what do we do if she's dead, Josie? Because of your foolish pride."

"Just give me a little more time, Mom."

"You have until twelve thirty, Josie Marcus. Then I call the police, and to hell with the consequences. I'd rather have a live granddaughter in Canada than a dead one close to home."

Josie hung up the phone and wept.

Chapter 29

Midnight.

Josie heard a church bell bonging somewhere, but the sound brought no comfort. Where was Amelia? Why would she do anything so foolish? She'd never run off before. Where did she get the idea she could investigate a murder?

From her idiotic mother, Josie decided. I've set a fine example for my child. After that pile of gifts we got when I solved the last murder, my daughter probably thinks she'll be richly rewarded.

Twelve fifteen. Josie drove aimlessly through Maplewood. Not a living soul was roaming the streets, not even a stray dog. The night grew darker as more house lights winked off. Maplewood was a city of people who worked for a living.

Twelve twenty. Ten minutes to go, and then Jane would call 911, and Josie knew that her life would be over. The police would broadcast an AMBER Alert. Amelia's grandfather would declare Josie unfit for motherhood and take her daughter to another country.

Josie's phone rang. She pulled the car over, took a deep breath, and answered it.

"Mom?" said a quavery voice.

"Amelia?" Josie said, relief flooding her. "Are you okay? Where are you? How are you?"

"I'm at Heather's place, Mommy, and I want to come home. She lives—"

"I know where she lives," Josie said. "Hang on. I'll be right there."

"Mommy? Be careful. She's mean. So is her mother."

"But I'm meaner than both of them put together," Josie said.

"Bring a gun or something," Amelia said.

"A gun? What the hell is going on? I'm calling the police, Amelia Marcus."

"No! Just get me out of here, please. She's crazy. You were right, Mommy."

"Okay, honey. I'll be right there."

There was no answer. Amelia had hung up.

"Mommy." Her daughter must be terrified. Amelia considered herself too old to use "Mommy."

Josie speed-dialed Jane and said, "Amelia called. I'm on my way to get her. She's all right."

"Thank goodness," Jane said.

"Mom, please call Mike and Stan and tell them I'll meet them at your place."

"Josie, where are you going?"

"I'll tell you shortly, Mom. You're breaking up," Josie lied, and switched off her phone.

Josie didn't have a gun. But wait—she had something she could use. She opened the trunk of her car and pulled out Alyce's Christmas present, the crème brûlée torch. With trembling fingers she inserted the butane cylinder. She put the torch on the seat beside her and drove to Heather's house, wondering why her daughter was visiting that "loser face."

Josie figured she was about ten minutes from the

apartment where Heather and her mother lived. She drove too fast on the freezing slush, grateful there were no other cars around in case hers spun out on an ice patch. She went into a long slide at a red light and forced herself to slow down.

You won't help anyone if you get into an accident, she reminded herself. You have a daughter to save.

Josie was a long block away when her phone rang again. She pulled over again and answered it.

"Amelia?" she said.

"Sorry," said the acid voice oozing out of her phone, "you've got me, Ms. Mystery Shopper."

"Who is this?" Josie asked.

"Doreen. The woman whose business you ruined with your lying little report. I've got a cash-flow problem, but you can help me."

"What?" Josie said. She wasn't sure she understood Doreen.

"I need money, bitch. That clear enough for you?"

"Money? Why?" This conversation wasn't making sense to Josie.

"I need twenty thousand in cash to keep my store alive through the end of January. That is, if you want to see your skanky daughter."

"But—but—I don't have that kind of money," Josie said.

"Then you'd better get it," Doreen said. "Ask Lover Boy. He's got lots of money. If he really loves you, he'll give it to you, no questions asked."

"At this time of night?"

"When better?" Doreen said.

"I'll be over as soon as I can," Josie said.

Her hands were shaking when she ended the call. Doreen had finally gone over the edge. She was holding Amelia for ransom.

Should she call Mike? Josie knew he'd go ballistic when he heard about Doreen. She also knew Mike didn't have that kind of cash on hand.

What about the police? No, Doreen really was crazy. She could hurt Amelia, even kill her. I have to save my daughter, Josie thought. The police will try to negotiate. I'll rip Doreen apart if she harms Amelia. This is up to me. I can call the cops when I have my daughter safe.

Josie wondered if she was behaving foolishly, and her mind went back to those movies she hated, where the scantily clad heroine ran unarmed into the haunted house when she knew the ax murderer was inside.

No, she decided. I'm not unarmed. She patted Alyce's Christmas present on the seat beside her. If she had to, she'd burn her way into Doreen's home.

Josie's car slid and skidded the short distance to Doreen's apartment. Doreen and her daughter lived on the second floor of a solid brick building from the middle of the last century. Doreen's faded blue VW was parked at the end of the U-shaped asphalt drive, as if she was the last resident to arrive home. Josie rammed the back of Doreen's VW, caving in the engine compartment. It made a satisfying crunch.

Josie's battered Honda shuddered. She checked the front end. The old car had a few new dents, but it seemed drivable.

Doreen came rushing out of the apartment's lobby. Her hair was nearly standing on end. Her baggy black sweater flapped like a manta ray in the cold winter air.

"What the hell are you doing?" Doreen screamed. Lights popped on in nearby apartments.

"Quiet," Josie said. "Unless you want the police here." She grabbed Doreen by the hair and flicked on the butane torch. "I want my daughter. Now."

"Where's my money?" Doreen asked.

Josie grabbed four strands of Doreen's hair on the left side of her head and yanked hard. They came out in her hand.

Doreen screamed in pain. Josie fired up the créme brûlée torch and set the four hairs on fire. They flared up and went out quickly, leaving the acrid scent of scorched hair lingering in the air.

Doreen's mouth dropped open in surprise.

"If you don't want to see the rest of your gray hair turn flaming red," Josie said, "get my daughter out here. Right now."

Doreen turned to go inside, but Josie grabbed her arm and dug her nails in.

"Ow, you're hurting me," Doreen said.

"Good," Josie said. She flipped open her cell, looked up her last received call, and hit SEND.

Heather answered. "Mom, is that you? What's going on? Freak face is a problem."

"You don't know what problems are, Heather, unless you let my daughter go," Josie said. "Now."

She handed the phone to Doreen. "Tell her," Josie said. "Before I set your head on fire."

"Let her go," Doreen said. She raised her voice. "I SAID NOW."

Josie took the phone back and said, "I'm counting to ten, Heather. If I reach it, I'll call 911 and you'll find yourself sitting in juvie."

Josie had gotten to eight when the front door of the apartment building opened.

"Mommy!" Amelia screamed and ran out. Her long dark hair was flying. Her pale face was flushed pink. Her hands were tied with some kind of elastic band.

Josie untied her daughter's hands, tossed the band in her car, and slapped Doreen across the face. Amelia ran for the passenger side, yanked it open, then locked her door.

"What about my car?" Doreen shrieked. "You hit it."

"Damn right," Josie said. "Let's call the police and report the accident. I'll also give them this band, which has your fingerprints all over it. Oh, and be sure to sue me. I'm guessing the Naughty or Nice franchise people will love to know how bad you've been."

"Mom," Amelia called. "We have to go now."

"Yes, we do," Josie said. She drove away in her battered Honda, with her daughter and the smoking créme brûlée torch.

Chapter 30

Josie backed out of the drive, nearly sideswiped a trash container, and barreled out onto Clayton Road.

Amelia was shivering and shaking in the seat beside her mother. "I'm sorry, Mom," she said between sobs. "It's all my fault."

Yes, it is, Josie wanted to say, but her daughter's shocked, pale face silenced her.

Josie waited for a red light, and speed-dialed her mother while her car idled. "I've got her," she said. "Amelia is safe."

"Praise God. How soon before you're home?" Jane asked.

"About forty-five minutes. We're stopping at Steak 'n Shake."

"Josie, come home now. I'll make you bacon and eggs. Mike and Stan are drinking coffee in the kitchen."

"Tell them thanks, Mom. Amelia and I need to talk first, so I can find out what happened. We won't be long."

"Josie, it's one thirty in the morning. Amelia has school in a few hours."

"See you," Josie said. She shut her phone and pulled into the Steak 'n Shake lot on Manchester. The stark black, white, and orange-red interior seemed oddly homey at this late hour. Even the glaring lights looked welcoming. The restaurant had a handful of late-night customers. Why did normal people look like derelicts in the early hours of the morning? Josie wondered.

In the harsh light she could see how tired her daughter was, but Josie was too angry to offer Amelia comfort.

They carefully avoided the subject while they ordered burgers, fries, and Cokes. When the waitress left, Josie said, "Now, would you care to explain why you stole six wine coolers out of my fridge?"

"I wanted to catch Daddy's killer," Amelia said.

"How were you going to do that?" Josie asked. "What if the police caught you with alcohol? You're underage. What were you thinking?"

"I was trying to help," Amelia said. Two tears rolled down her pale face.

"You scared your grandmother and me half to death," Josie said. "We thought you were kidnapped. You didn't have the courtesy to tell us where you were going."

"If I did that, you wouldn't let me go," Amelia said, with perfect kid logic.

"You're damned right I wouldn't, young lady," Josie said.

An unshaven man at the next booth stared at them, and Josie lowered her voice. She'd been worried sick at her daughter's disappearance. Now that Amelia was safe, Josie was seething.

"Explain yourself," she said.

"I took the wine coolers to give to Heather so she'd talk to me," Amelia said.

"Why would she talk to you?" Josie said. "She hates you."

"But she likes to drink," Amelia said. "It's hard for her to get booze. Her mother was going to be out all night with her boyfriend, so we had the place to ourselves."

"You used that girl's weakness to get information? I'm ashamed of you."

"But it worked," Amelia said. "It wasn't easy, Mom. Heather made fun of me at first, but she wanted those wine coolers. She chugged two real fast and started talking. Then she got sick. She barfed all over the bathroom. I had to help clean it up. It was gross."

"Good," Josie said.

"Heather started whining about how much she hated her mother's store. She's the one who turned the mice and roaches loose in it so it would close down."

"Where did she get the roaches?" Josie asked.

"From the Dumpster behind the school cafeteria. She made sure you got a piece of cake with a roach in it. She thought if you gave the store a bad report, it would close. She said you got a real sick look on your face when your 'raisin' had legs."

Josie's stomach turned at the memory of the insect-infested cake. Their burgers and fries arrived, but Josie wasn't hungry now.

"Heather nearly killed that lady, too," Amelia said.

"What lady?" Josie asked.

"The church picketer lady." Amelia dragged her fries through the ketchup. "Heather put on a Santa suit from the store as a disguise. She's big enough to pass for a guy. She went up a ladder and used a shovel to loosen the snow on the roof."

"Why would she do that?" Josie asked.

"Heather wanted to scare away the picketers, so the TV and newspaper stories would stop. She was afraid the kids at school would find out she was selling pornaments. She didn't realize the ice and snow would land on that woman's head and put her in the hospital. Now Heather can't sleep at night."

"So that old woman wasn't senile after all," Josie said.

"It really was Santa Claus up on that roof." She nibbled her burger. Amelia was eating her food like a famine was due in town tomorrow.

"It was really Heather, dressed like Santa Claus. She laughed her ass off when she saw that TV story."

"Amelia!"

"Well, she did." Amelia dipped another fry in ketchup.

"Did Heather poison your father and that other woman?" Josie asked.

"She swears she didn't. I got her really drunk, Mom. But Heather said her mother poisoned the dog next door."

"What dog?" Josie asked.

"The yappy dog that used to bark all the time so nobody could sleep. It kept me awake the whole night I stayed at her house. Doreen got sick of the mutt waking her up. She went to a Racers Edge car store, bought some antifreeze, poured it on a pound of hamburger, and threw it over the fence. The dog ate it and died the next day. Heather said she was glad. She hated that dog. That's cruel, Mom."

"Yes, it is," Josie said. Mike has a bigger problem than he knows with that girl, she thought.

"Heather had another wine cooler after she threw up. It made her sleepy. I waited until she passed out drunk, then checked her computer. She'd Googled poisons right before Daddy died. I found a bunch of sites about how antifreeze kills cats and dogs and some stories about a lady who murdered her husband with antifreeze. I know Heather killed Daddy. She's too afraid to say so."

"What did you do then?" Josie asked.

"It was after midnight, and I had to get out of there. I couldn't stay all night. What if Heather put poison in my soda or something? That's when I called you on the kitchen phone. I was sneaking out the door when Doreen came home early. She was supposed to spend the night with her boyfriend, but she didn't. She was in a bad mood."

I bet, Josie thought.

Amelia finished her burger, then finished her story. "Doreen wanted to know why I was at her home. I said I'd stopped by to say hello to Heather. She got real sarcastic and said, 'And you're such good friends you have to see her at midnight?'

"I was trying to figure out what to say next when Heather walked in the room. She was wasted, Mom, but Doreen didn't say anything about that. Heather told her, 'She's been snooping around in my computer. She left it on. She saw the antifreeze stories.'

"I said I had to get home and started running for the door. Doreen grabbed my arm. She left bruises." Amelia slid up her pink sleeve and showed a dark blue handprint. Josie burned with fury when she saw the damage to her daughter. She wished she'd really set fire to Doreen's hair.

"I tried to get away, but I couldn't," Amelia said. "Heather held me down and Doreen tied me to a chair in the kitchen. It hurt. I was scared she was going to kill me or something. Then Doreen called you and wanted a bunch of money. She saw your car pull into the driveway and ran outside. We heard you two arguing. Then you called Heather and said to let me go, and Heather did."

"Just how did you get to Heather's house?" Josie asked.

"Kelsey, a kid in our class, has an older brother who picks her up at school sometimes. He was out driving and saw me. He gave me a ride."

"And he didn't ask what you were doing roaming around alone at this hour?"

"No, he's cool, Mom. What are you doing with your phone?"

"I'm calling the police and having Doreen arrested," Josie said.

"No, Mom, you can't do that. I'll be a joke at school."

"You'll survive," Josie said.

"But she won't do it anymore, Mom. She's afraid of you."

"She better be," Josie said. "Amelia, promise me that you'll never do that again."

"Are you mad at me?" Amelia asked.

"I'm angry that you took off on your own and did something so careless. Yes."

"Am I grounded?" Amelia said in a small voice.

"Until you collect Social Security," Josie said.

"When's that?" Amelia asked.

"Fifty-six years," Josie said.

Amelia's lower lip quivered and Josie was afraid she'd start crying again. Their table looked like a battleground. Her daughter's pool of ketchup seemed like a bloodstain.

"It's late," Josie said. "We're going home and you're going to thank Mike and Stan."

"And then what?" Amelia asked.

"Then you're going to bed."

And I'm going to try to convince Mike that his daughter is a killer, she thought.

Chapter 31

"You think my daughter did *what?*" Mike shouted at Josie.

They were alone on her front porch at two thirty in the morning, and Mike's anger seemed to echo through the neighborhood. She winced at his shouting. Her neighbors had to work in the morning. They'd be calling the police any moment.

I've made a mistake, Josie thought. I should have told him this tomorrow, when he was in a more reasonable mood. No parent wants news like this, and there's no good time to deliver it. I wanted to wait until we were alone.

Stan had gone home, with Josie's thanks and a plate of her mother's brownies. Amelia was tucked into bed.

Mike was the last to leave, and Josie waited until they were outside to tell him what Amelia had discovered. Mike had not taken the news well. Even under the dim streetlight, Josie could tell her lover was red with rage. Mike was practically spitting, he was so furious. The muscles in his neck bulged.

"You really think poor little Heather killed two people and put that church picketer in a coma? Are you crazy?"

"Mike, please, keep it down," Josie said. "What if Mrs. Mueller hears you?"

"Screw her," Mike said. "That old biddy makes up half the gossip she spreads. Maybe we should move this fight to her porch so she can get the facts straight."

"Mike, please don't be angry with me. You need to know this or things will only get worse. Heather's already confessed that she put on a Santa suit and shoveled snow off the roof and it hit that church lady."

"Confessed?" Mike said. "Confessed to who—your delinquent daughter? The kid who roams the streets at night with wine coolers and gets Heather drunk? Amelia hates Heather."

"And Heather hates her," Josie said.

"With good reason," Mike said. "Amelia is making up those stories about my girl. Did she really tell you that Heather put on a Santa suit and climbed up on the roof?"

"Yes," Josie said.

"That's a lie. Heather wouldn't get up on a roof. She won't even climb the stairs to her mother's apartment on the second floor."

Mike paced Josie's porch like a caged animal, as if he couldn't contain his anger. He scratched the back of his neck, then threw his hands up in the air.

"I give up," he said.

"Mike, please, Heather didn't mean to hurt the church picketer. It was an accident."

"That's real generous of you, Josie. So if the woman dies, Heather is only guilty of manslaughter."

"I think the church picketer is going to be okay," Josie said. "But your daughter has a problem with alcohol."

"Only because *your* daughter gave it to her. What teenager would turn down booze? Amelia stole those wine coolers."

"I know she did, Mike. She's grounded for life. But this isn't the first time Heather was drunk. She sneaked beer out of my house and threw the bottles at the neighbor's fence."

"How do I know your daughter didn't give that beer to Heather?" Mike asked. "Every time something goes wrong with my girl, your daughter is in the picture. She's a troublemaker."

"Amelia wouldn't do that," Josie said. "She didn't give Heather beer. Heather took it."

"Oh, really?" Mike said. "So perfect little Amelia would hike miles to Clayton to get my kid drunk, but she wouldn't reach into her own refrigerator and hand Heather a beer?"

"No, I didn't mean that," Josie said.

Mike had his arms folded defensively in front of his chest. Lord, he was handsome. Those muscles in his arms were natural, not built at a gym. That wasn't designer stubble on his chin, either. Josie knew how good a slightly scratchy beard felt.

She longed for Mike to hold her. But Josie wasn't going to say her daughter was guilty of something she didn't do, even for Mike.

"Mike, please. I wasn't making accusations."

"Then what were you doing? You said Heather nearly killed that church lady. I bet you think she poisoned those people, too."

"I didn't say that. But I did say Heather Googled those sites about antifreeze deaths."

"And told your perfect little darling that her mother killed the dog next door. Now that I believe. Doreen is mean enough to kill an innocent dog. And here's my other problem: Why didn't you take me along to Doreen's house to get your girl? Don't you trust me?"

"I knew you wouldn't believe a word against Heather, no matter what my daughter said. Somehow you'd twist the information so it would be Amelia's fault. That's how you handle any criticism of Heather and that's why she's such a . . ."

Josie stopped, afraid to go on.

"Such a what?" Mike asked.

"That's why she has problems," Josie finished, proud of her diplomacy. "And I was right," she added triumphantly. "That's exactly what happened."

"Josie, I understand that you were worried about your girl," Mike said, "but my daughter was involved, too. You should have taken me along with you. Heather is living with that psycho Doreen. I want to marry you. We're in this together."

Mike should have taken Josie's hand by this point, but they remained apart. Some marriage we'll have, Josie thought. We'll be arguing about our kids till death parts us. The big question will be whose death.

Josie saw a light pop on in Mrs. Mueller's house, and lowered her voice to a near whisper. "Mike, your daughter needs help. She's drinking too much. She used her computer to look up information about how to kill people with antifreeze."

"Oh," Mike said, "so my daughter is a killer. Do you really think Heather murdered Nate and that poor radio contestant?"

Yes, Josie wanted to say. But she restrained herself again and gave a more reasonable reply. "Who else would it be?"

"Maybe it was me," Mike said. "Maybe I killed those people. Yes, that's it. I bought the antifreeze—the police will tell you that—and I went to Elsie's shop and poured it in the chocolate sauce. I wanted Nate dead so I could have you all to myself."

"Mike, that's crazy."

"Not as crazy as accusing a fourteen-year-old girl of killing two people. Why would Heather do that, Josie? Give me a reason."

"She didn't want to work at her mother's store," Josie said. "And I don't blame her. Heather planted those roaches at Naughty or Nice. She told Amelia that."

"Planted those roaches? Heather won't even kill bugs and spiders. She gets me to do it. She traps them under a glass. You really think she took a box, or a jar, of roaches to her mother's store and turned them loose?"

"Yes," Josie said.

"Funny no one else was around when that happened," Mike said. "Doreen watches that kid like a hawk, but she didn't notice her daughter carrying a box of roaches? She just let Heather turn them loose in the store and ruin her business."

"She could have hidden them under her coat," Josie said.

"Look, Josie, it's your daughter's word against mine. And I know who I believe. My kid has her faults, but Heather doesn't trap people with alcohol."

"Mike, please. I'm not saying Heather is a bad kid. But she has problems."

"She didn't make those problems, Josie," Mike said. "It isn't my daughter's fault that she has two bad parents—Doreen and me. I didn't help Heather when she needed me most. I didn't want her to live with me. I didn't fight for custody. I let her mother bring her up. I abandoned my daughter for my business, and Heather got stuck working at that terrible store.

"That's my fault, Josie. And my responsibility. I'm going to the police and confess, so Heather doesn't get blamed for those murders."

"Mike, you can't do that."

"Try and stop me, Josie Marcus."

"Mike, please. We can talk this out. Call me in the morning."

But Mike was already stomping down Josie's sidewalk to his truck. He was exactly the sort of man who would nobly—and uselessly—sacrifice himself for his daughter. Mike was burdened with love and guilt.

"Mike, please," Josie begged.

"Later," Mike said.

But Josie knew later would never come.

Chapter 32

Mike slammed the door to his truck. Josie slammed her front door, shot the bolt, then headed for the kitchen. Her fridge seemed strangely empty, until she realized the beer and wine coolers were gone. Josie guessed her mother had moved them, probably to the basement.

A bottle of cold Chardonnay glowed in the fridge light, an amber beacon. Josie picked up the bottle, started to pour herself a drink, then put it back.

A wine hangover would only make her feel worse—if that was possible. Instead she settled for a cup of chamomile tea at her kitchen table.

Josie mourned her lost romance. Mike was the first man she'd been serious about since Nate. She'd dreamed of being his wife. Marriage would have made things easier for Josie's mother. Jane had never accepted Josie's single status, and claimed that Nate was killed in a helicopter accident. Now the whole neighborhood knew the truth.

Josie loved Mike, but she loved her daughter more. *I made my choice ten years ago,* she told herself. *I can live without Mike. But I can't live without my daughter.*

I'm thirty-one. It's hard to settle into marriage at this age. I'm too independent. Where would we live—his house? My home? Would we buy another place? Would Heather live with us, at least on the weekends?

How would we handle the schools? My daughter has a scholarship to an expensive private school. Heather goes to a mediocre public school. She resents Amelia's education but has no interest in learning. Can I take care of two daughters? Heather won't listen to me, and Mike won't hear a word against her.

The situation is hopeless. I can't make Amelia like Heather. I can't stand the kid myself. This is one family that won't blend.

My romance with Mike is over. We need to end this gracefully before we hurt each other.

What's next for me? Josie wondered. More dates with men who have iffy pasts? The dating pool at her age was pretty scummy. She was looking at deadbeat dads, men hung up on their ex-wives, men with drug and alcohol problems, men who couldn't hold steady jobs, men who liked other men but thought they should marry to please their parents.

And Mike. Mike was perfect—except for his devious, drunken daughter. Heather was one problem Josie couldn't get around. She put her empty teacup in the sink and checked on Amelia.

Her daughter was asleep.

It was three o'clock when Josie hit the cold sheets. If I was married, she thought, I'd be climbing into a warm bed with a hot man.

And abandoning my daughter.

She was exhausted, but she couldn't sleep. The bedside clock seemed to taunt her as it moved through the night with digital slowness. The acid green numbers were burned into her brain. It was three 3:38 . . . 3:39 . . . 3:40.

Four twenty-two. At 4:23 Josie rolled over and faced the wall so she couldn't watch the clock.

She rolled back at 5:16 . . . 5:17 . . . At 5:18 she threw a T-shirt over the clock so she'd quit counting the minutes. But she still heard it click every sixty seconds.

At seven a.m., she was awakened by the buzzing alarm. Josie must have dropped off for at least a few minutes. She felt worse than if she'd sat up all night.

Josie put on a robe, made her groggy way to the bathroom, and splashed cold water on her face. Then she checked on Amelia. Her daughter was awake, flushed and feverish.

"I don't feel good," Amelia said.

"What's wrong?" Josie asked, feeling her daughter's warm forehead.

"My head hurts and I think I'm going to throw up."

Josie took her daughter's temperature—one hundred degrees.

"You have a temperature," Josie said. "I think you'd better stay home today. I'll e-mail the school."

"Before eight o'clock," Amelia said.

"I know," Josie said. "I'll get your assignments online, too."

"Mom, I'm sick," Amelia whined.

"Not so sick you couldn't hike to Clayton with a backpack full of booze," Josie said.

"Am I ever going to hear the end of that?" Amelia said.

"Not in my lifetime," Josie said.

Amelia sighed dramatically and threw herself back on the pillows. Josie went off to make toast, her one culinary achievement. Amelia had missed a week of school after Nate's death, but her grades were good, and Barrington was casual about letting parents take students on winter ski vacations and visits to grandparents in Palm Beach.

Josie was back in fifteen minutes with Amelia's breakfast on a tray. Even when she wasn't feeling well, Amelia methodically spread her toast with grape jelly, making sure all the corners were painted an even purple. Josie was in an impatient mood, and itched to take the knife from her daughter's hand and spread the jelly herself.

"Mom, did you e-mail the school secretary yet?" Amelia asked.

"Nope, I'd better do that now," Josie said.

Josie went into her office and tried to log on to the Internet. After the third time, she gave up and said, "Amelia, I'm going to have to use your computer to send that e-mail. I can't get online this morning."

Josie sent the e-mail, beating the eight o'clock deadline by ten minutes. "Still feeling like you might throw up?"

"No, my stomach is calmed down."

Josie gave Amelia two bubblegum-flavored Tylenol Meltaways for the fever and then crawled back into her own bed. She was asleep when her phone rang at nine thirty that morning.

"Hello," Josie croaked into the phone.

"Oh, Josie, did I wake you?" Alyce asked. "I'm sorry. I thought you'd be back from taking Amelia to school."

"I would, if she'd gone to school today," Josie said. "She's sick with a light fever. I hope it's not the flu."

"I'm sorry she's sick," Alyce said. "I have some good news for you. I've got your job back. In fact, Harry wants you to start working today."

"He does?" Josie asked. "How come?"

"I told him that according to your contract, you could work unless there was a judgment against you and you were found to be at fault in the dispute. I explained that he could either pay you the amount you made last year this time, or he could put you to work. Harry said as long as he had to pay you, he might as well get you to work."

"Alyce, that's amazing. Does my contract really say that?"

"No," Alyce said, "but Harry is too lazy to read it and too dumb to understand it if he did. Are you able to work today with Amelia sick?"

"Mom will watch her," Josie said.

"Expect Harry to call within half an hour. He wants you to mystery-shop Grandma's Country-made Biscuits."

"Oh, good," Josie said. "I like their food. Want to come with me?"

"I might as well apply the biscuits directly to my hips," Alyce said. "At least I can drink tea with you. That has no calories. I'll get a sitter to watch the baby. I'll pick you up at eleven if everything goes right."

It did. Harry called, cantakerous and crunching pork rinds. Through crunches, he ordered Josie to mystery-shop the country-biscuit restaurant. "You'll have to eat biscuits and honey," he said.

"I'm prepared to do my duty," Josie said.

By eleven thirty, she and Alyce were seated in Grandma's Country-made Biscuits with a pot of tea and a plate of "homemade 4 U" biscuits. The honey came in little plastic packets, which Josie wrestled open. "Wish my house was as hard to get into as these packets," Josie said.

"Can you mention them in your report?" Alyce asked.

"Only in the remarks section. I wonder why they don't serve those little glass jars of honey like you get on room-service trays." Josie bit into her first biscuit and said, "Damn."

"What's wrong?"

"My so-called homemade biscuit is cold in the center. It's been frozen and nuked."

"I doubt that 'nuked 4 U' would be a catchy slogan," Alyce said.

"I get so tired of having to turn in bad reports," Josie said.

"Couldn't you fudge it a little?" Alyce asked.

"It wouldn't be fair to the people who are paying seven bucks for a pot of tea and six defrosted biscuits," Josie said. She had her code. It was her job—her mission—to save innocent consumers from bad experiences.

"You're right," Alyce said. "I don't know why restaurants nuke biscuits anyway. They're easy to make."

"For you," Josie said. "Your biscuits are so light they need little anchors to keep from floating off the plate."

Josie pulled apart another packet of honey and sent a big glob squirting over the table and down the front of her shirt.

"Josie, are you okay?" Alyce asked.

"No," Josie said. "Everything's wrong." Her voice was wobbly with tears and she tried to hold them back. She didn't want to cry in the restaurant. Over another pot of tea, she told her best friend the story of Mike, her daughter and the wine coolers, Heather's alcohol problem, the rescue of Amelia, and the ruin of Josie's wedding dreams.

"Oh, Josie," Alyce said. "I am so sorry. Mike seemed perfect."

"He was," Josie said. "I mean, he is. His daughter is the problem that has no solution."

"Do you really think Heather murdered Nate and that poor radio woman, and then injured the picketer?"

"I do. That kid is the original bad seed."

"But Mike is so nice," Alyce said.

"Mike is too nice to see anything wrong with his daughter," Josie said. "And Doreen is a witch. I hate to see Mike make a noble sacrifice to save Heather. It won't help her. She needs treatment."

"So what are you going to do?" Alyce asked.

"Prove Heather is the killer and save the man I love—and Mike will hate me for it. I want to go back to Naughty or Nice. I think Amelia's poking around has scared Heather and she's going to try to get rid of some crucial evidence."

"Josie Marcus, you are not going to that store alone," Alyce said. "I'm going with you."

"Good," Josie said. "I was hoping you'd say that."

Chapter 33

"Are you sure you want to go into Doreen's store?" Alyce asked as they pulled into the Naughty or Nice lot. The asphalt was empty except for Doreen's faded blue Bug.

Josie felt queasy and wondered if she was coming down with Amelia's flu. She didn't like to admit—even to herself—that Doreen scared her.

"Of course I don't want to go in there," Josie said. "But I want to help Mike. Besides, what can Doreen do to me?"

"She's already suing you. As your non-lawyer, I advise against this," Alyce said.

"Point noted. You can say I told you so when the cops haul me off," Josie said.

Alyce punched in 911 on her cell phone. "All I have to do is hit SEND and the cops will be here," she said as she carefully closed her phone.

The picketers were still circling the building, carrying their condemnatory signs. The red GOING OUT OF BUSINESS posters plastered on the building looked like a judgment from God.

"Women!" screamed the preacher, running toward them. His black all-weather coat flapped like bat wings. "Remember your duty and your virtue."

He stepped in front of Josie, blocking her way.

"Move," she said. "Or I'll call the cops. It's against the law to prevent people from entering this store, and you have a duty to follow the law. Render unto Caesar and all that."

The preacher stepped aside.

"Josie, I had no idea you were religious," Alyce whispered when they were past the picketers.

"No man gets in the way of my shopping," Josie said. "I don't like being bullied. If those pornaments weren't so disgusting, I'd buy one."

"Jingle Bell Rock" jounced cheerfully out of the speakers.

"Here goes," Josie said. She took a deep breath and opened the shop door. The outside breeze made the red DRASTICALLY REDUCED tags rustle like a bloody snowstorm. A bell jingled and Doreen was standing in front of them with a feather duster. Josie thought the woman would look more at home with a black pointed hat and a broom.

"You," Doreen said, pointing the feather duster at Josie. "What are you doing in my store? Get your ass out of here."

"I need a Christmas angel ornament," Josie said, hoping Doreen couldn't hear the quaver in her voice.

"Buy it and leave," Doreen said. "I can't afford to turn anyone away, not even you. This is all your fault. You ruined my store with your false report."

Alyce guided Josie firmly by the elbow toward the winged ornaments before she could answer. "Here's a perfect angel for your tree," Alyce said loudly, digging her fingers into Josie's arm.

Josie didn't even look at it. "I'll take it," she said.

Alyce carried the ornament to the counter. Surly, lumpen Heather was at the cash register, once more wearing her "stupid" elf hat. Josie almost felt sorry for the girl. Why wasn't she in school?

Heather didn't acknowledge Josie. "That will be $26.58," she said.

"It will?" Josie asked. That was ten bucks more than she had with her.

"I'll buy it as your Christmas present," Alyce said. She put twenty-seven dollars on the counter.

Heather wrapped the ornament in red tissue paper. She moved a nearly empty plastic drinking bottle, the kind with a built-in straw, to spread out the sheets on the counter.

Doreen appeared over her shoulder. "Heather, what are you doing with that bottle?" she asked.

Josie saw a small amount of green liquid in the bottom.

"I found it in the trash in the back room," Heather said. "It's a perfectly good drinking bottle. We're supposed to recycle plastic. I learned that at school. It's important for the planet. You were throwing it out, anyway. I wanted it."

"And I said you couldn't have it," Doreen said. "But you don't listen."

Doreen slapped her daughter across the face and tossed the bottle in the trash. Josie saw a red handprint on Heather's cheek. Alyce winced at the violence of the attack.

"And you, quit gawking and get out of my store," Doreen said.

Alyce dragged Josie outside, not bothering to wait for her change.

Josie wondered why Doreen overreacted over a water bottle. What was the greenish liquid in the bottle? Limeade? Gatorade? A designer sports drink? Why throw out a perfectly good bottle when Heather wanted it? Josie practically threw herself in Alyce's SUV.

"Should we call the child abuse hotline?" Alyce asked. "Doreen hit that girl hard."

"Not yet," Josie said. "Not until we find out why Doreen went crazy over a water bottle."

Alyce wasted no time getting out of the lot.

"Thanks," Josie said. "I'm glad you were there with me. That woman scares the heck out of me."

"You and me both," Alyce said.

"I'd better call Mom and find out how Amelia is," Josie said. She put the phone on speaker so Alyce could hear the conversation.

"How's my girl?" Josie asked.

"Amelia's fever is just about gone," Jane said. "It's down to ninety-nine point one. We had chicken soup and grilled cheese for lunch. I'll give her some baby aspirin after she finishes."

"No!" Josie said. "No aspirin for children under eighteen."

"Josie, that's nonsense. I gave you aspirin and you turned out fine."

"Mom, they don't do that anymore because of Reye's syndrome."

"I never heard of that," Jane said.

"It's true. The latest surveys show that girls given aspirin instead of Tylenol grow up to be stubborn, rude, and have children out of wedlock."

"Don't play games with me, Josie Marcus."

"Mom, please, just give Amelia the Tylenol Meltaways. I'll be right home."

"I gather we're heading for Maplewood ASAP," Alyce said.

"You bet," Josie said. "Mom is in one of her stubborn moods."

Josie unwrapped the angel while Alyce drove. "She's beautiful," Josie said. "I love the dark hair. I'm tired of blond angels. And the freckles are so cute. She even looks like Amelia, though I'll be the first to admit my daughter is no angel—not lately, anyway."

"Amelia is just going through a phase," Alyce said.

"I'm afraid this phase is going to last nine or ten years," Josie said. "I was a trial to my mother at her age and I continued to be one until I was in college. Now I regret it."

"Josie, you turned out fine," Alyce said. "You have a career you enjoy, a beautiful, bright girl, and you get along with your mother now. I'd say you have an almost perfect life."

"Except for my love life," Josie said.

"I am sorry about Mike," Alyce said. "He's a lovely man. But you were smart. You won't jump into marriage because you had to have a man. You knew that living with Mike and his dreadful daughter would be misery for yourself and Amelia. A lot of women would choose a man—especially one making good money—over their own child.

"Lindsay in our subdivision did that. She was desperate to marry a lawyer. She even had a face-lift at thirty-two. Well, she married the man, but he controls the money. Her daughter goes to public school and wears secondhand clothes, while his child is a pampered princess. And he's fixed the prenup so Lindsay can't get a dime if she divorces him. Even if she does get out of the marriage, she'll be over forty. It's a nightmare."

"Well, I have managed to avoid that, anyway," Josie said. "We're at my place already. Come in so you can give Amelia her angel ornament."

Amelia was in her pajamas, sitting at her computer. "I'm doing my homework," she said.

"Alyce brought you a get-well present," Josie said. Alyce handed Amelia the bag with the ornament.

"Cool," Amelia said. "Can we have a real Christmas tree this year? I can hang my angel on it."

"We had one last year, remember?" Josie asked. "You wanted a live tree, so we wouldn't kill a tree to celebrate the holiday. We planted it in the backyard after Christmas."

"It's now my Charlie Brown Christmas tree," Amelia said. "Grandma and I hung suet and seed balls on it for the birds, but it's kind of sad-looking. The poor tree is almost dead. We might as well get a real one."

"If you ask me, it's a waste of good money," Jane said. "You can get a fake tree for a third of the price and use it year after year."

"But fake trees don't smell like Christmas," Amelia said.

"All you need is a can of pine spray and you can't tell the difference."

"Thank you, Mrs. Scrooge," Josie said to Jane. "Yes, Amelia, we'll go shopping for a real tree."

"A big one?" Amelia asked.

"As big as I can afford and still feed you. Unless you want to eat pine needle soup."

"Yay!" Amelia said. "Can we go tonight? Grandma said my fever is gone."

"If you're too sick to go to school, you are too sick to prowl a cold Christmas tree lot. Let's see how you're feeling tomorrow."

"I'd better get home," Alyce said.

Josie was pleased that Amelia remembered to thank Alyce for the ornament. She walked her friend out to her SUV. As Josie was waving good-bye, Mrs. Mueller came outside. Josie thought the old gossip looked uncommonly smug.

"Have you been watching the TV news?" Mrs. Mueller asked.

"No," Josie said.

"That man you had the loud fight with on your porch at two in the morning has been arrested."

"Mike?" Josie said. "There must be some mistake."

"I don't think so," Mrs. Mueller said. "The police said he confessed to two murders. He poisoned both those poor people with antifreeze at that Christmas shop."

"Are you sure?" Josie asked.

"Very sure," Mrs. Mueller said, not bothering to hide her triumph. "I heard those nasty things he said about me being an old biddy who made up gossip. This time I made sure I had my facts correct."

Chapter 34

"Mom, I have to run to the store. Can you watch Amelia for me?" Josie leaned against her daughter's wall so her mother couldn't see her shaking with anger after her ambush by Mrs. Mueller.

"Of course," Jane said. "Amelia and I will watch television."

"I can look after myself," Amelia said.

"Oh, no, young lady," Josie said. "I no longer trust you to be at home alone. You forfeited that privilege when you ran off with those wine coolers. Your grandmother will stay with you until I get back."

Josie grabbed her coat and was out the door before Jane could ask what she needed at the store.

Josie drove in a daze. Mike had done what he'd threatened to do—sacrificed himself for his daughter. He'd spend years in prison for a double murder he didn't commit.

Unless he really did kill Nate.

No, that was crazy, Josie decided. Mike wouldn't kill two people in cold blood. He might shoot, stab, or punch Nate, but he wouldn't use anything as sneaky as poison. Anyway, I'm not the sort of woman that men fight over.

Josie arrived at the Naughty or Nice shop five minutes before it closed. The picketers were still chanting and moving in a dispirited circle. Josie thought they seemed cold and weary.

She parked her anonymous gray car on the lot at the shuttered Elsie's Elf House and listened to a loose sheet of plywood slam in the wind. Ten minutes later, the back door opened at Naughty or Nice. Josie crouched down in her car and watched Doreen toss two trash bags into the overflowing Dumpster. Then the witchy-haired woman locked the back door. Her sullen daughter followed her to the battered blue VW. Heather's round shoulders and shambling walk made the girl even more unattractive.

Such an unlovely child, Josie thought. I wonder how Heather would look if I took her to a good stylist for a makeover and bought her decent clothes?

This is no time for mom fantasies, she told herself angrily. It's over. Heather is never going to like you or Amelia, no matter what you do. Mike is in jail. Heather won't appreciate her father's sacrifice.

And the real killer is free.

Josie waited for the VW to drive away, then sat in her car for another ten minutes, in case the two came back. She was so cold she could see her breath. She warmed her cold nose with her woolen gloves.

At last Josie turned on her car engine, grateful for the burst of warm air from the heater. She drove over to Doreen's Dumpster and threw the top two trash bags into the back of her car. She bought two *City Gazette*s from a nearby box and spread the newspapers on the floor and the backseat of her car. Then she opened the trash bags.

Soon Josie's car stank of garbage. Doreen must have saved her most disgusting trash for these bags—moldy takeout cartons, rotting salad containers leaking oily dressing, and a small smelly grocery bag tightly tied at the top. Josie pried open the knot and screamed. Inside

were four dead mice. The shriveled little creatures rested
next to a pile of gigantic roaches and the water bottle.

Got it!

Stuck to the bottle was a credit-card receipt, stained
with fluids Josie didn't want to think about. The receipt
was from the Racers Edge car store, dated two days before Nate was poisoned at Elsie's Elf House.

"Yes!" Josie said, and pumped her fist in the air.

Doreen's name was on the receipt. She'd bought two
gallon jugs of antifreeze, totaling $21.90.

Wearing her gloves, Josie opened the water bottle
and carefully sniffed the greenish liquid at the bottom.
That definitely wasn't lemon-lime Gatorade. She was
sure it was antifreeze.

This was it. Proof that Doreen was the killer. Why was
Doreen buying antifreeze? She didn't use it. She drove
an old air-cooled Volkswagen.

Josie photographed her find, then searched her purse
for the card of the homicide detective, the smart one
she'd nicknamed Detective Gray. He wasn't at his office,
but he did answer his cell phone.

"This is Josie Marcus," she said. "You interviewed me
the day of Nate Weekler's memorial service."

"I remember you, Ms. Marcus," the detective said.
"You had a lawyer with you."

"Yes, I did," Josie said. "You said to call if I remembered anything. Well, I did. I mean, I found the killer."

"We already have the killer, miss," Detective Gray
said. "Your plumber friend confessed. We have him in
custody."

"He didn't do it!" Josie said.

"Ms. Marcus, I know you want to save your boyfriend,
but we have a confession and a receipt. He bought a lot
of antifreeze. The case is closed."

"I have a receipt, too," Josie said. "Doreen, Mike's ex-girlfriend and the mother of his daughter, bought two gallons of antifreeze right before the murders."

"It's wintertime, miss. As your attorney said, everybody buys antifreeze this time of year."

"Doreen drives an old Volkswagen. She doesn't use antifreeze. She also poisoned the next-door neighbor's dog. She killed that poor animal with antifreeze-laced hamburger. Get the dog's body and check. After the dog died, Doreen put the antifreeze in a sports drink bottle, took it to Elsie's Elf House, and poured it into the chocolate sauce when Elsie was distracted by customers. She was in the store that morning. Elsie has the proof."

"Is that right?" the detective said. Josie could tell he didn't believe her.

"I have the drink bottle," Josie said. "I found it in Doreen's trash. It was in the Dumpster behind her store."

"So you're a Dumpster diver, as well as a mystery shopper. How do I know you didn't plant that bottle there?"

"Take a closer look at her teenage daughter, Heather. She pushed the snow off the store roof with a shovel and nearly killed that picketer."

"No witnesses saw her do that, miss," he said.

"They saw Santa Claus up on that roof. Everyone thought that old woman was senile, but she was telling the truth. Heather took a Santa suit from her mother's store. She's a big, strong girl. It would be easy to mistake her for a man in that Santa suit. Heather still has it, rolled up in the bottom of her closet. Did you take casts of the footprints in the snow around that ladder?"

"Are you telling me how to do my job?" The detective sounded angry.

"No, but if you check those casts against the shoes in Heather's closet, you'll have a match."

"And why should I do that, when the case is closed? I already have a confession," he said.

"Because it's a false confession. Mike confessed to save his daughter. I bet he didn't tell you how he managed to get the antifreeze into the store."

"The plumber said he sneaked inside when the place was quiet."

"Check the register transactions and credit-card receipts," Josie said. "Elsie was busy nearly every minute that day. That's what made Doreen crazy. Elsie's place was a success. Doreen's shop was a failure. She wanted to ruin Elsie's business, and she succeeded."

"Uh-huh." He was humoring her. "You don't like Doreen, do you?"

"No," Josie said.

"But you've got a thing for Mike. Your life would be a lot better if Doreen was out of the way and you had the plumber to yourself. You two women are fighting over him."

"No!" Josie said. "Have a vet check out the dead dog. I bet it's buried in the backyard next door. Then call me. I'll keep the bottle."

"I sure do appreciate getting orders from a civilian, miss," he said, and hung up on Josie.

Josie drove right through a stoplight and was rewarded with an angry blast from a horn. She knew she was too upset to be driving.

When she got home, Jane was waiting at the door. "I thought you were going to the supermarket," she said. "Where are the bags?"

"They were out of what I needed," Josie said. "Thanks for watching Amelia."

"I'm going upstairs," Jane said. "I've made chicken and dumplings. They're simmering on the stove. Although why I bother, I don't know."

"Thanks, Mom," Josie said. "GBH."

That was the family code for "Great Big Hug." Josie

folded her mother in her arms. "I appreciate all you do, Mom. I couldn't get along without you. Have I told you that recently?"

"No," Jane said, still stiff with anger. "You haven't done anything but complain, criticize, and cause trouble. I'll have to cancel the Christmas party after that fight you had with that plumber on the front porch. Now he's in jail. It's too embarrassing. I can't face the neighbors."

"I'm sorry, Mom, but he only confessed to save his daughter. Did you move the beer and wine coolers in my refrigerator?"

"They're hidden in the basement, where Amelia can't reach them. Mike and Stan helped me. And now, if you don't mind, I want to go upstairs and start calling people to cancel my party."

Jane marched out, back straight, head high. Josie could hear the television news. "A thirty-five-year-old plumber confessed to a double homicide today," the announcer said. Mike's photo flashed on the screen.

Josie turned off the TV. She couldn't take any more bad news.

Chapter 35

"I can't believe Mike killed those people." Alyce was so upset, she was shouting into her phone.

"He didn't," Josie said.

"Then why did he confess?" Alyce said. "It was all over the TV this morning."

"He wants to save his daughter."

"Oh, Josie, what's wrong with that man?"

"He's being noble," Josie said. "Mike blames himself for the way Heather turned out. He thinks by confessing to two murders he didn't commit, he'll save her. But Heather killed Nate and that poor woman—or her mother did. I fished a bottle of what I think is antifreeze out of the store's Dumpster."

"I'm sorry Mike is doing this," Alyce said.

"So am I," Josie said. "That kid's not worth it."

"Did I hear you right?" Alyce asked. "You searched the store's trash?"

"Searched it? I stole two bags and put them in my car."

"Good thing it's a cold day," Alyce said.

"Amelia complained about the stink this morning on the way to school. I moved the trash bags into the garage and put a note on them so Mom won't throw them out. Remember that police detective, the older, gray-haired one?"

"Sure, the smart one. You kept calling him Detective Gray."

"That's the guy. I told him Heather confessed to pushing the snow off the roof and her mother poisoned the neighbor's poor dog. I offered to give Detective Gray the bottle with the antifreeze. He turned me down."

"What a mess," Alyce said. "How's Amelia feeling?"

"Better, thanks. She went to school today," Josie said. "She's hounding me to buy her a real Christmas tree. We're going shopping tonight."

"Are you getting your tree at Ted Drewes's lot?"

St. Louisans flocked to Ted's frozen custard stand in the summer. In the winter they bought their Christmas trees off the lot there. They'd stand outside and drink hot chocolate and eat ice cream, even if it was two below zero. Ted's was a city tradition.

"I have to use the church lot or Mom will have a fit," Josie said. "The sales benefit St. Philomena's. They have good trees."

"Are you working today?" Alyce asked.

"Harry the Horrible hasn't called me yet. I'm hauling Christmas decorations out of the closet."

"Then I'd better let you go," Alyce said. "I still have cookies to bake."

Josie spent a nostalgic day going through boxes of ornaments. She had one ornament with the date on it for each year with Amelia, starting with her baby's first Christmas in 1999. She had china cherubs, tiny teddy bears, handblown glass globes, and dusty plastic poinsettias that clipped to the branches.

When Amelia was old enough to go to school, she made Josie ornaments that said I LOVE YOU, MOMMY in green and red crayon. Amelia was embarrassed by them now, but Josie still hung them on the tree.

Mixed in with the newer ornaments were old European glass ornaments that had belonged to Josie's grandparents—silver bells, blue glass fiddles, frosty snowmen, and Old World angels. Each came with a memory. Each was carefully packed away in cotton at the end of the holidays.

Josie unpacked loops of colorful glass beads to drape on the branches. The Christmas lights were stuffed in a box in a monster tangle. Every holiday, Josie swore she'd pack her lights more neatly, and the next Christmas she'd spend an hour or more unraveling them.

Josie didn't like the plain white twinkle lights. She preferred the fat colorful ones. She didn't have color-themed Christmas trees with the ornaments and ribbons all one tasteful shade of white, pink, or red. Josie's trees glittered with tinsel, bright lights, and offbeat ornaments.

When the tree was decorated, she'd wrap a sheet around the bottom for "snow" and put up the manger. Josie's manger had a camel, a cow, a horse, and a plastic dog. The dog was added when Amelia was five. She insisted that Baby Jesus wanted a puppy, and the dog had stayed next to the camel ever since. Baby Jesus had a chipped nose after Amelia dropped him one Christmas. Josie put a bit of straw over his face to cover that flaw.

The unpacked ornaments and sale boxes of tinsel were laid out on the couch and coffee table. The couch was moved to make room for the tree.

Josie's phone rang at two that afternoon, as she was finishing. It was Harry.

"Josie, I got some good news," her horrible boss said. "The lawsuit is canceled. That Doreen woman's lawyer called me. They dropped it, called it off, whatever they do when they decide not to sue."

"Harry! That's wonderful! I got my Christmas present early!"

"Yeah, yeah," Harry said. He sounded bored at her enthusiasm. Or maybe he was disappointed she wasn't in hot water. "Gotta run."

Josie called Alyce with the news while she put on a pot of chili for a quick cold-weather supper. She was arranging her Santa eggnog mugs on the mantel when she checked the clock. Time to pick up Amelia.

Josie pulled into the driveway at the Barrington School and gave the other moms a nod and a forced smile. They gave her fake smiles back. Most of them would never associate with her. Josie wasn't married, she worked for a living, and she waxed her floors, not her legs.

Ten minutes later, Amelia's name was called and she came running out, dragging her backpack. She slung it in the back, then hopped into the front seat. She sniffed the car.

"Smells better than it did this morning," Amelia said.

"I sprayed it with lemon air freshener. How are you feeling?"

"Fine. We're still going to the tree lot, right?"

"Right," Josie said. "After dinner."

"Can't we go now?"

"It's more fun after dinner," Josie said. "I like the smell of a Christmas tree lot after dark."

"You're weird," Amelia said.

"You should know that by now."

Amelia, eager to pick out a tree, put her backpack away instead of dropping it by the door. Then she set the table for dinner. Josie cooked macaroni so Amelia could have chili mac. She spooned the macaroni into a soup bowl, ladled chili on top of it, and put out shredded cheese and oyster crackers.

"Can we get a big tree this year?" Amelia asked.

"We can spend about forty dollars," Josie said. "That

should get us a nice six-footer. Don't shovel your food in so fast. You'll get sick."

Amelia slowed down a notch. Dinner was finished and the dishes were cleared away by six p.m. "Can we go now, please?" Amelia asked. "It's dark."

"I've tormented you enough," Josie said. "Let's go."

"Yay!" Amelia said, and bounced around the house.

"Get your coat and scarf and wear a hat," Josie said. "It's cold out."

When Amelia was bundled up, Josie grabbed her coat, an old blanket, and some bungee cords to tie the tree to her car's roof. Amelia raced ahead and was already seated in the car when Josie slid in on the driver's side.

St. Philomena's trees were under a big white tent, with a giant inflatable Santa outside. Two men in puffy winter coats sat around a barrel burning newspapers and wood. The trees were propped on racks. Bare light-bulbs were strung overhead. Needles crunched under-foot. The lot was just the way Josie remembered from her childhood.

"Breathe in," Josie said, and took a deep breath of the pine-scented air. "It's delicious."

"I don't want a tree with fat needles," Amelia said.

"You mean a Scotch pine?" Josie said.

"Yeah, one of those. They're not real Christmas trees."

"How about a blue spruce?" Josie asked.

"I don't want a blue tree, either," Amelia said.

Josie began singing, "I'm dreaming of a blue Christmas . . ." until Amelia howled, "Mo-om!" The kid looked embarrassed. Josie stopped singing.

"How about a Douglas fir?" Josie asked. "Does that fit your exacting standards?"

"That's a real Christmas tree," Amelia said.

"Our price range is over here with the six-footers," Josie said.

She held out a tree.

"Too skinny," Amelia said, giving it two thumbs-down. "How about this one?"

"Looks like somebody took a bite out of it," Amelia said.

Amelia rejected more than a dozen trees. Their search took them to the dark shadows at the edge of the lot, where the rejects were stacked. Many of these trees had been cannibalized to fill in bare spots on the more expensive ones. Amelia held up a skinny tree, a broomstick with three branches.

"What if we used this tree to fill out the hole in the second tree we looked at? You could cut off these branches, make holes in the other tree's trunk, and fill it in."

"Amelia, I want a tree, not a do-it-yourself project."

Amelia screamed, and Josie turned in surprise.

Doreen had leaped out between the rows of trees. This was the horror-movie version of Mike's ex. Her hair was a wild gray-black corona. Her eyes were red and blazing. She was dressed all in black, and her skin was sallow.

"You!" Doreen screamed. "You killed my shop. My lawyer dropped the case because you had that cake with the roach. You blamed my daughter."

"Your daughter put the roach in it," Josie said.

"She told me," Amelia said. "Heather was bragging about it."

Doreen was beyond listening to reason. She held a scrawny tree like a lance and charged Josie, trying to run her through. Josie dodged the crazed woman, tossed her cell at Amelia and yelled, "Run! Get away from here. Call 911."

Doreen came back down the aisle and nearly hit Josie with her tree. Josie picked up her tree and tried to swing it at Doreen. It was too heavy. She missed Doreen on the first swing. On the second, she clipped her on the shoulder.

Doreen made another charge with the skinny tree and Josie threw herself into a pile of trees to keep from getting impaled.

She saw Amelia's skinny tree leaning against a rack, and swung it at Doreen. She hit her in the chest, then used the tree trunk as a battering ram and hit her in the stomach.

"Oof!" Doreen said, and staggered backward, dropping her tree.

Doreen quickly found another tree from the reject pile. The two women fought, using the trees as clubs. A whole rack of trees toppled over.

Josie heard a man call, "Hey!" Then Doreen was on her, crazed with anger, determined to wipe out her enemy. She backed Josie into a display of decorative wreaths and garlands and pounded her shoulders with the tree trunk. Doreen's tree hit a string of lights and they snapped off. The corner went dark.

"You killed my store, bitch," Doreen shrieked like a madwoman. She hit Josie so hard with a wreath that it dazed her. Blood ran down Josie's forehead into her eyes. She could feel Doreen's fingers around her throat. Josie's world started to go black. As she sank to her knees, Josie felt something against her leg—a thick roll of evergreen garland.

That gave Josie one last surge of strength. She slung a loop of garland around Doreen's neck and pulled.

"Gotcha," Josie said.

She pulled the garland tight while Doreen clutched at it. Doreen was choking. Josie was still pulling on the garland when the tent was illuminated by flashing red lights.

Two uniformed police officers shone their flashlights on Josie and Doreen. Josie was blinded by the bright light.

"Merry Christmas, ladies," said one officer.

His partner loosened Josie's fingers from around Doreen's neck.

Epilogue: Christmas Eve

The lighted Christmas tree glowed in Josie's living room. The six-foot tree was bright with fat lights, shining with homemade and store-bought ornaments. The oldest were safe at the top of the tree. The ornaments Amelia had made in grade school were discreetly tucked toward the back, in deference to her new maturity. The angel ornament from Naughty or Nice was in the middle. The tinsel was distributed the way Josie liked it, starting at the ends of the branches and working back.

"It's perfect," Amelia said.

It wasn't perfect, and Josie knew it. The tree tilted sideways, no matter how much she fiddled with the stand. But Amelia liked it, and that was what mattered at Christmas.

Josie had had to buy the tree "with the bite out of it," plus the tree she'd used to clobber Doreen. It was part of the deal Jane worked out. Josie's mother pulled rank as the second most powerful church lady at St. Philomena's and prevented the tree lot from filing charges against Josie for destruction of property. Josie had agreed to pay for the trees and volunteer four nights at the lot as an informal community service program.

Stan the Man Next Door had offered to set up the tree. He'd spent an entire evening drilling holes in the trunk of the "bitten" tree, then filling in the bare spots with branches from the reject.

While he worked, Josie noticed for the first time that Stan had serious muscles. His arms bulged. So did his pecs. His belly flab was gone.

"Have you lost weight, Stan?" Josie asked.

"About twenty-five pounds," he said. "Another twenty to go. My mom got me a home workout center for my birthday. I exercise while I watch TV. I added a used treadmill I bought at a garage sale. The equipment takes up most of my living room. I was a nerd in high school gym class, but I like working out now. The only problem is my clothes don't fit right anymore."

He grabbed the front of his dingy beige T-shirt and said, "See, it's too big." Stan lifted the shirt slightly to demonstrate, and Josie saw a major six-pack above his belt. Whoa. Where was the nerdy Stan she knew?

"You need Mom to take you shopping for some cool stuff, Stan," Amelia said. "You dress like a grandpa. You could be a hottie if you tried."

"Amelia!" Josie said. "Go to your room."

"No, don't punish her," Stan said. "She's right. I mean, I don't know if I'll ever look hot, but I do dress like an old man. That's the truth. Josie, I know you're busy, but would you do a makeover on me—hair, clothes, glasses?"

Josie had prayed for this moment for years. Stan was sweet: kind, loyal, handy around the house. Unfortunately, he was about as sexy as a glass of warm milk. Stan had always resisted her tactful suggestions to dress his age, and clung to his dull wash-and-wear shirts and baggy pants.

"I'd be delighted," Josie said. "We'll start after Christmas, when men's clothes go on sale."

But Josie kept thinking about those pecs and that

six-pack. Muscles like those should be shown off. The next day she bought a good black T-shirt in a size she was sure would fit the new Stan and added it to the wrapped packages under the tree. A big green box with a holly-decorated ribbon held a pair of new skates from Amelia's grandfather. He wanted to take her to Steinberg Rink before he went back to Canada. Josie bought Amelia a RAZR phone. If the kid had had her own cell phone, help would have arrived much sooner. Maybe Josie wouldn't have needed four stitches in her forehead.

Josie knew her family wasn't the same. She and Amelia were still mourning Nate's loss. But the changes weren't entirely bad. Josie had faced her own lies and cover-ups. Amelia now knew she had a father who had loved her—and who'd told her so. She had a grandfather who cared about her and was there to help when she needed it. Josie had made some stupid mistakes, but that's what parents do. She hoped someday her daughter would understand.

Now it was Christmas Eve. Stan was drinking eggnog in Josie's living room, eating Alyce's Christmas cookies, and checking the water level in the tree stand. Bing Crosby's "White Christmas" sounded better in Josie's home than at the mall. The lights were low enough to hide the stains on the carpet and the sags in the couch. The living room didn't look bad at all.

"I like your tree," Stan said. "It's homey. Every ornament has a personal meaning."

"That angel on that middle branch has real personal meaning," Amelia said. "It came from that loser face Heather's store."

"What happened after Doreen attacked you in the Christmas tree lot?" Stan asked.

"The detective reopened the case," Josie said.

"He must be quite a man to admit he was wrong," Stan said.

"Definitely. Heather, Doreen's daughter, had already told Amelia that her mother had poisoned the dog next door. The detective had the dog dug up and autopsied. The body was preserved by the cold weather we'd had. The poor dog had died of antifreeze poisoning. Then the detective checked out Doreen. There was a receipt in her trash—"

"How did he get that?" Stan asked.

"I went digging in her Dumpster to find it," Josie said.

"You really are remarkable," Stan said.

"You should have smelled the car," Amelia said. "Mom had two bags of trash in it. It stunk for a week."

"I also found a water bottle in the same trash with some greenish liquid in it," Josie said. "Doreen wouldn't let her daughter keep the bottle. She went ballistic and slapped the girl. That didn't make any sense. The detective had the bottle examined, and the liquid turned out to be antifreeze. He got the security videos from the Racers Edge auto parts store showing Doreen walking to her car with two gallon jugs. She was by herself. Doreen bought the antifreeze two days before Nate and that woman were poisoned—and Doreen has an old VW that doesn't use antifreeze. The police got a search warrant and found one jug still in Doreen's storage locker, with her fingerprints all over it.

"Elsie, the owner of the Elf House, said Doreen had been in her store the morning before the poisonings. Doreen gave her a poinsettia as a gift, and she'd never demonstrated any other signs of neighborliness. Elsie thought Doreen poured the antifreeze in the chocolate sauce when Elsie was busy with customers. Elsie remembered Doreen carrying a sports drink bottle because it was so odd—Doreen never worked out, and she drank beer or coffee. Elsie didn't use the poisoned chocolate sauce until the next day

"The detective arrested Doreen for two counts of murder and assault with a deadly weapon. The deadly weapon was the Douglas fir she swung at me."

"I bet he wanted to give you a medal for solving the case," Stan said. His brown eyes were wide with admiration, and would look good if they weren't hidden behind those ugly glasses. Maybe he should think about contact lenses, Josie told herself.

"Not exactly. He really chewed me out. He said, 'Who do you think you are, Jessica Fletcher? This is real life, not a TV show.'

"I told him I was trying to help. He said I was a great help—to the defense. 'How do I know you didn't plant that bottle?' he yelled at me. 'That's what they'll say and the real murderer will get away.' That's when I told him, 'Check it for fingerprints. I wore gloves the whole time. You won't find my prints on it.' "

"You're amazing," Stan said. "Most women would burst into tears if a detective yelled at them."

"I doubt that," Josie said. "My friend Alyce can stand up to the cops. I've seen her."

But Stan's praise soothed Josie's hurting heart. Mike had been angry and called her a "meddler." He'd hardly spoken to her since the police let him go.

"Still, you got Mike released," Stan said. "He must have been thrilled."

"He was surprised," Josie said. That was the truth.

"So the charges were dropped against him?" Stan asked,

"Mike's free. He has full custody of Heather, now that her mother's in jail."

"That's good news."

"It means big changes in Heather's life," Josie said.

"With her mother in jail, she's going to live full-time with Mike and his dog. Mike's mother offered to take her, but Mike refused. 'Grandma is just a little too easy to fool,' he said."

"So was Mike," Amelia said. "Heather walked all over her dad and he never knew it."

"Ameliaaaaa," Josie said, drawing the word out to warn her daughter that her patience was nearing an end. "Heather is in counseling now."

"That's good," Stan said.

"I hope so," Josie said. Secretly, she wondered how much good it could do.

"So Heather didn't get in any trouble with the law?" Stan asked.

"She's on probation. The Santa suit was found at Doreen's house, rolled up in Heather's closet. Heather confessed that she wore it and shoveled the snow off the roof to scare the picketers 'because Mom made me, but I didn't mean to hurt anyone.' "

"Do you think that's true?" Stan asked.

"I think Heather was lying. But I don't care if Doreen serves time for a crime she didn't commit. She shouldn't have made that poor kid sell pornographic Christmas ornaments."

"So Doreen killed those two people—Nate and that radio lady—for no reason."

"She killed them for a big reason," Josie said. "She wanted to ruin her rival's business. She didn't realize that she would also kill her own store. But, no, she didn't know Nate or Sheila, and didn't care."

"That's cold," Stan said.

"She makes the North Pole look like Nassau," Josie said.

"I forgot to ask in all the confusion," Stan said. "How did Doreen know you were at the tree lot?"

"Her new boyfriend worked there. He called her as soon as he saw me. Doreen came over and attacked me. Oh, here. I wanted to give you a little thank-you gift."

She reached under the tree and handed Stan a package wrapped in shiny red paper.

"For me?" Stan said. He tore it open and saw the T-shirt.

"Thought we'd start that makeover early," Josie said.

Her doorbell rang. "You have company," Stan said. "I'd better go."

"No, you were invited," Josie said. "That's someone who dropped by without an invitation."

"Go put the shirt on," Amelia said. "You can change in Mom's bedroom."

The doorbell rang again and Stan vanished with his new shirt. Amelia led the way to Josie's room.

Mike was standing on Josie's porch. He looked at her candlelit living room and said, "Sorry, I didn't know you were having a party."

"Come on in," Josie said.

This was the Mike she'd first met at Alyce's—drop-dead handsome and a little shy. He looked uncomfortable, like a schoolboy asking out a girl for the first time. "Josie, I owe you an apology."

Ah, she thought. That explained the attitude. Mike hated apologies.

"I was angry at you for meddling, but you were trying to get at the truth. It's better for Heather, too. I know that now. Heather's counselor said you did the right thing. I came to tell you that I'm sorry and to give you this."

He handed Josie a blue box. Josie opened it. A diamond ring in a platinum setting glittered on the dark velvet.

"Oh, Mike," she said. "It's lovely."

"So will you marry me?"

"No, Mike." There was regret in her voice.

"I thought you loved me," he said.

"I do love you," she said. "But—" *I can't stand your daughter* was the rest of that sentence, and Mike knew it.

"But I think we'd have problems with our daughters," Josie said. "Heather comes first with you. Amelia comes first with me. The girls don't get along, and we have two different ways of raising them. Mike, we can't get married now. It wouldn't work." She handed the ring back.

He shuffled his feet and said, "I'm sorry, Josie, but . . ."

"I'm sorry, too, Mike," Josie said, and she was.

"Is there someone else?" Mike asked.

His question angered her. "Right," Josie said. "I have so much time for men. I have them stashed in every room."

The door to Josie's bedroom opened and Stan came out. This was the new Stan, wearing a tight, sexy shirt that showed his improved physique. "Hi, Mike," Stan said. Mike practically bared his teeth.

"What do you think, Josie?" Stan asked.

"You look hot," Amelia said. "But you need to lose the pants."

"Amelia!" Josie said.

"I didn't mean right this moment," Amelia said.

"Good-bye, Josie," Mike said. Josie didn't hear him leave.

Shopping Tips

Black Friday, the day after Thanksgiving, is the busiest shopping day of the year.

Or is it?

The mall may be crowded as a mosh pit the day after Thanksgiving. But surveys show the real retail buying may take place closer to Christmas. The International Council of Shopping Centers (ICSC) reports that between 1993 and 2002, Black Friday was a sluggardly seventh or eighth place, occasionally rising to fifth. In 2003 and 2005, Black Friday jumped to first place, but that's only twice in nine years.

So what's really the nation's busiest shopping day? The one you can count on?

The Saturday before Christmas. Or, if Christmas is on a weekend, December 23 is the big day.

Shopping protest: When you stay home from the mall on Black Friday, you could be choosing to avoid the crowds—or engaging in a protest. *Adbusters* magazine declared Black Friday "Buy Nothing Day" back in 1997.

But if you do go to the mall: Josie feels Christmas decorations have been up since Labor Day, but the ICSC says most retailers begin decorating November 1.

The song Josie is most likely to hear in the malls during the holiday season?

"Jingle Bells" is the mall favorite, followed by "White Christmas."

Have your eye on special holiday decorations? January is the best time to buy them on sale, especially expensive ornaments or china. They can cost fifty to seventy-five percent less after the holidays. If you can't wait a whole year, check out the Christmas decoration sale all year round at www.christmaspeople.com.

Worried about unsafe toys? Be a label reader. "Look for toys that give age and safety recommendations and use that information as a guide," the U.S. Consumer Product Safety Commission says. The CPSC suggests buyers avoid "building sets with small magnets" for children under six years old. Ditto for toys with small parts for children under three. Those can be a choking hazard. Air rockets, darts, and slingshots can cause serious eye injuries and are best enjoyed by older children. Some stores have online safety and recall information. One is Toys R Us at www.Toysrus.com/safety. It's tough when you have to take away a Christmas gift because it's unsafe for your child, grandchild, or godchild.

Bargain hunting is not for the timid. Some brave souls get up at four a.m. the day after Thanksgiving and shiver in the cold for those special holiday prices. Just make sure you're waiting for something that's there. Call the store before the sale and find out how many units are in stock of the items you want. If the store only has four or five flat-panel televisions at that incredibly low price, you may decide you want to sleep late that day.

Better yet, sit tight until the last two weeks before Christmas, when you'll see real deals on TVs, computers, electronics, and other gifts. The lines are shorter, too, except maybe on December 23.

So you want to be a mystery shopper: As in all professions, you need to look out for potential problems. Be careful before you sign on with a company as a mystery shopper. Go to David Grisman's www.2006topscams.com/mystery-shopping. He says some of those "get paid for shopping" Web sites want you to buy a mystery-shopping directory that may contain outdated information.

What should a wise mystery shopper do?

Grisman suggests you ask this key question: Does the site offer a money-back guarantee? Some promise that you will "get paid to shop" if you give them money but never give you anything in return. Look for Web sites that include a way to get your money refunded.

Not sure if a mystery-shopping company is legitimate? Check with your state attorney general's office or the Better Business Bureau. Check out the Mystery Shopping Providers Association at www.mysteryshop.org and make sure your potential company is a member of MSPA. Check the same site for mystery-shopping scams.

Now, let's go holiday shopping. Out of fresh holiday gift ideas? Consider these:

Hot flash: When a friend sent my husband, Don, an LED penlight, I expected it to wind up in a junk drawer. Don isn't crazy about gadgets, and I'd never find him wandering the aisles at the hardware store. So I was surprised when he liked the penlight. Don keeps it in a place of honor by the TV. He uses his new flashlight to tease the cat, find the object that rolled under the bookcase, and help operate the remote.

I started asking around and learned an important lesson: Most men love flashlights, from skinny penlights to macho titanium tactical lights. Check out a Web site called Cool Flashlights, www.coolflashlights.com.

Extra scratch: There's a nifty telescoping back-scratcher from C. Crane and Co., www.ccrane.com, for around ten dollars.

Gifts for women that are easy on the wallet but send the right message: There's something about that Tiffany & Co. blue box that makes a woman's heart flutter. If a five-figure necklace is out of your price range, Tiffany has gifts for less than one hundred dollars, from earrings to Elsa Peretti charms. They all come in that distinctive Tiffany blue box. Check them out at www.tiffany.com.

Put some sparkle in her life: You don't have to give her diamonds. If your favorite female plans to hit the beach this holiday season, consider sparkling crystal-trimmed flip-flops from Deborah Evans. They're less than $100 at www.funfeet.com. Hey, if they're sexy enough for Eva Longoria, chances are the woman you know will be pleased, too.

Take her career seriously: An engraved card holder will keep a businesswoman from presenting a dog-eared card pulled from the bottom of her purse. Tiffany has those, too, but if you're on a budget, consider JCPenney's engraved business card holders for about thirty dollars or less. Check out www.jcpenney.com.

Sex and chocolate: Red Envelope has offbeat gifts, including Truth, Dare or Chocolate. This game has racy questions: "Where is the kinkiest place you've made love?" and gives you chances to tattoo your partner with Chocoholics Body Frosting. The game includes paintbrushes, cards, pawns, and two tiny jars of body frosting. www.redenvelope.com.

Cook your heart out: This romantic staple from novels works in real life, too. If you're a man who knows his way around the kitchen, fix her a meal. If you can't cook, stop at your favorite deli or supermarket, pick up a roast chicken, a salad, veggies, and flowers. Hardworking moms and working women all appreciate having someone else cook for a change.

Like Josie, I'm not a good cook. Fortunately, many of my friends are. Every year I wait for my Christmas present from Janet Smith. Janet mails a big box of home-made Christmas cookies. Liz Aton sends the ingredients for delicious holiday dips. All I have to do is add fresh sour cream, and I can bring something homemade to a holiday party. It wasn't completely made in my home, but they don't have to know that.

Give your time and talent: Short on cash but want to do the right thing? Offer your services as a babysitter, an errand runner, or car washer. If you're handy, a couple of hours of fix-it service are a welcome surprise. Volunteer to hang pictures and repair that dripping faucet.

For one-of-a-kind dogs: Pure Mutt is a company that celebrates one-of-a-kind dogs. After all, there's no pet quite like the collie-Lab mix you adopted at the shelter. Pure Mutt has matching shirts for dogs and their human companions, as well as leashes, key chains, collars, and other apparel. A portion of the proceeds benefits a no-kill animal shelter. For information, orders, or to find a Pure Mutt supplier near you, go to www.puremuttinc. com.

Gifts that give back: If a family member says, "Please don't buy me another useless holiday present, I have too much stuff," give a gift that gives back. Buy a better future with groups like Kiva. Where else can a pig farmer in Bali get help from a socialite in Boca Raton?

Kiva is a global organization that lets you sponsor little loans that make a big difference to people in developing nations. The amounts may seem small by our standards. Many are twenty-five to seventy-five dollars. Most loans are less than fifteen hundred dollars.

At the Kiva Web site, you can pick your beneficiary, lending one hundred dollars to help a man sell fish, or twenty-five dollars to a seamstress who wants to expand her business. You can also buy Kiva gift certificates, so your family can choose the person they want to help. For information, go to www.kiva.org.

Make sure you get the right kind of red for the holidays: Red is a good Christmas color, unless it's in your bank account. Here are three easy ways financial experts say you can avoid the wrong shade of holiday red:

1. Know how much you're spending: Sure, you want to get Mom a nice gift for a hundred bucks. But write down the total cost. Add up all your holiday gift expenses, including wrapping paper, ribbon, cards, gift bags, and shipping costs.

2. Leave your credit cards at home: Shopping with cash means you can't overspend—when you run out of money, that's it.

3. Cash in twice: Carrying cash may put you at risk for theft, but it has another advantage: It may keep you off new mailing lists. To remove your name from mail or e-mail lists, visit the Direct Marketing Association at www.dmaconsumers.org/EMPS.

Shop in your pajamas: Shopping online is a good way to save gas and avoid the crowds. "E-tailers" must follow the same rules as retailers. Online companies must ship the item during the time they advertise on their Web site. If their site promises, "We'll have it to you by December 24!" then they'd better do it.

If the company can't deliver on time, it has to give the shopper notice, with the revised shipping date. If there's no promise of a special shipping date, the company must ship the item within thirty days of receiving the order. Protect yourself by making a copy of your confirmation order.

If calling the company for help gets you nowhere, you can file a complaint with the Federal Trade Commission at www.ftc.gov. You can also protect yourself by checking the Web site with BBBOnLine, www.bbbonline.org before you order.

One more tip: Some consumers prefer to use major credit cards for online purchases rather than store cards. The major credit cards are often more responsive to consumer needs.

Two- and four-legged bandits: One year I sent gift baskets for the holidays. Two friends did not call or write that they'd received their gifts. It turned out one gift basket was delivered to the porch of a friend's suburban home. He was at work, and returned to find that squirrels, raccoons, and other critters had gnawed through the box and eaten the fruit, cheese, smoked salmon, nuts, and cookies. All he had waiting for him was a jar of preserves and some apple cores.

Another friend lived in a large apartment complex with no doorman or security guard. A "good neighbor" signed for her gift basket and helped himself to the feast.

To its credit, the company re-sent the baskets at its expense.

Happy holidays.

Two tiny women in their sixties stood outside the door to Miguel Angel's salon on Las Olas. They were both about five feet tall and wore pantsuits, one pink, the other blue. Their hair was short and gray. They looked like little round twins.

Helen Hawthorne towered over them as she opened the salon door. "May I help you?" she asked.

"Is this where Miguel Angel works?" Ms. Pink asked. She pronounced his name *Mig-well* and said "Angel" with a flat Midwestern accent.

"*The* Miguel Angel," said Ms. Blue.

"Yes, he's the owner," Helen said.

"Wow, you're tall," Ms. Pink said, looking up at Helen.

"Six feet," Helen said.

"Are you a model?" Ms. Blue asked.

"I'm only a gofer," Helen said. "I go for drinks and magazines for the clients, fetch lunches and run errands for Miguel Angel. I'm too old to model."

"You don't look old," said Ms. Pink. "Your dark hair is pretty."

"Thanks," Helen said. "Getting my hair done by Miguel Angel is the best perk of this job."

"We saw the *People* magazine article about how he

changed LaDonna and gave her a new look. It saved her acting career," Ms. Pink said.

"From 'street' to 'elite,'" Ms. Blue said. "We'd love to meet him. He's a real artist."

"He's here," Helen said. "Come on in."

"Can we actually come inside?" Ms. Pink asked.

"Sure, why not?"

"Because we're fat," Ms. Blue said. She said the F word as if being slightly chubby were shameful.

"We like fat," Helen said. She didn't add that the salon really liked fat wallets.

The two women entered cautiously, as if they expected a supermodel with a flaming sword to banish them. They surveyed the sculpted black and chrome client chairs, the chic black dryers, the outrageous bouquets of flowers. Billie Holiday was crooning "Stormy Weather."

The salon's softly lit mirrors were designed to flatter. The floor sparkled as if sprinkled with diamond dust.

"Oh, my," Ms. Pink said.

"It's beautiful," Ms. Blue said.

"Everyone here is beautiful," Ms. Pink said.

Black-clad stylists were working on two models in the sculpted chairs. Paolo worked on the blonde. The woman's head was crowned with tinfoil for highlights. Richard was adding extensions to the glossy hair of a brunette. You could have built condos on the models' jutting cheekbones.

Ms. Blue ran her hands over the leather scrapbooks on the salon's rosewood center table.

"Those are Miguel Angel's credits," Helen said.

Ms. Pink opened one book. "Look at that. Miguel Angel has been in *Vogue*, *W*, *Glamour*, *Vanity Fair*, and *People*. He did the MTV awards show. He's worked with so many celebrities."

"May we have his autograph to take back to Pittsburgh?" Ms. Pink asked. "Our friends won't believe we actually had the nerve to walk in here."

"Let me see if he's busy," Helen said. "Would you like some water or tea?"

"Oh, no, we can't afford to stay," Ms. Blue said. "We just wanted to say hello. Everyone talks about his work. He's famous."

"And handsome," Ms. Pink said. "Even if he won't be interested in us."

They giggled. Helen wondered if they knew Miguel was gay, or if they were talking about their cute, frumpy figures.

"What would it cost us to get our hair done here?" Ms. Blue asked.

"Three hundred for a color and cut," Helen said. The price tripped off her tongue as if everyone paid that much for hair care.

"Oh, dear," Ms. Blue said. "I don't think I can manage that. I'm still paying off my Saturn."

"Besides, we don't have much hair to work with," Ms. Pink said.

"Never underestimate Miguel Angel," Helen said. "Let me ask if he's seeing visitors."

Miguel Angel worked in his own alcove at the back of the salon. He was blow-drying the tawny-haired Kim Hammond, this season's top model. Miguel looked dangerous in his trademark black leather pants and black shirt with the collar turned up.

He wore his two enormous blow-dryers in black leather holsters, like six-guns. Why not? The man produced killer hair.

"Two nice women from Pittsburgh want to meet you," Helen said. "They admire your work. They want your autograph."

"That's sweet," Miguel Angel said. He was an international celebrity stylist, in a class with Frédéric Fekkai and that hunky Brazilian Oribe. Cuban-born Miguel Angel specialized in making aging beauties look glamorous. Actresses swore his touch could revive their lagging careers, and flew into his Fort Lauderdale salon from around the country. Ordinary women paid big bucks for his remakes.

Miguel asked Kim, "Do you mind if the ladies come back to meet me?"

"Really, Miguel. Are you giving tours now?" the model said in a bored voice.

"It's good for business," Miguel Angel said.

"But Pittsburgh?" Kim said with a sneer.

"There's money everywhere in America," he said.

"Then bring them back," Kim said. "Give the little people a thrill."

What a snob, Helen thought. In a few years, she'll be begging Miguel Angel for a new look.

Helen gave Ms. Pink and Ms. Blue the good news. "Is Angel his last name?" Ms. Pink asked.

"No, it's part of his first name," Helen said. "Cubans are partial to double names, especially the men. They prefer combos like Marco Antonio, Juan Carlos and Miguel Angel."

"Sort of like my Southern cousins," Ms. Blue said. "I have a Billy Bob and a Larry Joe."

"Yes," Helen said. "Let's go back and meet him before his next appointment."

Helen took off across the salon with her long, loping stride. The two women struggled to keep up. "Stop! I mean, slower, please," Ms. Pink said. "Our legs aren't as long as yours."

Helen slowed. Ms. Pink and Ms. Blue stopped when they saw Miguel Angel brushing Kim's long mane.

"Look at her hair," Ms. Pink said in an awed voice. "It's like a silk curtain."

"You do such beautiful work," Ms. Blue said, handing Miguel Angel an old-fashioned autograph book. "Would you sign this?"

"I'd be delighted." When Helen had first started working at the shop last month, she'd expected Miguel Angel to sneer like Kim, but he was surprisingly kind.

"Did anyone ever tell you that you look like a young Elvis?" Ms. Pink said, handing him a sheet of hotel stationary.

"Thank you," he said as he signed it.

Ana Luisa, the salon receptionist, came back. "Excuse me, Miguel Angel. Honey is here for her final appointment before the wedding."

"We'd better leave," Ms. Blue said.

"Thank you," the two women chorused, then toddled toward the door, trailing girlish giggles.

"Be careful what you say around Honey," Miguel Angel whispered to Helen.

"Why?" Helen asked.

"Because her fiancé is Kingman 'King' Oden. He writes the Stardust gossip blog and hosts the TV show *Stardust at Night.*"

"Yuck. He's King Odious, right?" Helen asked.

"That's his nickname, but we never use it in this salon."

"But he is nasty," she said. "The man makes fun of older celebrities who've put on weight and young ones who are too skinny. He enjoys revealing who is in rehab. Didn't he out a couple of actresses as lesbians?"

"That's him," Miguel Angel said. "King is mean. Lots of people hate him. But even more read his blog and watch his show. Two weeks ago, someone gave King a photo of Bianca Phillips without her makeup, and he posted it on his blog. Poor Bianca looked about a hundred years old. She nearly lost a movie deal because of King."

"Isn't Bianca back in rehab?"

"*Shhh.* That's supposed to be a secret," Miguel Angel said.

"Did Honey take the Bianca photo here?"

"I don't know," Miguel Angel said. "But if there's a rumor that King got that photo at my salon, it could ruin my business. Go help her."

Helen approached Honey, then handed her Miguel Angel's signature black silk robe embroidered with his name. Honey took the robe and a hanger into the changing room. She was a honey blonde, like her name, with a pale oval face and small, delicate features. The heels on her shoes were high and skinny, and her long legs were encased in designer denim.

Honey carried a large, flat white box. She presented it to Miguel Angel as if it held the crown jewels. "That's my bridal veil. It's silk illusion. That's very soft tulle."

Miguel had done enough weddings to recognize illusion of all types. He opened the box and gently lifted out the veil. "It's long," he said.

"It's a ninety-inch circle veil with silk-edged stitching." Honey handed him a smaller white box. "This is my tiara. It's crystal stars, in King's honor—for Stardust, you know. We're also getting Swarovski crystal stars for the dinner guests' place settings. We got a good deal on them—only seventy dollars a star."

"How many guests?" Helen asked.

"Two hundred," Honey said.

Helen did the math. Honey was spending fourteen thousand dollars on wedding favors alone. She'd already spent nearly every cent of her savings to be one of Miguel's Angels. He'd transformed her from a practical nurse with thick-soled shoes into the spike-heeled consort of King Oden.

"We'd better get started," Miguel said. "The wedding is Saturday, and we still haven't decided on a hairstyle."

"I'd like to try my hair up this time, in a French twist," Honey said. "Sort of Grace Kellyish. King will like that. Very classy."

"Phoebe, wash Honey's hair," Miguel Angel commanded his assistant.

"But I washed it this morning," Honey said.

"It will look better after my treatment," he said.

Many customers thought they'd save time or money by washing their own hair. But they usually didn't get out all the soap, and their hair looked flat and lifeless when it was styled.

"I use something special that will brighten the color," Miguel said. "You don't need your roots done yet."

Phoebe tucked a towel around Honey's neckline and washed her hair. The two women chatted like old friends. Phoebe usually didn't get along well with the women customers, but she knew how to flatter and flirt with the older men.

The hair washing, from soaping to a mini scalp massage, took almost ten minutes. When a wet-haired Honey was installed in Miguel Angel's chair, Helen asked, "May I bring you a drink? How about a magazine?"

"Just water," Honey said.

Helen went back to the prep room and poured ice and cold water into a crystal glass, added a thin lemon slice, then wrapped the glass with a paper napkin so the bride's delicate fingers wouldn't be chilled.

When she returned, Miguel Angel was blow-drying Honey's hair. In half an hour, he had it up on her head in a golden twist.

"Now the veil," he said. "Stand up."

Honey stood. Miguel carefully draped the veil over her hair, pinned it in place, then added the tiara. The crystals caught the light and gave Honey an angelic halo.

"Beautiful," he said.

"This is how I want to look," Honey said. "Now will you brush out my hair? I want King to be surprised on Saturday."

Miguel Angel unpinned the veil, and Helen carefully folded it and packed it away. The tiara went back in its small box. When Miguel finished brushing out Honey's shoulder-length hair, the bride-to-be gave Ana Luisa her credit card, wrote a check to Miguel Angel for his tip, handed Helen five bucks and gave Phoebe a thick wad of money.

But she still didn't leave. "I'm worried about Saturday," Honey said. "All of King's celebrity friends will be there. What if something goes wrong?"

"What can go wrong?" Miguel Angel said. "We're supposed to have beautiful weather, and you're a beautiful bride."

"What if I trip and fall going down the aisle?"

"King will only love you more," Miguel Angel said. "Do you love him?"

"Of course," Honey said. "His first marriage was a mistake. He'd knocked up Posie and they had to hurry up and get married by a judge at city hall. Posie was so desperate, she signed the worst prenup agreement ever. But we're doing this marriage right. King wants a traditional white wedding with all his friends there and a real honeymoon. He loves me. He tells me so all the time. And I love him to death. I mean, till death parts us."

"You're just having a case of bridal nerves," Miguel Angel said. "What could go wrong?"

"I guess we'll find out on Saturday," the bride said, and kissed him lightly on the cheek.

LOOK FOR THE BOOKS BY
ELAINE VIETS
in the Josie Marcus,
Mystery Shopper series

Dying in Style

Mystery shopper Josie Marcus's report about Danessa
Celedine's exclusive store is less than stellar, and it may
cost the fashion diva fifty million dollars. But Danessa's
financial future becomes moot when she's found
murdered, strangled with one of her own thousand-dollar
snakeskin belts—and Josie is accused of the crime.

High Heels Are Murder

Every job has its pluses and minuses. Josie Marcus gets to
shoe-shop—but she also must deal with men like Mel
Poulaine, who's *too* interested in handling women's feet.
Soon Josie's been hired by Mel's boss to mystery-shop the
store, but one step leads to another and Josie finds herself
in St. Louis's seedy underbelly. Caught up in a web of
crime, Josie hopes that she won't end up
murdered in Manolos...

Accessory to Murder

Someone has killed Halley Hardwicke, the hot young
designer of Italian silk scarves—and the police have their
eye on Jake, the husband of Josie's best friend. Josie
decides to do what she does best—go undercover and see
if she can find some clues. Because this time, there's a lot
more at stake than a scarf, even if it's to die for...

**Available wherever books are sold or
at penguin.com**

**The seventh book in
ELAINE VIETS'
nationally bestselling
Dead-End Job series:**

CLUBBED TO DEATH

Helen Hawthorne's latest dead-end job
is in a country club's complaint
department, dealing with the gripes of
the rich and spoiled. Then Rob, her
deadbeat ex-husband, sails back into her
life aboard the yacht of his new lady,
Marcella—known as the Black Widow
for her string of dead spouses. The next
day Rob's reported missing. If the Black
Widow has such a murderous reputation,
then why is Helen led from the
club in handcuffs?